BUSY DYING

BUSY

CHAX

HILTON OBENZINGER

DYING

ISBN 978-0-925904-73-7

Library of Congress Cataloging-in-Publication Data
is on file and available from the publisher

CHAX
650 East 9th Street
Tucson, Arizona 85705
www.chax.org

Editorial production for Chax by Stephen Vincent at
Book Studio, San Francisco Copy editing by Elissa Rabellino
Designed by Jeff Clark at Quemadura, Ypsilanti, Michigan,
and composed in Electra, Bank Gothic, and Trade Gothic
Printed on recycled paper by Thomson-Shore, Dexter, Michigan

FIRST EDITION

CONTENTS

... and he not busy being born ... BOB DYLAN

It was April 1968, and I was occupying the president's office to protest Columbia University's complicity in the Vietnam War and the administration's insistence on building a new gym in Morningside Park despite the objections of Harlem, the city government, faculty, and students. I would spend nearly a week in President Grayson Kirk's second-floor office in Low Library—despite the name, the building with the iconic rotunda no longer held books, just administrative suites—until the cops broke down the barricades and we were all beaten up and hauled off to jail in the final bust.

We were young, righteous, and full of fervor, and our days together in Low Commune were deliciously utopian. We were about 125 students making decisions through participatory democracy, through consensus, changing the world by example. Although we were nonviolent, it was also dangerous. The right-wing students were charging the building again and again, and they set up a blockade to prevent the anti-war students from sending in supplies. Fists were flying, and the scene around the building roiled with constant near-riots.

The faculty decided to set up their own line in an attempt to prevent the situation from getting even more out of hand. Professors took turns standing on the lawn outside the building beneath the second-story window ledges to form a protective cordon to keep the right-wing students from bursting through the windows of Low Library to get at the "pukes" inside. The professors were attempting to be fair, which meant they also stood on the lawn to prevent our supporters from bringing supplies to the communards.

In the midst of this siege, I was assigned to a shift standing guard at one of the windows. Behind me and out of sight was one of those long poles with a hook used for opening the tall windows—a possible weapon to pry from the ledge any right-wingers, including some very large jocks, if they made their charge.

On the grass below stood the line of professors, and among them was poet Kenneth Koch, doing his stint on the faculty cordon. He was looking up at me, smiling in his affable way. He didn't preach or wail or gnash his teeth, and he offered a friendly wave at me, Les Gottesman, and Alan Senauke, the other editors of the literary magazine.

He couldn't keep from enjoying himself, couldn't take things too seriously, which was in its own way unnerving. But it was good to see him, in all his goofiness, and we waved back. He had thrown his lot in with the rest of the feeble faculty who were futilely trying to impose themselves between the student factions when they should've joined us, which saddened us, although I couldn't be mad at him. His humor lent him some transcendent grace.

"Did you write any poems?" he chuckled up at us.

No, we hadn't. We set right off to punch out a bunch of spontaneous three-way-collaboration poems, each of us taking a turn on the typewriter we had liberated from President Kirk's secretary.

So terrible, so embarrassingly idiotic were these poems that we threw them away almost immediately. The muse of André Breton and Tristan Tzara and Frank O'Hara had failed us, and moment-to-moment rhapsodic bop would sound like Allen Ginsberg—and there was only one Allen Ginsberg. We couldn't bear to write tedious Fight-Team-Fight anthems or lugubrious, boring manifestos. All we could knock out was intense, manic gibberish when what was needed was something entirely new written in a language no one had yet invented.

Still, I marveled at Koch's sweetness, his unwillingness to change his peaceable demeanor in the face of chaos and violence, his chuckle, and his question, "Did you write any poems?"

Whenever times have been tough in my life, I've remembered Kenneth Koch's chuckle, seen his sweet grin, recalled the pleasures of peace, and heard his question: "Did you write any poems?"

That moment stuck in my memory.

This little book is one more attempt to write that poem.

BUSY DYING

FIRST SUITE

GOD IS A DUCK

God Is a Duck
2003

I was drying myself off with a towel after a shower, alone in my bedroom, when I heard a loud quack. I looked around. It was evening and the lights were all off. No one was there, certainly not a duck.

But the quack was unmistakable; I could not deny it. I had heard a quack, for sure. I looked down the hallway from my bedroom, but no one was there—all dark. There was nothing to do but finish drying myself off.

I am going crazy, I thought to myself, the time has finally come, and I am now hearing auditory hallucinations. That was all there was to it. I was delusional. I didn't feel bad, and I shrugged. Next I would probably believe that the quack was the voice of God. Such an idea made me giggle: The voice of God is actually a Quack, and God is a Duck. I dressed, laughing to myself: *God is a Duck!* This was strange, indeed. People who are delusional are actually in pain—they don't laugh at the voices they hear, at least not with real joy—so I didn't know what to make of this. Maybe I really did hear the voice of God.

I spent more time giggling to myself. After a while, I passed the bedroom we use as an office at the end of the hall, and I noticed my oldest son sitting at the computer in the dark. I hadn't realized he was there, and I asked him, "Did you shout out something?"

He nodded.

He had been frustrated by the machine, and he exclaimed, "Crap!" which had become "Quack!" to my ear. The voice of God was not even a delusion, just a misapprehension.

Still, I kept giggling, and the rest of the day I chuckled to myself: I had heard a Cosmic Quack, and the Quack was the Voice of God. *God is a Duck!*

A few days later I read a newspaper story about a talking fish. The Hassidic fishmonger and his Honduran helper had tossed a carp onto the cutting board to prepare for gefilte fish. But the carp twisted and flopped around, and started making strange noises. The assistant called over his boss, who was astonished to hear the fish speaking in Hebrew, delivering apocalyptic utterances from its gills. The fish eventually revealed that the soul of a recently departed rabbi was speaking through it. The rabbi-fish asked about members of the congregation, and described himself as doing well, considering, and the fishmonger was amazed.

However, his Catholic assistant insisted it was the Devil. He grabbed the carp by its tail and clobbered it to death.

The Author Describes His Job
2007

I work with Stanford students on their research writing. It's like I'm managing a stable of detectives of sorts. I help students to write their theses from all the different fields—natural sciences and humanities and social sciences—consulting with them on their writing, egging them on to challenge themselves, giving them tips on how to corner their prey. They are all sniffing out the truth, "creating knowledge," as we like to say, rather than passively "consuming" it in the classroom. (Who wants to be a "consumer" when it's so much more exhilarating to be a "producer"?) Stanford students are sharp, and precocious until it hurts, and they can decipher literary codes or DNA or Russian foreign policy with great aplomb.

They're so smart it's scary.

Most of the time, they're on to fascinating discoveries. True, some of the knowledge they "create" makes me ill—rationales for "targeted assassinations," for example—but I help all who come through my door. Students untangle knots of genes and viruses and proteins, or they carefully observe the habits of seagulls far from human garbage in the wilderness of Kamchatka. They dive deep into *Moby Dick*, and they run MRIs to locate where in the brain love and laughter and cocaine buzz reside. They determine things I can't even fathom, like "the sensitivities of a microwave cavity experiment to various forms of Lorentz violation that can occur in an extension to the photon sector of the Standard Model." Sometimes they can be funny, as in the thesis on cultural attitudes toward Michelangelo's statue of David called "The Most Famous Penis in the World."

So much knowledge still waits to be "created," while the supply of raw materials never seems to end. And here are all these detectives, these brilliant young brains, ferreting out the jewels of the past and the chemical compositions of the future, year after year, and they come to me for help in unraveling the mysteries of documentation, interpreting the strange behavior of their advisers, strengthening their arguments, writing with expected clarity and unexpected eloquence. I help them stay on track, I pound at their procrastination, and I blow up their writing blocks. I tell them they already got the guts, they're tough: All they got to do now is see it to the end.

It's satisfying enough, marshaling this small troop of detectives. But sometimes something even more special happens; sometimes the research goes beyond production and moves into another realm—and the student is changed beyond any expectation. There's the Chicano student who studies Paul's epistles in the original Greek, which causes him, unintentionally, to journey backward from Damascus, and he ends up converting to Judaism, to everyone's astonishment and his parents' dismay. There's the girl who observes the lives of Indian villagers in Chiapas, and soon after graduation she dissolves into the jungle to join the Zapatistas. But most of the time something hits inside so deeply it shakes them up in ways that don't seem so obvious, in ways that escape formal religion or politics, even though there's no visible change.

It's not a bad job.

Hilton Obenzinger Magazine
2003

Victor Seidel was a doctoral student in management at Stanford. He contacted me to confirm that I was indeed Hilton Obenzinger. And then he came over to my office to explain. It seems that in the mid-eighties, when he went to Schreiber High School in Port Washington, New York, he was editor of the humor magazine, which was called *Hilton Obenzinger*. Just a few sheets of eight-and-a-half-by-eleven paper folded over, it was filled with more than the usual wisecracks, silly jokes, and mild gross-outs expected from high school students.

The magazine had been in existence since at least 1982, and from the first it had been called *Hilton Obenzinger*. No one by the time Vic became editor in 1984 knew where the name had come from—he assumed that it was made up, that someone came across "Hilton" somewhere and was intrigued, and then made up "Obenzinger" or saw it somewhere, and decided that fusing the two would make a bizarre combination. He thought that the editor in 1982, Josh Berman, might know the true origins of the name, and certainly the faculty adviser, Robin Dissin, would know. But this was more than twenty years earlier, and he had no idea how to find either of them.

Vic didn't even have any copies to show me, although months later he accidentally bumped into Carol Blum, who had worked on the magazine with him, on an airplane. They reminisced, and he told her that he had found the real Hilton Obenzinger at Stanford, and she was amazed. From her he obtained several copies, which he passed on to me.

"And now a message from the president of *Hilton Obenzinger* . . ."

"*Hilton Obenzinger* prints an article mocking every major religion and no one gets offended."

"The Official *Hilton Obenzinger* Watch!"

"Call the *Hilton Obenzinger* Complaint Hotline."

"MAKE-IT-YOURSELF #1: *Hilton Obenzinger*'s Rotor Beanie."

My hunch was that Josh Berman or someone had come across one of my books or an article I wrote, cracked up at the strange name, and claimed it for the magazine. After all, how would the real Hilton Obenzinger ever find out about it?

So, there I was: a brand name, a byword for laughs, and I hadn't even known about it for all these years. Only by coincidence had I discovered the existence of my doppelganger. But the facts were clear: For over twenty years, I had led a double life. All the time I had gone about my business—family, job, words, God, war—there was another Hilton Obenzinger going about his own affairs, someone entirely on his own: "Never before has *Hilton Obenzinger* printed a statement of policy, and it may not be a good idea this time either."

When I told Paul Auster about *Hilton Obenzinger*—he appreciates these sorts of things—he laughed so hard that he nearly fell to the floor.

Casket

2001

It was time to bury my mother, and I was at the cemetery, and the hearse pulled ahead of the few cars waiting for it to arrive. The driver stepped out and waved to me, and I walked to the back of the black wagon.

"I need to have you identify that we have the right body," he said.

I was taken aback. We had just buried my father two months before with the same funeral home, and they hadn't asked for such a thing. Why were they sure then but needed to check now?

I just nodded, and he rolled the simple pine casket partway out of the hearse and opened the lid. I had been with my mother for her last breath, had held her hand as she struggled, unconscious, singing to her as her mouth sucked in air, her tongue reaching out one last time. I had seen the last quiver of life in her eighty-seven-year-old body, so I knew what she had looked like—and I dreaded to view the first hints of decay.

But when the driver opened the casket lid, I saw her wrapped in the white gauze of her shroud, her hair sweeping across her face. I pulled her hair back. It was her, and I nodded. She looked transformed—her skin was taut, no longer wrinkled, her hair delicate and auburn, and she had a slight, wispy smile. It was as if she had become young again, a pretty little girl. How beautiful, such a pretty little girl. She was the daughter of the highest Jewish official in the Polish government before the war, from an assimilated family of culture, and she came to America to marry and have kids and become an artist. And now she looked like a young girl at peace, excited with the prospects of the world.

The revelation was a shock, and I was speechless. I just nodded that the body in the box was indeed my mother so that the driver could get his paperwork done and the burial could begin.

I quickly recovered and felt more at ease having seen her that last time, knowing that she had become the beautiful little girl whom I saw in the photos of her in Warsaw wearing her sailor-suit school uniform. Like her, I felt at peace.

I hope that one day my son will look down at me in my casket and will be amazed at the handsome little boy stretched out before him.

Jazz

2001

After my mother's funeral, I went to a bar on Broadway near my brother's apartment. At night they offered jazz, and on that chilly December afternoon, as chance would have it, the pianist of the house band was getting married.

He was balding, had been around the block a few times, and his bride was a young girl from Colombia who stood next to him with her mother by her side. A woman in a minister's robe presided over a very spiritual non-Christian ceremony, tasteful and not too heavy on New Age blather, and the groom played a song on the piano that he had composed for his bride. Seeing him tickle the keys and sing, she glowed with deep satisfaction.

I watched, stirring my scotch, on the other side of the horseshoe bar. I felt sadness and joy, a moment of gentleness and grief, smiling at the newlyweds. Of all things, I bury my mother and end up at a wedding. How sorrowful, strange, and sweet.

After one more drink, I went up to the couple on my way out.

I shook their hands. "I buried my mother today, and I'm just back from the cemetery," I told them, "and I only stopped in for a drink. I had no idea you were getting married." They gasped, offering condolences, and I continued, "No, that's OK, she was very old, and it was time. I only want to congratulate you, and to say that it was wonderful to see this. This little coincidence means that the spirit of my mother has come to bless both of you. It was no accident."

We all three hugged, and I walked out, feeling lucky.

Revelations
2003

How many revelations do I get in life? Am I born with a fixed number? How many first encounters, how many true loves? How often do I discover a piece of the past that so many years later can open like a blossom? How often do I understand something—have a mystery explained, a flash of insight? How often do the scales of history fall off? How many times does the immensity of the universe reveal itself in all its splendor or terror or ordinary blandness? How many joys, how many sorrows? How many truths unveiled, how many lies of the powerful exposed?

I may be born with a fixed number of revelations, like a set number of eggs or sperms. But what if I leave myself open like a radio, a great antenna stretching into the daily workings of life, and I harvest the enlightenments of multitudes—well, at least a few others? Should I restrict my dreams to the borders of my soul?

So I have decided to tune in to the revelations of others, good or bad, as I pick through my own scratchy reports. I will work through the files of my own moments—at least those that made my heart tender and filled with hope, my eyes open, or brought me grief, rage, love, particularly when I was very young, a college student like the ones I teach now.

I may not have too many more occasions to take account of such moments as I get older, so I leave my spiritual radio on, day and night. Mostly I get static and fragments—again and again I get the revelations of my students—and I get memories. All together, these will be the sum of something bigger, although I can't tell what that sum of all awakenings will be.

I invite you to share your flashes of awe.

I look forward to reading your inklings of truth, your instances of startling comprehension, those scenes of mystery and illumination — anything that gave you a peek through the fleshy gates of wonder.

I will print them here. You can send your stories to

Hilton Obenzinger Magazine

SCHREIBER HIGH SCHOOL

PORT WASHINGTON

NEW YORK 11050

TRY TO REMEMBER

1962/1965

When the day of the contest came, I waited for my turn on a wooden bench in the lobby of the Carnegie Recital Hall right next door to the big Carnegie. Mrs. Williams, the young black woman who led the chorus in spirituals and Gershwin at JHS 59, had suggested that I enter the WQXR–New York Times Young Performers Contest. Even though I was only in the ninth grade and would be competing against high school seniors, the contest would be "good experience" for a young pianist, she said, as well as practice for the test to get into the High School of Music and Art.

The sound of crashing Brahms drifted through the door, and despite the plush coolness of the lobby, I began to sweat. I had only a low-caliber Chopin waltz, no virtuoso bombshell, and I agonized through the tumult of Brahms until finally there was silence and my turn had come. Pushing through the doors, I shuffled down the maroon carpet and up the stairs to the stage. From there I could barely make out Abram

Chasins, the famous pianist, *New York Times* music critic, and WQXR radio host who presided as judge. He sat by himself in the darkness of the little hall, a gray man in a gray suit. He had a small lamp on a podium that lit up his hands so brightly that it left the rest of him, particularly his shadowed face, in even deeper gloom.

"Milton?"

"No, it's Hilton, Mr. Chasins."

"Like the hotel?"

"Yes, like the hotel. Hilton, Hilton Obenzinger."

"Well, what will you play, Milton?" His was that elegant, cultured voice for announcing Beethoven symphonies. I realized that I really didn't want to see his face.

"The Chopin waltz, opus 69, number 1, in A-flat major."

I sat on the bench and stared at the Steinway keys too long. A great fear swallowed me, terror battered my eardrums, and I felt myself fluttering and trembling like a leaf. You know how the A-flat major waltz has that wonderful opening phrase—E-flat, D-natural, D-flat, E-flat, D-flat, C, on and on—which makes your fingers go up down up down like you're hiking up and down hills and valleys? To my horror, I began to crank out that lovely little phrase like it was pistons on a Model T, while my left hand started shaking so much that my hand began to stutter, hitting two, even three chords for every one Chopin had intended. I could not hold the three-four time to save my life.

"*STOP!*"

I turned to the illuminated, disembodied hands jutting out from the darkness.

"You're a little nervous," he spoke from the black depths. "Take a breath and start all over again." His illuminated palms turned up in a gesture of reassurance.

I took a deep breath. I thought, "Soon this will be over; soon I will be out on the street." Then I recommenced hammering and stuttering.

"*Milton!*"

I looked up again, still shaking. Chasin's hands exploded in and out of the circle of light as he spoke.

"Do you like to go to the schoolyard?"

"Ex-excuse me?"

"Do you like to play baseball?" he asked, in a studied calm.

That was a strange question. "Sure, I do—sometimes."

"Then I suggest that you go to the schoolyard and play baseball as much as you can, *because you will never, never play the piano—ever!*" he spat out. Then, returning to his calm, businesslike tone, he concluded: "You may go now. Thank you."

I'm not sure how I made my way out to the street, but by the time I reached the automat near Sixth Avenue, I became aware that I was crying and muttering to myself like some crazy kid derelict as I careened across town to Sloan-Kettering Hospital.

"*Drop dead, Abram Chasins!*" I howled. "*Drop dead!* They threw Verdi out of the conservatory—told him he was no good," I muttered to myself. "Look how Verdi turned out, you bastard! You won't stop me, Abram Chasins. I'm a—*I'm a Verdi, too!*"

I thought about all the times I had turned down invitations to play baseball with Joe and the other kids in Laurelton because I needed to practice, rolling on the bench with that lilting sad melody traveling up and down the hills and valleys. Besides, Mrs. Covello, my piano teacher, told me to take especial care to keep my hands safe. Yes, I'd played ball a few times—but I did make sure that my fingers didn't get twisted or slammed, and I wasn't some athlete like my brothers Ronnie and Mark, throwing shot put on the Andrew Jackson track team. No, I had practiced that Chopin waltz every day, the sad melody rolling up and down the hillside like my *touchas* pivoting along the bench.

"*Drop dead, Abram Chasins!*" I mumbled through tears, all the while a small voice whispering, "*He's right, he's right. You're not a Verdi, you're not a Verdi.*"

By the time I reached the hospital, I was able to calm down. It was early March, and in the darkening chill of late afternoon the air felt icy, and I stood there gulping down deep Frigidaire breaths, gathering myself by the front door. I didn't want Ronnie to see me like that.

Ronnie had been home for months recuperating from his operation. He seemed to be getting stronger, but a few days before, he had turned slightly yellow, and the doctor had him sent back to the hospital. I hadn't seen him since, and I didn't want to walk into his room blubbering like a baby. That was the last thing I wanted to do.

He didn't look too bad, really, just oddly yellow. "How are you, Ronnie?"

"I'm doing OK. I'll be all right soon. What about the contest? How'd you do?"

I choked back, looked down. "OK."

"What happened?"

I didn't say anything. He seemed tired, weary, distracted. Maybe he wouldn't ask again.

"Something happened. I can tell. What was it?"

I told the story in jerky half-sentences, told him what Abram Chasins had said.

"He said that?"

"Yeah."

He sighed, and I looked at his yellowish face. The thick shadow of his beard on his cheeks. His watery blue eyes. I looked in his eyes. "Pretty mean, huh?"

He put his arm up to give me a pat. "Just try again."

I noticed a blue plastic band circling his wrist. "What's that, Ronnie?"

"This? Oh, it says the patient's name, his religion. In case I die, they'll know I'm not Catholic so they won't need a priest to say last rites."

"In case you die?"

"I'm not going to die, Hilton. I'll be all right. But everybody has to wear a wristband for identification. Otherwise they might cut up the wrong person."

Dad and Mom came in, and I just stood in the corner at the foot of the bed while they talked until visiting time was over.

A few days later he was dead, and I stood in the same room in the very early morning hush, his lips slightly parted and his eyes open too wide. I stared at his watery blue eyes until they burned into my own, until I could see nothing but those transparent eyes.

Ronnie had said he wouldn't die, yet he was dead. And the last time I saw him, he felt sorry for me, and I didn't even want to believe he was that sick.

■   ■   ■

The memory keeps coming back.

I don't know how long I had been looking into Jimmy's eyes. The dawn light was barely gray, but I could still see Ronnie's eyes as Jimmy peered straight up at the ceiling in the bed across from mine. I was working at the Hampton Bays Dinner Theater out on Long Island, and they had cleaned up the barn to use as a dormitory for the actors and musicians and members of the stage crew like Jimmy and me. Our beds were parallel to each other, one on either side of the door. Jimmy had a strict wake-up ritual, and he was doing it again this morning when I found myself half-dreaming, half-remembering Ronnie as I looked into his wide-open eyes.

I pulled myself out of Jimmy's eyes to watch him go through his ritual.

Jimmy would open a warm bottle of Coke that he had left by the side of his bed the night before, then he would light a Lucky Strike, and he'd drink and smoke and stare at the ceiling on his back as he gathered his soul in one last quiet meditation before beginning the day. He was doing the same this morning.

The women who worked at the theater were luckier. They got cabins in the abandoned motel across the road. But most of the men — about a dozen — had to put up with mass intimacy, snores, and all the other charms of barracks life. I didn't mind it too much, though. I enjoyed working on the tech crew hanging lights, switching gels, changing sets. And I enjoyed working with Jimmy, who was not a theater person at all but a handyman from when the restaurant only served food without side orders of Rodgers and Hammerstein. I liked his loose-limbed walk, his slight drawl, the slow calm way he made his way through any job. In a room full of prancing tenors and pirouetting sopranos, Jimmy seemed wonderfully unpretentious — the only one in the barn who wasn't acting.

I ended up out at the Hamptons a couple of weeks after graduating from Andrew Jackson High School, excited about starting Columbia in the fall. A few days later, I thumbed through *Backstage* at the candy store down Broadway, and when I saw the ad for the tech job out on

Long Island, I figured I would just pick up where I had left off in show business.

I had worked one summer at the Woodstock Playhouse in upstate New York as an apprentice painting sets and playing small bits—I dozed as a Mexican in *Night of the Iguana* and called out telegrams as the messenger boy in *The Skin of Our Teeth*—and I had worked as a tech in my high school—we called the crew the Amp Squad. I'd acted for a few small companies off Broadway, and I had even taken acting lessons at Circle in the Square. Even so, I was a little surprised that I got the job. But considering how low the pay was after deducting room and board, even by summer stock standards, I suppose I shouldn't have been. In any case, the owner, a Jewish guy who called himself Ian Leloir, just glanced at my application, offered that the guy who had last held the job had just quit, asked me if I could start in two days, and then hired me on the spot.

Ian Leloir's schtick seemed like it could work: The sophisticated Hamptons audience would come and eat a steak and enjoy some dinner jazz. Then, while nibbling sweets and sipping coffee, they'd catch the revue-style versions of musicals on the theater-in-the-round stage on top of what looked like a sawed-off *Titanic* smokestack. The entire place was decorated with all sorts of buoys, lifesavers, and nautical flags, all in keeping with its previous incarnation as a seafood restaurant. A tall mainmast right out of *Moby Dick* loomed outside, and that morning I was supposed to climb up the pole with Jimmy to change the movie marquee letters on the sign attached to the mast. Today was the last performance of *Oklahoma*, and we had to add beneath it "Starts Friday—*The Fantasticks*."

This would be a rough day, an all-nighter. After the performance we had to strike the set, put up the new one, and then hang the lights in time for dress rehearsal. But that morning I wasn't thinking of work as I peered across the barn door at Jimmy's eyes. I wasn't thinking of anything until I remembered Abram Chasins. I had just drifted from dream to memory to grief in the enormity of those oceanic eyes without any awareness of what I was doing. When I jolted fully awake, I realized that I had been staring at those eyes all along.

I was transfixed by Ronnie's dead eyes again, and he was dead, really dead, and all the dominoes in Southeast Asia could fall and he would still be dead. All I could do was keep on staring and remembering and weeping—I was eighteen years old, and I still couldn't shake the ghost, and the eyes from four years ago looked out at me from Jimmy's skull.

Suddenly Jimmy snuffed out the butt, shot up in bed, threw his feet to the floor, and sat on the edge of the thin mattress to cradle his face in his hands, the whole quick combination of moves exploding silently in the dim light. This was the next station on his ritual schedule. He would sit like this for five minutes or so, thinking or praying, I suppose, after which he'd open the Bible he kept under his pillow and read a little, his lips slowly, silently forming around each word one by one like some awkward Saint Jerome. Then he'd grab his shoes and slip out the barn door. Jimmy slept fully dressed—I'm not sure why—but when everyone else was working the show, he'd take his shower and change for the next day and bed down by curtain call. He wasn't at all interested in the musicals, and his handyman chores always started early in the morning before breakfast, so he would inevitably blow his cloud of smoke and get up before the rest.

No one would sleep too much longer, though, since breakfast was served in the empty dinner theater no later than ten. The entire crew would assemble over watery scrambled eggs, and no matter how cottony their mouths, they'd get into singing, mugging, and hamming around. I had worked on some musicals at the Woodstock Playhouse when I apprenticed two years before, but I'd never before worked with a troupe that did nothing but musical comedies. Sure, actors always love to act and tend to fall into any role at the drop of a hat, but bundle together a bunch of musical-theater freaks and coop them up in old barns and dilapidated motels, and you descend into ham hell. They were unrelenting, anything and everything was a cue for a chorus, and not one moment passed without some one or other belting out "Pass the butter!" like Ethel Merman.

This morning, in addition to the usual complaints about the liquefied eggs (Gershwin: "*It Ain't Necessarily Eggs*"), the fact that paychecks had not arrived as expected the day before erupted into a version of "Try to Remember" from *The Fantasticks* ("Try to remember our pay by December / Or we will strike and cut your member"), in the middle of which Ian Leloir shuffled in and waved for silence. Donald, who was playing El Gallo, waved back and intoned in his vibrant baritone, "And what do you say for yourself, my dear Monsieur Leloir? Will we get our due, or shall we indulge in a *real* rape at the end of Act One?"

Leloir smiled wanly. He was chubby and balding, but you could still make out the outlines of a skinny kid on his face. "You can rape anyone your heart desires, Donald, but I'm afraid the accountant said the checks will be ready by tomorrow morning at the earliest."

This was met with a chorus of boos. "I'm sorry, but I've told you all that I've arranged for additional loans, which haven't cleared the bank yet. You don't want me to write bad checks, do you?"

"*Nooo, Mr. Leloir*," they responded like a chorus of second-graders.

"Now, you're all doing great. We're beginning to get some full houses, and word of mouth is just starting to do its stuff. The season is early, and you know and I know *we're gonna be stars.*"

"*Die, Mortimer, die!*" Donald retorted, and Alvin, who played Mortimer in *The Fantasticks*, reeled out of his chair, stumbled with his hands over his heart, and began one of his overcooked vaudeville death scenes, twirling and writhing until he flopped on the floor with his feet sticking up in the air.

"With acting like that, we can't lose," Leloir quipped back. He was no actor, but he knew he had to let his kids play to keep them quiet.

"OK, so the checks come tomorrow," Annie chimed in. "How about we get some real eggs *today?*" This elicited a raucous chorus of "*Egglohoma!*" and laughter. The actors wanted to open *The Fantasticks* as much as the producer did—only through some fluke or under-the-table deal had the company been given permission to mount the show for a short run, despite the fact that it was still drawing people to the tiny theater on Sullivan Street in Greenwich Village—so giving Ian Leloir the benefit of the doubt was a foregone conclusion.

I sat silently in the back by the kitchen doors drinking coffee with Jimmy. In my career in the theater—if you could call it a career—I had started studying to be an actor, but then I found myself hanging out more and more with the techs, the stagehands, the lighting crew, the unseen people whose lives were always behind the stage, not on it. Besides, I didn't really want to be an actor. I wanted to be the words in an actor's mouth. I wanted to write poems, stories, maybe even plays. But I loved the work and watching the musicals—and I figured I could play along with overbearing manic giddiness easily enough for a while. I liked to goof, and I liked everyone at the Hampton Bays Dinner Theater, but it was just that the songs and the bits all seemed to be masks with nothing underneath. There was a lot of screwing going on—although no sex came my way, naturally—and there were plenty of artistic jealousies, so the sniping and gossiping would get acted out in scenes from old movies and musicals. I suppose I gravitated toward working as a quiet tech sitting in the shadows by the kitchen door because it felt calmer. Besides, the real world had become theater enough lately.

Soon after breakfast Jimmy and I were climbing up the whitewashed mast, stepping on one metal spike after another to the signboard. A bag like the ones used by newsboys was slung over my shoulder with the plastic alphabet stuffed in the pouch on my chest. As Jimmy stood on the little catwalk that ran along the signboard, I handed each plastic letter to him, one giant black letter at a time. Each letter took a few minutes to position, so I could hold on tight to the mast and glance out over Sunrise Highway and the dunes to the beach before Jimmy called for the next.

What a kick, to stand on a mainmast and survey the rolling immensity below. I am usually terrified of heights. High up someplace—like when I tried to climb the Eiffel Tower steps but only got up to the first level, or when I stepped to the edge of the cliff at Ashokan Dam two summers ago—I would suddenly be filled with an overpowering, perverse desire to throw myself off, hurl myself over the edge or the rail. It was like something right out of Edgar Allan Poe. Usually I would have to fight back the dread urge to fling myself into the void with no little difficulty. Up high I would panic, not so much because of the height but because of myself: I knew I couldn't trust myself, that I was my own worst enemy.

But this time I felt at ease in Jimmy's shadow. I could trust the way he stepped, so deliberate, yet with poise that seemed casual, easygoing. He worked without effort, without even needing to think, and I felt drawn into the circle of his grace. I mimicked him, aped him completely. This time, high above Long Island, I would be safe, just so long as I became Jimmy's double.

After about an hour we climbed down and admired our work from a distance—yes, "Starts Friday—*The Fantasticks*"—and we took a break and sat drinking Cokes at the base of the mast.

"Have you ever seen this musical, Jimmy? *The Fantasticks?*"

"No."

"You might like it. A couple of guys from Texas wrote it. It's kind of corny, but the music's great, terrific tunes, haunting."

"Is that so?" he responded to my quick review. "Perhaps the Lord has brought me here just to see *The Fantasticks*."

And we lapsed into silence.

Jimmy was a loner who was never lonely. I yearned to know the secret of Jimmy's life, to plumb his heart. He never talked about his religion—and he certainly never preached. He only did as he was doing now, couching all his desires in terms of God's will. I figured I would have to ask him directly.

"Jimmy, how did you come to be a churchgoing man?"

He took a swig from the bottle, eyeing me with his face tilting up at the sky.

"If this is too personal or something, just forget it, I understand." I wasn't so curious that I would risk losing his friendship.

"I don't mind," he said, wiping his mouth with his sleeve, "so long as you don't mock me. Even if you do mock me, it don't matter much. Anyway, I'm not a churchgoing man."

"But I see you reading your Bible every morning."

"Sure," he nodded. "I read the Holy Book, but I'm not a church man. Every church sooner or later turns into the Whore of Babylon.

The Lord gave us His Book, everything He wants us to know is in that Book, and His Book is all I need."

"Did you learn how to read the Bible from your parents?"

"My parents? Not hardly at all. My dad was drunk, mostly." He chuckled slightly. "No, I was told by God Himself one day. I know the place, the date, even the time. I was told, that's why." He confided such a tremendous occurrence in his typical matter-of-fact manner.

"Jimmy, do you mean that you talked with God?" I was the one who was starting to get agitated.

"No, I didn't talk to God, God spoke to me."

"What do you mean?"

Then Jimmy told me the story of his conversion.

A few summers before, he was working in northeast Pennsylvania, near Carbondale, repairing appliances. That whole part of coal country is a little strange because they've had so many coal fires. The veins of coal underground had somehow caught fire—maybe from a mine fire, originally—and they would slowly smolder and burn, the fires lasting for years, maybe decades. The nagging, persistent burning had worked its way for miles underground through all the coal veins, meandering even under Carbondale and other towns, releasing odorless invisible deadly gases all along its course. A family had died as they slept in their beds unaware that the earth beneath them was on fire and spewing poison. Parts of towns had to be evacuated, and an army of steam shovels and bulldozers constantly labored at clawing up huge pits and building great heaps of smoking anthracite slag. That was the only way to put it out, by digging it up; and over the years, as the steam shovels pursued the runaway fires, the land all around had become marked with blackened, smoldering scars.

One day Jimmy was driving alongside the coal-fire works when he felt the ground begin to move. It wasn't like an earthquake but as if the road wasn't quite staying in place. He pulled over and looked out the windshield at the heaps of slag and the dismal houses of the ghost town down the road. He saw the ground undulate in the heat more than usual, heaving up and down, swelling like a giant dragon snorting fire and brimstone. He thought he was going crazy, he rubbed his eyes, but the vision of Hell remained. He became terrified, began crying, called out to God. He felt an all-powerful presence of a malicious being beneath the earth vomiting up fire from its entrails, and he screamed for God to save him, to keep him from the burning pit.

"That's when I saw the finger of God," he said. He held his right forefinger across my eyes and stretched the length of the finger with his other hand. "I saw a giant finger filling the sky. It was a huge finger right across my eyes. Just like this." Then Jimmy turned his hand and, pointing his finger directly toward his eyes, almost whispered, "It was the finger of God. Then the great finger slowly turned and pointed right at me. A finger—and I felt lost, and I begged for mercy. That's when I felt God's command."

He halted, dropped his hands, and looked out across the traffic coming down Sunrise Highway.

"So what did God want? Can you tell me? Is it a secret?"

"No, it's no secret. Probably the same thing He would say to you, I figure. He told me to live His Book and to witness for His Son. And He told me to wait until He called me again. I seen the finger of God! It was a giant finger like a whale or a blimp right in front of my eyes. Sort of funny, huh? But after that, I began to read and pray and wait for the time, His Time, when God would decide to point at me again.

"That was July 17, 1962, right outside Carbondale, three years ago, almost to the day. That's when I saw the finger of God." He stopped again.

"Well?"

"Well, what?"

"What does God want you to do?"

"That's just it. I won't know until it happens," Jimmy explained. "I only know that God has a plan for me. God will show me what to do in His time. I'll know it when it happens—there won't be any doubt—but it hasn't happened yet. It will, though, I'm sure of it—although I suspect that you don't believe me."

I don't believe in God, not even in His Finger, but I do believe in visions: There was no doubt in my mind that Jimmy had seen a giant finger. How could I object? Why not a finger?

"I totally believe you, Jimmy. I mean, I believe you saw what you saw and He was real." I paused, and we could hear the mainmast creaking in the sea breeze over our heads. "Do you think you'll have to go to Nineveh—like Jonah?"

Jimmy actually liked it when I teased him a little.

"Maybe so," he grinned. "And is Long Island Nineveh?"

■　■　■

After we struck the set that night, we positioned tall ladders underneath the leikos, and we switched lamps and changed gels, hauling lights up and down, teetering with wrenches, while John Batchelder, the lighting director, called his instructions up to us. *The Fantasticks*, skimpy on sets, relies on lighting a lot, so this was not easy work.

It gets pretty hot high up, dangling from the light frame, but we kept at it in steady workmanlike fashion. Occasionally, members of the cast would sit drinking beers and watch us work late at night, which we didn't mind. This was our show, and the actors appreciated it. But tonight everyone else had gone down Sunrise Highway to a rock-and-roll bar to celebrate the closing of *Oklahoma*, and we hadn't seen anyone in the dining room around the stage for hours.

I first noticed Norman out of the corner of my eye by the front door, watching us as we hung from the light frames and ladders. I don't know how long he had been standing there. I hadn't heard him come in, yet he seemed to be standing with dead weight, as if he had been rooted to that spot for ages, his knees bent, ready to dance or pounce.

"Hey, Norman. Cast party over yet?" I called down to him.

He just stood there glaring up at us, his arms slung by his side and a beer bottle dangling from one hand. Suddenly he stumbled a few steps forward, swung his arm slowly behind him, and flung the beer bottle directly at my head. I ducked as the empty Budweiser smacked against the ladder.

Norman played trombone in the band—and he was also a full-blooded Indian of some kind, a Cherokee or an Apache, I don't know. I had never met an Indian before, and he seemed ordinary enough, although he was also a little bit of a Dr. Jekyll and Mr. Hyde. He was a sweet and polite and gentle man by day, and he made up much of the audience for each of the cast's mealtime performances. Just this morning at breakfast, he'd sat back with a broad smile and laughed as the cast sang their way through their labor dispute with Ian Leloir. He even clapped and guffawed when Mortimer—who gets dressed up like a vaudeville stage Indian in the show—died for the boss. But by night, after each show, Norman became something different. He'd start to drink, and he'd get angrier and meaner with every snort. Everyone would leave him alone after a couple of beers, and he'd mainly go off by himself to feed his rage in back of the barn, guzzling and muttering and cursing until he passed out.

Norman grabbed another bottle on a table beside him, intending to toss it at Jimmy's ladder.

"Hey, Norman! It's me! Jimmy! Don't shoot!"

Batchelder started for him, but the Indian let the bottle fly, spun around, and swiftly shot out the door.

I knew Norman wasn't really angry at us. I could tell he wasn't seeing me in his eyes. He was looking at some demon or fantasy—maybe the first ugly White Man, I don't know—although his beer bottle could still clobber the shit out of me. Freaked out, the two of us scuttled down our ladders to await the results of Batchelder's scouting party.

We stood in the dark offstage, half ducking behind chairs, not saying a word, listening to the silence and surveying the whole dining room, eyeballing for signs of attack.

Three of the girls from the cast party suddenly burst into the dining room, laughing and shouting. The group was led by Alice Boyar, who was playing the Girl in *The Fantasticks* the next night, and we jumped up to run, thinking Norman had come back for the next barrage. Alice was just a couple of years older than me, so thin and with long, dark hair and a great voice—everyone thought she would be a real star someday, a new Audrey Hepburn. Right now she was drunk, winding down from a big party night.

"What's a matter wi' you? You don' like me? Why you run away fro' my love, baby!"

We told her of Norman's rampage and the lighting director's pursuit.

"My God, we bein' attack by Injuns! Protect me, darlin', and save th' chil'—" She fainted back into my John Wayne arms, and I could feel her taut, thin waist in my hands.

Just then Batchelder strolled through the kitchen door with a smile on his face, so we straightened up for his report. "Take it easy, there's no problem. Norman threw up all over the barn, puked and passed out. That's all there is to it. You can un-circle the wagons now and get back to work, and I'll talk with him in the morning. For sure, Norman can't keep on doing crap like this."

"What do you mean he threw up all over the barn? His bed is just at the foot of mine. *You mean he puked on my bed?*" I inquired with some concern.

"I didn't do an inspection. But it looked like he could heave almost as far as he could pitch a beer bottle and with aim just as bad."

Batchelder had to let me go check my bed just in case Norman had totally fouled it, and I walked through the dark across the road to the barn. It was late, maybe three in the morning. I climbed upstairs and quietly stepped through the door. Almost all the beds seemed to be occupied, the barn filled with soft snoring. Norman was stretched across his bed in a puddle of vomit that had filled his blankets and oozed down to the floor. It seemed he had fouled only himself and no one else. Still, it was hard to see my own bedding in the moonlight, so I bent down to feel gingerly around my blanket and pillow to double-check that everything was cool.

A giggle from behind startled me. I turned, and there in the doorway poked the heads of Alice and her friends, all three choking with stifled laughter and pointing their fingers out into the darkness of the barn. At first I couldn't see the source of their merriment, but then I made out a bed in the gloom sticking out perpendicularly from the back wall behind mine. Two heads were leaning together on the pillow. Holy shit—Donald and Vargas were in bed together! They played El Gallo and the Boy in the musical, but now they were sleeping like two innocent babes, the Boy sweetly nestled into the crook of El Gallo's arm.

Alice kept pointing and cracking up at the two men in bed. I was taken aback, too. I knew there were plenty of queers in the theater, but I didn't expect to see two men sleeping together in the barn just like that. It would be like having sex in Penn Station. Alice couldn't get over it, and just pointed and choked back her laughter until her girlfriends pulled the giggling starlet away from the door and down the stairs to the cabins.

No one stirred in the barn, though. I waited for the silence to close over the soft breathing of the sleepers again. Then I made a final check of my bedding, glancing one last time at the sweet and dreamy smile on the Boy's face as I left.

"Disaster averted," I reported to the crew when I got back. "He just puked all over himself."

I kept my mouth shut about the little love scene in the barn, just climbing back up the ladder to finish the job.

By four or so we put our wrenches down and did a quick run-through of the light board. Batchelder figured all the fine-tuning would wait for the dress rehearsal, and he called it a night.

"How about an ice cream sundae?" I suggested.

Batchelder declined with a wave and went off to his cabin on the women's side of the road (as lighting director and a married man, he received better accommodations than the barn). Jimmy and I headed past the darkened stoves with their greasy hoods to the long, low freezer locker where the kitchen staff kept the ice cream. Technically, we weren't supposed to pilfer eatables from the kitchen, but we just took it as one of our prerogatives for doing an all-nighter to grab a little treat — it was our just reward. No one would notice, and it wasn't as if we didn't have "board" coming to us with our barnyard "room," anyway. Still, we were always discreet whenever we raided the icebox, and we kept quiet as we knelt down to fumble with its latch in the dark.

I heard voices. I looked up in surprise as Jimmy put his finger to his lips. Maybe Norman had gotten up? We peered into the blackness beyond the meat locker and the shelves of bulk cans and sacks and boxes to the corner next to the rear door. There, Ian Leloir had his small office, and we could see that the light was on through the plate-glass window's closed Venetian blinds. I could make out Mr. Leloir's voice but not what he was saying. There were other voices as well. Instinctively, we stayed down. The voices kept rising then falling, sounding like ordinary conversation, until suddenly they buzzed into anger, sounding a tone of malice, even of evil. We crept closer to the office, crawling alongside the meat locker and the bulk pantry.

A few of the blinds were bent back, and through the chinks we could see two men standing by the producer. Mr. Leloir was wearing a white polo shirt and a captain's hat, while the two strangers stood in dark suits with their backs to us. We could only make out fragments of what they were saying. I heard "money" several times and a "Mr. Pellegrino" or something invoked with insistence. Suddenly one of the visitors, the taller one, let loose a swift punch into Mr. Leloir's gut. We could see Ian doubling up in pain, then they pulled him up straight, and the tall one punched him again, then again.

"Goons," Jimmy whispered. "Mr. Leloir got himself some gangster trouble."

"Let's split," I mouthed in his ear. "We don't want to end up in the meat locker." Then I began to slide back on all fours.

Jimmy stayed put. I tugged at his pants leg insistently.

He wouldn't budge, and I slid back up to his face. "Jimmy, let's get outta—"

I cut off when I saw how his eyes had fixed on the gleam of light from between the bent Venetian blinds. He seemed to be focused on something far off, like a mountain or a cloud, his jaws flexing tightly, his eyes widening into moons, and in a flash I realized what he must be seeing.

"Jimmy—stop!" I hissed at him, grabbing him by the hand, but he yanked it away and stood up. Pausing a moment, he knocked on the door.

"Excuse me, Mr. Leloir, it's Jimmy," he said with a casualness that belied the lateness of the hour and the weirdness of the situation. "Do you have a minute?"

The angry voices broke off. There was only a hole of silence in the night. As soon as I heard the doorknob turn, I scampered away, careening on all fours, not even looking back until I reached the ice cream locker.

Jimmy was gone. I suppose he had been invited into the office, but I wasn't going to stick around to find out. When I reached the kitchen doors, I got up and ran as fast as I could through the darkened dining room and out across the street. I bolted for the field behind the barn, to the clump of trees and piles of rocks where Norman would hide out drinking.

Jimmy must have seen The Finger. But he would only get himself killed trying to save Mr. Leloir on account of it. It was a fake, a delusion. It was the finger of Death, not God, and I was chattering with fear, trembling as I leaned against a sycamore.

I didn't want to go into the barn, so I just stood there holding on to that sycamore, breaking its crumbly bark in my hands, quivering and quaking, torn by my fear of the Mafiosi and my guilt for leaving Jimmy to his fate. "Oh, shit! Oh, shit!" I chattered over and over. I heard a car motor—and then another. Maybe the goons were going, but I stayed hugging my tree until the first light of dawn.

When finally I sneaked into the barn, I could tell that Jimmy hadn't been to bed. Norman and his puked-on sheets were gone, though, while El Gallo had made his way back to his own bed. I only stopped shaking after I showered and changed clothes. I was living out of my backpack, so it didn't take me long to toss in my dirty clothes and tie it up.

I waited until the kitchen staff was cleaning up after breakfast to talk with Eric Christianson, the stage manager, who lingered over his coffee, looking over the score, trying to apply his Yale Drama School brains to all the show's nuances. I told him I had called home that morning and learned my mother had suffered a near-fatal heart attack. I would have to leave that day to take care of her and my aged father. My brother was in the army on his way to Vietnam, and my only other relative, my mother's sister, was flying in from Caracas, Venezuela. My eyes were red, and I looked haggard, fatigued from work and terror, so I didn't need to put on an act. In an instant, Christianson believed my lie.

He sighed and expressed his condolences—and that he was pissed to lose yet another tech—but he told me to just go on and talk to Mr. Leloir when he came to sit in on the dress rehearsal that morning. I told Christianson that I would at least stay through the run-through and catch the late-afternoon train. Fortunately, once *The Fantasticks* was set up, it was easy to play. Batchelder could run the lights by himself, so I didn't feel like I was leaving the company too much in the lurch.

It didn't matter, anyway. I was splitting no matter what. I could smell the danger, could feel it in my palms and in the way my balls shriveled up like they were dipped in ice. I was not interested in getting killed over Ian Leloir's shady money deals.

I sat nervously by the maitre d's podium to await the rehearsal. Alice Boyar made her entrance laughing — it seemed she hadn't stopped tittering from the night before — with Carlton Downing. Downing was a genuine big name, a real Broadway performer. He had played with Helen Hayes in *The Skin of Our Teeth*, and opposite Tallulah Bankhead in *House on the Rocks* — he was the closest thing the Hampton Bays Dinner Theater had to a star. Sporting the checked vest, bow tie, and straw hat of his part as Bellomy, the father of Luisa the Girl, Downing strode in with his arms around Alice's waist, a giant grin lighting up his face.

Barnyard gossip had it that Downing was fucking Alice, and anyone could see why he would want to. Alice wore a short black skirt with smooth white panties, and as she jumped up to the low stage, she twirled and climbed the ladder in a move from one of her solos, her skirt floating tantalizingly above her panties. Exposing them was an innovation of the director, Ed Randall, who figured that a little tease would buoy the show without spoiling its bittersweet innocence.

"If we were really bold and not chickenshit," one of the actors cracked, "we'd do the whole fucking play totally nude — and on roller skates to boot!"

Still, *The Fantasticks* was very sexy, in its own way. The fact that it has only one female part draws all eyes to Luisa, making the Girl even more alluring. That the role was played by the beautiful starlet only made the titillation of her short skirt even more mesmerizing. I stared at the rehearsal, tormented, my delight at peeping at Alice's white panties distracted by the icy fear tightening around my nuts.

Mr. Leloir hadn't shown up as expected. Worse yet, I still hadn't seen Jimmy. Usually, he would check in before the rehearsal began to see if we needed to switch lights or anything before going out to mow the front lawn or do some other chore. His absence made me shiver. Was

Jimmy out changing the letters on the sign on the mainmast? Or was he with Mr. Leloir, hanging from blood-soaked hooks in the meat locker? Was he at the bottom of the Long Island Sound? I didn't even know if I wanted to find out. Surrounded by people at the rehearsal was probably the safest place to be, so I watched, assured that I had no choice but to wait.

I knew *The Fantasticks* inside and out. After the high school acting lessons I took at Circle in the Square on the weekends, I would hang out with a hulking Italian kid from Staten Island, a Golden Glove boxer who wanted to act, a sweet, gentle guy built like steel. We would slobber over Italian sausages and green peppers on MacDougal Street and maybe catch a matinee. We saw *The Fantasticks*, just around the corner from Circle in the Square, perhaps a half-dozen times. We went so often that we even got to know the two little girls who lived in the apartment above the theater who came to every Sunday matinee. We would bow politely and offer solemn greetings, and they would curtsey back at us in their crinoline dresses before taking their front row seats. We liked to study the show, how Word Baker directed it to take advantage of the cramped space of the Sullivan Street Theatre, how he made the intimacy of the place a theatrical experience in itself, how Tom Jones and Harvey Schmidt took the slight Edmund Rostand play and molded a sad-eyed Emmett Kelly quality out of schmaltz.

In Act One, two neighboring fathers, desiring their children to marry, practice reverse child psychology. Bellomy and Hucklebee feign a feud, build a wall, and forbid their offspring from fraternizing with the enemy—which of course provokes just the opposite response, enticing the kids into illicit romance. With the help of El Gallo the Latin Lover, the fathers agree to create the conditions for matrimony by arranging for Luisa's mock abduction—they call it "rape"—so that Matt the Boy can come to her rescue, save the day, and win her hand.

With the exception of Alice's panties, the production kept close to the Sullivan Street original—yet knowing the amours of the cast made the gossamer fluff very weird. When Luisa and Matt mooned at each other, it was hard to suspend disbelief knowing that El Gallo was actually sleeping with the Boy, while the Girl was fucking her own father. The whole show became a loony Freudian joke, and I almost laughed out loud when I realized it, although I guess I was just giddy from my fear of gangsters.

But when El Gallo did his "It Depends on What You Pay" number, singing of the full menu of "rapes" from which the fathers could order, the joke seemed too strange. A rape could be "emphatic," or you could get "the rape polite," the one with Indians, "a truly charming sight." There was one on horseback, "new and gay." And it all added up to one grand sales pitch:

> So you see the sort of rape
> Depends on what you pay.
> It depends on what you pay.

How light and coy and cute the whole thing was, but I began to feel dizzy at the crisscrossing between the libretto and the cast. What if the two dads and the Latin Lover were actually singing about arranging a real rape, like the way Donald joked over breakfast? How about a knife at the throat and a cock shoved into a tight cunt? How about Mississippi Delta rape? I felt myself getting more and more nervous as I watched the show. Bellomy rapes Hucklebee, El Gallo rapes Mortimer, and everyone gangbangs Luisa.

Just then, Ian Leloir glided past the maitre d' podium and took a seat next to Randall.

He was alive—and he didn't even seem to be bruised!

I felt relieved, quieted, soothed. After all, if Mr. Leloir was all right, then Jimmy was probably fine, too, and I had just worked myself into a frenzy for no good reason. For a moment I even entertained the idea of my mother suddenly recovering—but then I remembered the gangsters and decided to keep her in the oxygen tent. Those guys would be back, and the tall one would probably work his way around the producer's body, breaking legs, then arms, eventually getting to his skull like the practiced artist he no doubt was. I could be his next recital. At the end of the act I went up to the boss to tell him my story.

Leloir just stared at the stage with no expression, then got up and signaled me to follow him into his office so that he could write me my last check.

In the daylight his office didn't seem too frightening. Nothing was messed up, papers were neatly stacked, everything looked normal; even the Venetian blinds were raised.

"Have you seen Jimmy, Mr. Leloir? I wanted to say good-bye to him."

"Jimmy took off for a few days," he replied in a monotone, his head down over his checkbook as he scribbled his signature. "Some personal business." He tore off the check and looked up with a smile. There wasn't a scratch on his face.

I felt a chill run through my body. "Personal business?"

"Can you figure that? He came in the middle of the night to tell me. He needed a few days to do something, I don't know what. He's a little nuts maybe. Now with you taking off, too, I'm going to have to pay one of the waiters extra to fill in. But the show must go on, am I right?" The fat circling his boyish face wobbled like a halo. "I hope your mother does well, Hilton," and he extended his hand with the check. "By the way, it's post-dated. I hope you don't mind."

Personal business? What did Ian Leloir mean? Maybe Jimmy split on "personal business" the way my mother got a heart attack. If Leloir was telling the truth, then . . . but what if he wasn't? What if "a few days" turned into a week, a month, until the end of the season, and still Jimmy didn't come back to his job? Who would give a shit? Jimmy was just a drifter, and the cast would be too busy with itself to remember a handyman. But what if Jimmy had actually set out to quit right that instant when he knocked on Ian Leloir's office door? What if the vision he saw in the gleam of light was really a warning? What if The Finger told him to run?

I had promised to stay for the rehearsal, so after switching a few gels and realigning some of the lights, I took my seat again and numbly stared at the stage as *The Fantasticks* came to its end.

In Act Two the lovers fall out, Luisa is seduced by El Gallo, and Matt is pummeled by the misfortunes of a cruel world before the two lovers, made wiser by pain, come back to each other.

I hardly paid attention to any of it, my brain swirling with conjectures about Jimmy's fate. But after El Gallo fights with the Boy over Luisa's love, then abandons her to her own loss of innocence, he addresses the audience about "a curious paradox." Suddenly I tuned in to El Gallo's poem, listening to the words as if they had come from somewhere else, a message meant only for me.

Who understands why Spring is born
Out of Winter's laboring pain?
Or why we all must die a bit
Before we grow again?

That was it. Jimmy must die a bit. I must die a bit. But then we'll come back, all my friends, all of us. We'll fly away, visit crazy places, then come down. But first we must die, and then we'll grow into something the world has never seen before, something truly amazing.

Jimmy will return. Just wait and see. Maybe I'll see him in Carbondale fixing washing machines and watching the planet burn. Or I'll run into him suddenly in upstate New York working in the kitchen at a resort in the Catskills. No matter where I come upon him, he'll be smoking Lucky Strikes and drinking Cokes and staring at the ceiling, and he'll tell me the truth: The Finger actually told him to disappear; it told him to split for Nineveh.

Jimmy can't be dead.

I went up to Alice after the rehearsal, complimented her performance, and gave her my line about leaving.

She beamed, too excited about the opening night coming up to think too much about a mere tech making farewells. But I forced myself on her. "Alice, listen to me. Can you say good-bye to Jimmy for me when he comes back—and give him this?" I held out a slip of paper with my phone number on it.

"You mean—*you* and Jimmy? You guys been *doing* it?" she teased back at me.

"C'mon, Alice—not everyone's a fag."

She smiled and took the piece of paper back to her dressing room.

"I worked with him, you know, and he's taken off for a few days," I called after her. "I just want to see how he's doing, and I didn't get the chance."

She whirled around and grabbed me. "Kiss me good-bye so I won't think you're a fag."

SECOND SUITE

THE LAUGHING DISEASE

The Laughing Disease

2004

Dear Hilton Obenzinger,

A friend's daughter goes to Stanford, and she told me of your project to gather revelations, which sounds like a wonderful idea. I want to add another story to your collection, if I may. It's my aunt's story, actually, so I hope you don't mind if I tell it for her. She passed away some time ago, so there would be no other way to tell it. I didn't know this story until she was quite old, and when she told it to me, it was, for me, a little revelation in itself. But she was the one who had the experience, even though she admitted that she never quite understood what it was all about or what it truly revealed. She did say it changed her life, and I believe her.

My Aunt Elizabeth was a proper British lady, and she moved near my family in Seattle to live by her younger sister for the last ten or so years of her life. She hadn't married, and she was alone. She liked my brother and me, but she was not especially fond of children, particularly if they were loud and rambunctious. And kids' laughter would make her wince. She spent her time visiting the park and feeding the ducks, living a quiet life, and if a little troop of children came by squealing and giggling and chasing the ducks, she would quietly retire until they were gone. She never talked much, either. But one day, she told me the story of the laughing madness.

In 1962, Auntie had been a teacher in a missionary school for girls between twelve and eighteen in Kashasha in the Bukoba district of Tanganyika. The country had just become independent from Britain, but it had yet to merge with Zanzibar and rename itself Tanzania. There was much excitement in the air, everyone was expecting big things to happen as a result of independence, and everyone felt that the children, including the young girls of my aunt's class, were part of a generation that would change Africa forever. It was exciting, of course, but everyone was nervous, especially those little girls who were given the big burden of the future to carry.

One day, she was teaching geography—the idea of the isthmus. *Isthmus* is one of those funny little words, and one of the girls giggled, understandably. Another girl said some kind of witticism or joke—Auntie did not remember what it was—and more girls began to laugh. Soon the whole class was laughing. There was nothing remarkable about this: Twelve-year-old girls, even shy, well-behaved girls, can find themselves giggling over the smallest things. And there was nothing remarkable when, after a bit, she hushed the class, and they fell silent; but as soon as she said, "And now, back to the isthmus," they burst out laughing once more.

They would laugh, and then settle down and compose themselves, then someone would giggle, and they would burst out laughing again.

At first, Auntie joined them for a giggle or two, but after a while she became stern—something difficult for that gentle lady to do. Well, her scowl just provoked more howls of laughter.

Finally, it came time to dismiss the class, and the giggling bunch headed out, where they met other girls who got swept up in the contagion and started laughing themselves. Soon the entire school was laughing, and off they went, heading home, where they met children from other schools, and once they met up and cavorted, these students began to laugh as well.

The next day started normally enough, but then again, for no apparent reason, one of the girls started to giggle, and once more the entire class was swept into the maelstrom. The uproar caused girls in the neighboring classes to burst out, and soon the entire school was overtaken. The teachers poked their heads into the courtyard and held a quick conference. One after the other tried to quiet the children, but as soon as the girls contained themselves, the effort to be serious would cause one of them to burst out, and the whole school would start up again.

All of this is remarkable enough. Now comes the point where the whole episode took on a character so bizarre, so unbelievable, that my aunt became afraid. This is the time when, as she said, all of Tanganyika seemed to be swallowed by the Laughing Disease. Laughter took hold of all the schools in Kashasha, and then it spread to schools in neighboring villages, and soon the entire region was filled with laughter.

Everything pretty much came to a stop. It was impossible to conduct classes at school or to attend church. Mostly it was children who were affected—and mainly, but not only, girls. Yet adults would get swept up from time to time, too. And, you understand, this was not laughter without end—it's impossible to laugh without breathing, eating, or sleeping. But after a brief interlude of respite, something would trigger it again. A sweet fourteen-year-old girl at home, helping Mum prepare dinner, for example, would suddenly burst out again, for no apparent reason. Risible waves would sweep over whole villages and then recede, and then flow back again. And this was not always mirth, my aunt assured me. The laughter would often overwhelm, and a little girl would burst into tears or she would scream in pain. Rashes broke out, headaches pounded, tears flowed—but then the laughter would begin again.

Auntie became really concerned, and she was not alone. The teachers and village adults would meet, whispering, afraid that any noise could trigger another bout, trying to figure out how to subdue the epidemic. The new government was terribly embarrassed. I could imagine some government official thinking, "This riot of giggles is the response to the great expectations of independence—how shameful!" They prevented reporters from coming to see the afflicted, to keep the shame within bounds. One of the results of the news blackout was that there were no outside witnesses, so the whole episode became murky and took on the character of a legend, even as it occurred, and its reputation only kept growing the more it receded into the past.

No effort to stop the laughter seemed to work, and repression only seemed to make it worse. Days, then weeks, then months passed. Auntie told me that the madness lasted at least six months, but she doesn't really know anymore. Others told her that it lasted twice or even three times as long. Aunt Elizabeth lost track of time. She stayed in her cottage listening to guffaws and howls and screams erupt from time to time and sweep from one end of Kashasha to the other.

Eventually, the government surrounded each village with grim, humorless troops. Every village was sealed off from the other villages and the outside world. They were effectively quarantined. The isolation prevented the contagion from renewing itself, and one village after another grew quiet, returned to calm, and the great Laughing Disease came to an end.

As soon as Aunt Elizabeth could, she left Kashasha. She never returned, and she never taught again, anywhere. She told me that, while she did not lose her faith in God, she had seen something that shook her to the bottom of her soul. She realized that there is some weird force in people. We usually train ourselves to control this strangeness or it is kept hidden, but the fact of the matter is that something utterly inhuman is hidden in the human soul, and this chaos or whatever it is can erupt at any time.

Auntie grew terribly frightened of people, especially children; she knew something that made her mistrustful, and she shrank back at children's laughter, in particular. I can't tell you how being in the presence of crowds would throw her into a panic. She told me that a single person possessed the famous "herd mentality"—no one needed a mob to become irrational; the madness was hidden in each breast, full-blown. The actual mass of individuals at a carnival or at a rally or on crowded downtown streets amounted to an atom bomb in her eyes.

To me, laughter is wonderful, a gift from God. But to her, it meant something else, and the Laughing Disease changed her life forever.

I was very touched by what my aunt told me, and I thought you might be interested in this little story and add it to your files.

Yours,
M_____ Y_____

Canal Street

I maneuvered around trucks and crowded loading docks, pushing across Canal Street to stand outside my father's storefront at the corner of Broadway and Walker. I opened the door—the automatic doorbell clacking weakly—then moved down the narrow tunnel of cardboard cartons and textile rolls that filled the entire length of the long loft to spot my father standing beside his desk with Mrs. Lopez and her two husbands haggling over a deal.

"Well, hello! Look who's here! *It's the boss!*" he exclaimed as I stood at the door of the glass-enclosed office.

My father had named his business the Hilton Textile Corporation after the birth of his youngest son (as well as to escape creditors by means of incorporation), and it was his standard joke to make me "the real boss."

"He's the one with the money, not me! Do you remember Mrs. Lopez, Hilton?"

I did. The lady from the Philippines was one of his regular customers. She didn't really have two husbands, I suppose, but every time she came into the Hilton Textile Corporation, the two well-dressed Filipino men followed after her, holding attaché cases and sitting silently behind her. Mrs. Lopez did all the bargaining; and then, when it seemed a deal was struck, she would go off and consult with her two husbands, then return with her counteroffer. I could never tell whether she fronted for the businessmen, doing all the talking while they were the real brains behind the operation, or whether she turned to the men as a ruse directed at my father or as a ritual to offer her two husbands

SECOND SUITE: THE LAUGHING DISEASE   44

all the appearance of power while she was really the one to call the shots.

I greeted Mrs. Lopez and her two husbands, and then retreated to the back of the loft to tuck myself in between two cartons to wait.

Mrs. Lopez's ways were no more curious than those of Mr. Nehrula, my father's client from New Delhi, who really did have two wives. Jews, Indians, Filipinos, the whole world would cross his threshold to haggle. Here was a place where buying and selling was the real Esperanto, and no matter if the gentleman from Haiti only spoke French, terms could always be reached. It was a business, also, that took risks as a matter of course, as trade twisted and turned with all the vicissitudes of life—especially wars, coups, revolutions. My father used to do business with Cuba, the Belgian Congo, the Dominican Republic, Laos, Vietnam, but history closed up shop in each of those places one by one, and he lost plenty of money as a result. Yet the world is large, and he still managed to sell goods to Chile and Argentina, to Lebanon and Israel, even to Texas. He had even sold all the khaki to outfit the entire Moroccan army.

As a kid I'd climb over the bales and cartons and the big tubes of goods clogging up the whole floor. When I got to some place way off in the corner or in the back, I would shout out the numbers scrawled on the tags so that my dad's assistant, Saul, a short, balding Orthodox gentleman who always wore a cap with a visor as his secular yarmulke, would repeat them. Then Dad would punch in the numbers, crank the noisy old Remington adding machine, and yell them out again to confirm the yardage bought or sold.

It was a constant task, this keeping track of inventory, and with the vast accumulation of cartons leaving only a narrow path to the office space in the back, it was one way a kid could help. Otherwise, my dad and Saul, along with Albert, the black trucker who was an ex-coal miner with lung problems from West Virginia, would have to take the hand truck and shuffle cartons from one side to the other like one of those number puzzles on a keychain in order to reach the right ones. I would climb over mountains of khaki and denim to call out each number, feeling important, but soon I would begin to choke on the acrid textile dust. I'd feel hemmed in, claustrophobic, and no matter how much I tried not to, I would begin to hate the place and the gray dust of commerce and fidget until it was time to go.

This time was no different. I couldn't bear suffocating in my nook any longer, so I climbed up on the cartons, careful not to trip on the metal strapping bands, to perch against the rear wall. From my lookout on the carton tops a sea of cardboard stretched before me, my father's windowed office like a lone ship locked in the Arctic ice. Way in the front, close to the door, Albert kept his eyes peeled for friends and clients passing up and down Broadway. I watched the bargaining, the give and take, eyeing my father as he laughed and bickered and cajoled.

My father, Nat, was born in a small town outside of Lublin where his own father, a used-shoe merchant and pious rabbi, did his business and his prayers. After the rabbi left for America to buy old shoes to sell back in Poland, World War I broke out, and at the age of seven or eight Nat became a refugee to avoid the carnage. His mother packed all she could into a cart to Lublin, where they rented a small single room with only a dirt floor in the basement of a large apartment building. There the five of them — mother, three sons, daughter — were squeezed in two beds to form an L, leaving room for barely anything else. When Nat slept, curling up against his older brother's feet, he put a board over his eyes to keep the rats from scurrying across his face. They used their beds for tables to eat what little they could find.

His sister had gotten badly burned from a pot of boiling water while working for the landlord, his older brother was a rabbinical student and was useless for anything practical, and his younger brother was still too small, so it was up to Nat to help forage for food. Early each morning he joined his mother, who bundled up with layers of dresses and overcoats against the chill, to wait on line for their ration of terrible bread made from chestnuts and hay. At eight o'clock the little door over the tiny window of the bakery would slide open, a hand would take the coins in exchange for the bread, and the frenzied crowd, no longer a line, would press wildly toward the tiny opening. With the hungry mob packed tightly together into a solid mass, Nat could only reach the window by jumping up on top of the crowd and stretching out on the sea of heads to wriggle and float with his hands extended until he reached the window to grab his prize.

He would grab in other ways, too. When the landlord's son came down the steps with a roll and butter, Nat would snap it from his hands. Then he graduated to guarding other kids who were afraid of getting jumped, agreeing to protect them through dark alleys and hallways in exchange for a part of their loaves. He put a nail on the end of a stick and walked through the open market, spearing an apple and then dashing away at top speed. He had no shoes, but he even got a job hauling a cart like a rickshaw loaded with firewood, cutting his bare feet on stones and glass as he delivered the sticks to different buildings.

But no matter what he did, the hunger grew, blotting out thoughts of anything else. A nibble of chestnut bread never satisfied, only kept the pain at bay, and all he could do was work and steal and stand outside in the warm sun to try to forget the gnawing worm of starvation. His little brother could not, however, and Nat sat at the foot of his bed, rubbing his feet and hands, watching him grow weaker day by day. One night, he sat at Aaron's feet crying and begging that the boy hold out, but he was too young, too frail, and as Nat stared into his eyes, Aaron smiled back at his brother and gave him his last breath.

Reckless, Nat climbed to the rooftop to see the Germans and the Russians battle, shells whizzing overhead. Eventually the war ended, money from his father in America began to arrive, Trotsky marched near Lublin briefly, and then normal life began once more. His father returned, by this time an American citizen, although he loathed the country, a place where they worked on Shabbas, where a Jew lost his faith even before he could finish wrapping the *tefillin*.

All of Nat's friends had begun to leave—to Paris, to Palestine, to a technical institute in Belgium, anywhere, just so long as they could flee Poland—and, with U.S. citizenship bestowed upon him by his father's misfortune of becoming marooned, Nat began his own campaign to go there, fed up with fighting the goyim whenever they lost their soccer matches to the wiry Jewish boys. Why fear the boy going to America, his uncle interceded, "he's already a goy." Finally, his father relented and Nat raced to buy the next Cunard ticket, only to discover afterward that the ship would arrive on Yom Kippur, although he took it despite the transgression. His father, already in New York on another business trip, awaited his arrival, but since his ship came to dock on the Day of Atonement, Nat wandered for a day until his father was done with his prayers to collect his son. The rabbi arranged for a job at a factory, owned by a man from Lublin, that fired watch cases, and then his father returned to Poland and his piety.

Nat's progress was like that of so many immigrants—at least the ones who lived to tell the tale—that it almost does not bear repeating. He soon left the watch factory, choosing lower pay in the garment business rather than risk losing a finger in the metal press. First he went to night school to learn English, then on to Seward High School, and finally to Columbia's Textile Institute to learn how to become a converter, a designer of weaves and fabric patterns, all the while working for a shop that manufactured ties. After starvation in Lublin, the Depression in New York seemed painless, and he continued to prosper, marrying my mother—"a *tchachka* right off the boat," as he described her. Only in America could there be such a match: the Yiddish-speaking son of the pious rabbi with the cultured Polish-speaking daughter of the modern, assimilated gentleman.

The newlyweds traveled to Poland to visit both families in 1938, and Nat tried to convince them that Hitler was more than the usual Jew hater, that the families had to flee, and he could make it easy for them in America. But his father still disdained Moloch, preferring to outlast yet one more Jew-hating monster to cling to his piety, while my mother's father—who had fought with Pilsudski and was the highest Jewish civil servant in the country—was too much of a patriot to abandon his Polish homeland.

From America, Nat watched his family perish, all of them, with the exception of his cousin, a rabbi who had fled with his wife into the forest outside of Lublin. A peasant had just had a vision of the Holy Virgin Mary, and the Blessed Lady told the poor, uneducated man that he must save a Jew, anyone. And so it came to pass that the rabbi and his wife were the ones to stumble across his field just then, and for five years the man hid the couple in his attic, saying his rosaries, fighting off his own son's cowardly threats of betrayal. Everyone else from Nat's family perished in Majdanek, only mounds of shoes and eyeglasses and gold fillings left behind, and he cursed first Hitler then his father's stubborn piety for the evil.

After the war, he prospered more, entered the wholesale trade, and raised three sons, and life seemed gloriously happy in the big Tudor-style house in Laurelton, Queens, until that day when Ronnie stretched his arms over his head and my mother screamed at the lump in his armpit. Nine months or so and it was over—surgery, recovery, treatment, death. No Virgin Mary appeared to save Ronnie. Nat sat by his bedside watching, just as he had watched his brother, holding Ronnie's hand as he died. *"Daddy, I'm afraid, I'm afraid,"* Ronnie had whispered, but Nat could do nothing to lessen the fear and the terrible certainty of death.

After the tears of the funeral, he would cry only when he drove. With the road hypnotically unrolling before him, perhaps he felt no one was watching—although we all did, each silently staring out the window, each making believe we didn't see—as he would lose himself in grief and rage. Picking me up at the subway at Kew Gardens or going shopping at Green Acres, he would mumble to himself and slam the steering wheel, his eyes glistening, arguing with fate, cursing God. I would watch him pound the Buick's steering wheel, the man who had seen everyone he loved die again and again while all he could do was prosper. But money meant nothing, could do nothing, when death mocked him, took all that he cherished while always leaving him behind.

He would always be left to watch, to witness, and to suffer in his success.

The Legend of Hilton Obenzinger
2004

Vic Seidel, the Stanford graduate student who had been an editor of
Hilton Obenzinger, contacted me again. This time he had a copy of a
page from the 1983 Port Light Yearbook, Schreiber High School, Port
Washington, New York:

> *Hilton Obenzinger,* a magazine founded by Josh Berman, helped
> add laughter to the sometimes boring Schreiber halls. Its editors and
> panel of writers included Bruce Jacobs, Jason Diehl, Matt Healy, Bill
> Geller, Lisa Greenstein, Chris Lauricella. Miss Dissin was the faculty
> adviser.
>
> *Hilton Obenzinger,* named after a legendary Columbia student,
> was created to give student writers a new option. It fills space between
> *The Schreiber Times* and *Kaleidoscope.*

So it wasn't simply the oddness of my name—I had assumed that
someone had seen one of my books and found the name a laugh riot:
"What a ridiculous name—perfect for our humor magazine!" But "a
legendary Columbia student" meant that someone had found a connection to my college days, even the "legendary" part, whatever they
meant by that.

But who unearthed that connection—and why? The students were
too young—even the parents would have been the wrong age—I graduated in 1969. Was it Miss Dissin, the adviser? Or did the key to the
mystery rest in the hands of Josh Berman? Would I ever find out how
Hilton Obenzinger came to be my alter ego?

Writers' Week

2006

Every spring I'm invited to speak to students at Los Altos High School, close to Stanford, as part of their Writers' Week, a time when they invite writers of all sorts to visit the school. The students read excerpts of whatever I'm working on; then I come and share some thoughts about the writing life and explain what drives me to do something so frustrating yet exhilarating.

I talk to them about how stories keep me going, and how they can make sense of their own lives if they tell stories to themselves, and if they find out about each other's stories, and if they ask their grandparents for theirs and any ordinary person they meet out on the street— that they would discover wonders, and the stories of their own lives would join up with all of theirs to be part of something really terrific, something greater than any one of us.

They think I'm nuts.

But then I ask them if any of them like to write. Writing is too much a school thing, so many of them are caught by surprise by the strange idea that they might actually like writing. Most of them can't conceive of enjoying something they are forced to do, although I know there are those, too shy to speak up in class, who write secret poems or stories or cook up hip-hop eruptions for their friends.

After a moment of blank stares I ask them if anyone sends text messages on their phones. They all smile and nod. Nothing like ubiquitous cell phones to make new art.

"So, you're really all writers, after all," I exclaim.

Afterward, I receive letters and emails from the students: the usual thank-you notes they're egged on to write by their teachers, but sometimes I get questions, and from time to time a sample of their own true stories.

After one of these visits, I received a letter with a story that was so remarkable, I could hardly believe it. I had asked for such stories, but I didn't expect to get something like this.

Dear Mr. Obenzinger,

I am a student at Los Altos High School, and you came to my English class during Writers' Week. We had read your story about hearing a loud quack and thinking that God was a duck, and you described your project of collecting the stories of people who realize something surprising or learn something new, and collecting what you remember too. I didn't want to say anything in class, but I have a story you might find useful in your collection. I hope you can use it.

You see, I survived the tsunami that devastated Thailand and Indonesia and the other parts around the Indian Ocean. That's a big story everyone's heard about, I know. But the story I want to tell you is one that a lot of people don't know about and it's a little bit odd.

I was with my parents, spending Christmas vacation at a resort in Thailand. There were elephant rides at this resort, and I loved to watch all nine of the elephants. As many as eight people would climb up on one of these giants, and they would lumber off into the forest and on to the beach and over to the lagoon and back again, with everyone on their backs rolling from side to side, and then they would be done and all the passengers would step off onto a little platform and climb down to the ground. When they weren't giving rides, the elephants would stand around, chained to little posts, and kids would come by to feed the elephants peanuts and stuff. It makes a big impression to see nine elephants all lined up in a row throwing their trunks from side to side. I loved it.

The morning after Christmas I was watching the elephants. Besides snorkeling, this was my favorite part of the trip. All of a sudden four of them that had just gotten back from giving rides got very agitated. I thought this was a treat—rampaging elephants—at least from a safe distance. The handlers hadn't chained them up yet, and they bumped into the other elephants to help them tear free from their posts, and then all nine of them stampeded up the little hill. This was awesome—I didn't know what to think, and neither did the handlers, who yelled after the beasts and did everything they could to make them come back. Instead, the elephants gathered up on the hill and they started bellowing with their trunks, and it was so loud and so demanding that people at the resort started to run up the hill to see what they were bellowing about.

That's when, looking down from the hill, we saw how the water had pulled back so far from the beach, how weird that was, and then we could see the gray line in the distance come closer and closer as the wall of ocean raced to the shore. The elephants kept trumpeting, and more people raced up the hill, but when finally the tsunami hit, not everybody had listened to the warning of the elephants. The force of the wave was astounding—it seemed to fill up the sky and destroyed everything in front of it with such huge power that it made you feel that you were helpless, and everyone was filled with fear and horror—but we were the safe ones on top of the hill. The elephants had known that the wave was coming, and they had saved us just because we were curious about why they were bellowing so much.

When the water receded, the elephants charged down the hill, and I could see them pick up little kids with their trunks and put them on their backs and then run back up the hill. They did this over and over, and when they could find no more kids, they started to help with the adults, pulling them out of the debris and lifting them up on their backs and carrying them up to the hill. They ended up rescuing over forty people, and then they carried up the bodies of three dead grown-ups and one little boy. I had never seen elephants move so fast, and they seemed so graceful stepping through the wreckage, scooping up one survivor after another.

The elephants wouldn't allow their handlers to jump up on their backs again until all of this was done. And then they began to use their trunks to pull apart the trees and other debris, going to work as they always did with people mounted on their backs, slowly and methodically hauling away logs and boats. They were beautiful and solemn in their hugeness and devotion.

Anything about the tsunami is an amazing story, I know. But I felt very special—to be there at such an event, to survive, and to see what the elephants did. When I saw more of the wreckage around Phuket—and especially when I saw the films on TV of all the other places, and the videos of the huge wall of water—I felt that I had really seen something, and I was so lucky. I knew how powerful nature was, how big the universe was, and how little humans are. In fact, humans are puny but we think we have big heads.

We think we're so special, but we can be swallowed up by a wave in an instant, just like that. These are just words, I know, but the feeling is something else. When what you know is deep inside of yourself, when you stand right next to the hugeness, you change the way you look at things. It's not just that I'm more serious now or I'm afraid or I've become a religious fanatic. It's something more: I know that I don't know.

Maybe I would have learned that just from the tsunami. But seeing the elephants mixed it up, and made everything even more complicated. They are so big and so powerful themselves—and yet they came to the help of us pitiful humans. Why did they help us? In all of that bigness of nature, and in all of that not caring and the way humans get tossed around like twigs, it's not as if nature was mean or malicious; it just does its work, and people don't really count. But in all of that, there was the possibility that elephants could love humans, the idea that animals could feel sorry for us—and especially after all the terrible things we do to them, how could such a thing be? And can love be more powerful than a giant wave?

Sincerely,
Kevin _____

Buffalo Bill
1966

I stayed in 617 Furnald Hall during my freshman year at college. Many years later I learned that this was the very dorm room in which Federico García Lorca lived when he studied briefly at Columbia, which may explain the visions I entertained there.

More important for this story were the "parietal rules": Girls could only be up in a Columbia student's room during certain hours, and only if your door was open at least the space of a book. Students, of course, interpreted that measure in our own narrow, letter-of-the-law fashion, readily squeezing books—thin matchbooks—into closed doors.

I had gotten to know Buffalo Bill when I worked at the Woodstock Playhouse as an apprentice two summers before I started college, and we met up at a Japanese restaurant. Her name was really Wilhelmina Cody, but everyone called her Buffalo Bill—and after we crunched down some tempura, she came up to my dorm room to slow-dance to Johnny Mathis, matchbook properly in place. I was aware that the slow-dance bit was a very clumsy routine from junior high school, but it was the only art of seduction I knew, and after a while of grinding we started to make out. Wrobolewski had the bottom bunk, but the football player was off at a game. Even so, we climbed up to my own top bunk to do it under the sheets.

I was a little disappointed, of course, given how furtive it was to have sex in a narrow dorm-room bunk bed. It didn't seem to take very long—yet that didn't matter: The moment had come, and I had lost my virginity at last.

There was a knock at the door.

"Who's ther—"

The door swiftly pushed open before I could finish, the matchbook tumbling to the floor, and there stood my father, his thin brown face tilted up expectantly. "Hi—why do you have this in your—?"

"*DAD! GET OUT!*"

He looked up to see Buffalo Bill sliding under sheets, squealing, and got the picture in a flash. Very quietly he shut the door and fled. "I'll meet you downstairs in the lobby!" I called out after him.

I could hardly believe it. My dad had just barged into my room the very first time I got a chance to have sex. It was too much like a joke: "A funny thing happened on my way to losing my virginity . . ." It was too funny, really, and all I could do was laugh. Buffalo Bill was not laughing at all, and she had turned deathly pale as we both jumped down to clamber into our clothes. I instructed her to leave first—just go out the elevator, and walk right through the hall and out the door with her eyes straight ahead. Don't look to the right or to the left—don't even look at anyone in front. She did as I said, while I walked into the lobby a few moments after her, trying not to giggle. My dad caught a glance of Buffalo Bill as she rushed past him, her head bowed, her eyes fixed to the floor, her face the color of Mao's Little Red Book.

"Dad, why didn't you call first?"

"Is she Jewish?" he asked, skipping the pleasantries or explanations.

"I don't know. I didn't ask."

"Is she a prosti—"

"Please, Dad," I stopped him. "I know her from working at the Woodstock Playhouse. She's a friend."

"Are you, uh, protecting yourself? You know, you can get a disease . . ."

Here was the roaring beast of sex itself, and his son no less. Yet all he wanted to know was if I had a Trojan: Health, not prudery, was the first item of business.

"Don't worry," I replied with an involuntary grin.

He was treating it as natural, as wild oats, and I suppose he was happy that at least it was a woman he had caught me in bed with; and then he forgot the whole thing, starting to talk about school and everything else. Awkward as he was, he was kind and gracious and concerned.

As we walked to get a little lunch at the Chock Full O' Nuts on the corner of 116th Street, I chuckled to myself: *My first time, and that's just when my dad walks in . . .*

I had sex for the first time. But as a result, I discovered something completely unexpected: how much I loved my father.

Memory
1967

"I don't want to remember," Amy shot back. "If you remember everything, then there's no more room for anything new. You have to forget. Even if it's painful, it's best to forget."

"That's just what I mean," I continued. "It's gone. Forgetting is getting old—it's death, oblivion—and you don't even know what's happened to your life. You just forget."

"You're wrong. Getting old is not forgetting—remembering is."

"Remembering? That doesn't make sense."

"Of course it does," she went on. "If you forget, you forget. That's it. How can it matter if you've forgotten? But when you remember, that's when you know life has slipped right by—and telling the story over and over to fill up the hole in your heart is bullshit. It's a bottomless pit, an endless garbage dump.

"Sure, telling stories is wonderful, but only if it's a way to let them go, to give them to someone else, pass them on, forget. You don't want to remember pain. Only victims have to repeat the horror over and over, and remembering just makes you more of a victim."

Amy was my girlfriend, we had just met that summer, and we began to argue over the respective merits of forgetting and remembering. It was a stupid, fractious argument, and the heat generated from our differences seemed way out of proportion to the issue at hand. Somehow, it seemed to pertain to how we felt about being in college and the idea that maybe we would go off together to find our lives. Did it matter if we would remember our college days?

"You know what my dad said?" she continued. "My dad told me he knew he was getting old when—you know how he could tell he was getting old?"

"No, how?" I delivered her cue.

"He could tell he was getting old when he would remember something."

"So? Getting old is memories?"

"No, that isn't all of it, let me finish," she snapped. "He said he would suddenly remember something, anything—some kind of pain, even some happy time, his first kiss, a fight in high school—anything at all. You know, walking down the street, reading a book, no matter what you're doing, and all of a sudden you get zapped by a memory?"

"Yeah?"

"Well, first he would have a flash of recognition, a quick realization, that typical thrill of recall, then—well, the memory would sink in, and he would remember the event. Yes, that was his old experience—yes, he recalled the old familiar feel of it, the comfortable fact of it, no matter how distressing or awkward or embarrassing it might have been when he first experienced it. Then he would settle in to savor the details of it all—that usual way memory opens up like a flower, the way the original moment is kind of born again—when all of a sudden he would be overcome by a strange thought."

"Which was?"

"*How boring.*"

"How boring?"

"Exactly. How boring. No matter what the memory was, no matter how painful or how delightful, it was still his old memory. It was still that same, used-up, squeezed-out experience he had been dragging around in his skull for twenty, thirty, forty years. After he made that realization, the memory simply felt tedious, and then he just nodded recognition to himself and let the whole thing go."

"That's it?"

"Isn't that enough? He knew he was reaching old age when he got bored with the same old stories of his own life, and ever since then he says he's stopped bothering to cultivate his memories. He simply got bored with himself, just couldn't be interested anymore. That's one of the reasons he went back to acting, his passion when he was young that he left to become an insurance executive. He wanted to discover someone else's memories, to enter a character's past, so that he wouldn't be so damned bored with his own."

"Weird."

"I don't think so. Don't you get it? If you forget more, maybe the events in your life that you do remember won't be so boring. Did you ever think of that?"

Knots

1968

It was a few years before it became popular for artists to occupy lofts around Canal Street, sharing space with the garment factories and textile businesses, and Beatrice's place was one of the first.

Other than a few stools, a folding table, and her easel, the only pieces of furniture were a bed and a dresser pressed up close to the door.

The rest of the darkened hall stretched to a bank of windows that covered one entire wall, the cavernous loft filled with a jungle of ropes and strings hanging from the steel beams, all knotted and trussed up and noosed. Dozens of large paintings of knots, every imaginable kind of knot, shared the space with coils of nylon cord, bristling twine, sailor's hemp, spools of string.

Her canvases displayed knots with luminous intensity, tan or dark brown ropes set against off-white backgrounds, some knots so convoluted, so tightly drawn, that they gave off pain, anger, sorrow, the hairs from the ropes shooting out like spikes. Others were threaded loosely, as if the ends were yet to be pulled tight or they were coming undone, so you could easily follow the bends of the ropes, and these paintings seemed playful, even comic. I barely remembered a square knot from the Boy Scout handbook, so I couldn't tell what kinds they were, except that many were complicated, and the more I stared at them, the less I could figure how the ropes looped in and out to form such strangely hypnotic mandalas.

Some paintings had inscriptions along with the knots. One small pattern of red ribbon had a quotation from somewhere painted alongside it: "The Primary Object and Expected Result of Every Magic Knot Is Some Form of Prior Restraint." A silver string bowed around a bulging blue bag with the title "Wind Bag." Another canvas showed the coils of the *tefillin* wrapped around a very hairy arm, the follicles themselves twisted and knotted, alongside the words from the Torah in Hebrew and English: "Bind them for a sign upon thine hand." Next to that, a vertical series of knots as if they were all coming undone at once was captioned with the words: "Mohammed untying the Jewish magician's knots." A fuzzy thread of blue wool was twisted in another series:

This knot I knit,
This knot I tie,
To see my love
As he goes by.

"Beatrice, you're totally out of your mind!"

She smiled broadly, happy that I was pleased, my mind genuinely blown.

"How did you come up with such a crazy idea? What drove you to this mania?"

Beatrice told me of her dream.

A large black snake had slid around her neck, and then it coiled into a knot in front of her eyes. The dream had been deeply engrossing yet not at all frightening: just the standard phallic emblem is what she had thought when she awoke. But when she bent to tie her sneakers that morning, she felt inexplicably drawn into the knot her hands had begun to form, watching the laces loop and bow with increasing fascination, repeating the operation she had done automatically from childhood again and again. Soon she began to play with ropes, twisting and pulling them into endless patterns, sensing some kind of meaning locked in each coil and loop. In the days following, she went to the library to dig out old mariner-knot catalogs and folklore charm-knot compendiums, always twisting and tying one or another noose, Turkhead, slipknot, four-loop plinthios, all sorts of oddly named knots. Inevitably, knots began to fill every one of her canvases. She had no idea why she had become so obsessed, only that she found the expanding mystery of knots endlessly fascinating, her obsession filling her studio with one version after another.

Then she went behind her easel to pull out her latest work.

On a very large canvas was a huge, hideous bulge of intestines boiling into a convulsion of knobs and knots, a twisted, undulating blob that appeared to have been sliced horizontally just a split-second before—I could sense the saber whizzing just off the edge—both halves of the blob tilting slightly to the left with the momentum of the cut, blood and guts momentarily suspended before splattering to the floor. Next to the blob Beatrice had inscribed "Gordian Knot."

"Holy shit," I whispered.

Beatrice began to chatter excitedly about her ideas for new paintings: molecular structures, surgical knots, umbilical cords, math formulas, lassos, testicles, highway interchanges. The whole world seemed to have opened before her as an imprint of one or another kind of knot. It was as if she had discovered the secret double helix of all being.

Quietly I pushed the swaying ropes and macramés off to the side to make my way to the window. Across the narrow street I could see only another dark commercial hulk, just like Beatrice's building, with drifts of soot blackening its gray sills. Each floor was darkened with cardboard cartons or other marks of storage except for the one right below ours. Its row of windows was filled with bright fluorescent light, an illuminated belt across an otherwise blank torso.

Through the windows I could see a little factory still busy in the early evening. Women bent over sewing machines, about ten rows of them. I could only see the four or five sitting closest to the windows as they angled the textiles around their Singers, stitching cuttings into blouses or pants, but I imagined the ones hidden from view were also Puerto Rican or black. Against the far wall I could just make out the pale hands of a man with long shears that swung from overhead wires as he sliced through thick piles of goods on a great table. Occasionally, young black men patrolled the aisles handing out piles of cut fabrics or picking up finished goods. Not a sound escaped, yet I could sense the clatter of the machines.

I could see down Broadway almost to my father's storefront, and it felt very odd to stand among these paintings to look out at the world of business.

"But . . . why all these knots?" I asked Beatrice.

Her eyes drooped. She didn't really know, only that she had begun something important that seemed to have no end, and one canvas would be completed and another would be started, like the bolts of cotton chugging through the sewing machines across the street.

I noticed that Beatrice was standing right beside me as I looked out the window at the factory. I could feel her soft, ample breasts gently pressing into my arm. Taking my hand, she tied a fuzzy piece of blue wool around my index finger.

"Remember me," she whispered.

Reflect on Me

1962–1966

Nothing was ever the same after Ronnie's death. I would shun every Saint Patrick's Day celebration, even though technically Ronnie expired in the early hours of the following morning. I would wear no green, and his death in the awful green of the hospital room was marked by my revulsion to all shades of green (except in trees and plants, where the color of life belongs). All public sorrows began to carry hidden messages of the private one. When Kennedy was assassinated, I too wept at little John-John's salute, but it was for my brother that I cried in front of the TV.

Instead of riding my bike to Andrew Jackson High School, I would from time to time veer off and cut school, spending the morning at the tiny patch of the Springfield Cemetery. The colonial graveyard was surrounded on three sides by acres of Montefiore's newcomer Jews, a whole city of dead Jews who were regularly visited by live ones, but no one visited the tilted copper-colored headstones of the early settlers. I would open the iron gate, walk through the tufted, unkempt, scrawny grass, and visit Abigail Hendrickson, dead in 1794 at the age of nineteen.

> Those who pass reflect on me.
> In time this grave shall be for thee.

To have a 170-year-old dead girlfriend is morbid, of course. But I would see visions of her short life, read poems out loud to her, or simply sit in the sun beside her tombstone and find peace in inventing her life, somehow keeping her memory alive when no one else would. Two hundred years from now, would a young girl do the same for Ronnie?

But most of all there were the eyes. My idle doodles during classes were no longer intricate maps of cities and peninsulas and contours of mountains on which I would sketch complex, shifting battle lines of make-believe wars. They became faces, endless faces, each with pronounced, deep-set eyes. I would even just draw the eyes by themselves, circling around and around their pupils until the ballpoint dug through the paper. Large eyes, small eyes, round, oval, all sorts of eyes. I realized I was just repeating Ronnie's death stare over and over, never able to get enough of his wide-open gaze burning into me. The fact that I was obsessive was obvious, even to me, but I could not stop.

Remembering was not enough, is never enough. At Columbia I began to have strange dreams, to hear voices implore me to jump out of the windows of Furnald Hall. I began to see Jesus perched on his cross, and I unzipped his flesh and crawled inside through meat and fat, muscle and blood. I started to see shrinks. Through talk therapy (and unofficial sessions of LSD) I dug Ronnie up from the depths of my inner self. The ache I had felt had been secret, something to be kept to myself, from myself, the guilt hidden, but I was able to draw him out, feel how my life was forever distinguished from others as a result, although even such distinction was tinged with guilt. After all, others had been dealt pain far worse than mine.

Even at the funeral I had felt the guilt mix with grief, so the shrink's archeological excavation of hidden shame came as no surprise. I realized I had colluded with my parents to keep myself from knowing the truth. My mother explained that my father's cousin, the rabbi—the one who had survived the Nazis when a Polish peasant came upon him fleeing with his wife as they stumbled into his field just after the peasant had seen a vision of the Holy Virgin Mary, who had told him to save one miserable, hunted Jew—this rabbi explained the wisdom of the Talmud: In order to preserve the Law or to keep family peace, one can tell a lie, a white lie, a small one from the heart, and God will forgive you.

My parents never did lie, not really. They simply plugged up my ears with Polish. They had avoided the truth, they had papered over reality—I was the one who had lied. I could have known if I had wanted to, but I had kept at my piano contests, my junior high school parties, my horniness, all in a distracted haze, glad not to know.

"What Were You Students Thinking?"

1999

"Are you the Hilton Obenzinger who went to Columbia?"

"How many Hilton Obenzingers are there?"

Elisabeth Hansot taught political science at Stanford and saw my name. Columbia had its famed Great Books program, and she had been my Contemporary Civilization teacher nearly 40 years before.

Now she was on the phone, trying to identify a surprising find from her past. "Do you remember me?"

"Of course I remember you," I responded.

At a time when Columbia students were all men, and so were all the professors, Elisabeth Hansot was the only teacher I had who was a woman. The boys in her class relished that fact—and we all had shared one keen observation: She had great legs. There was hardly a glimmer of women's liberation at that time, and we enjoyed the presence of a female, *any* female. But she was also brilliant, and she cultivated her students with rigor and warmth and concern. I certainly remembered her.

I went over to Elisabeth's house on a wooded street of the Stanford campus. She was older, her hair gray, yet I recognized her instantly when she opened the door. She had the same alert eyes and clear face, and the same sonorous, cultured manner of speaking I had remembered, and we soon caught up on our lives over the last few decades, sipping glasses of beer.

She had left Columbia—not surprising, considering the hidebound attitudes that the first woman ever hired in the political science department had had to face. She went on to do education policy research for a senator in Washington, and married, taught at various schools, wrote books about female utopias and education. Eventually, she landed at Stanford with her husband, a professor of education.

I gave her my own thumbnail sketch: fleeing to the Yukon, teaching on the Indian reservation, working at the preschool, operating printing presses for the movement, radical activist, Indians, Mission District, Philippines, Palestine, poems, peace, technical and business writing, and on to Stanford.

"You know, I remember things about you," she said with a wry smile, after my story. I felt that queasiness that everyone who reconnects with their past must feel: Someone knows things about you that you no longer do.

She described how intense I had been, how I searched for the wisdom of those Great Books with burning zeal. I did remember that intensity; how I even parsed each of Thomas Aquinas's logical propositions—an absurd task—wrestled with Aristotle, lunged at Locke. Her class fed my freshman dreams of what the university would be: the grand quest, intellectual delirium, nights with chums in taverns posing Ultimate Questions over beer.

But then she went on to describe something more. In one class, we were studying Hegel, and I got so upset that she thought she might have to call for medical help.

I could recall the scene, vaguely. We had been reading *The Phenomenology of Spirit*, with all its wackiness about masters and slaves. I freaked out at Hegel's invented myth of everyone set on dominating each other, wrestling to see who would be on top. I couldn't remember precisely, only that I became agitated, began to visualize the text and to act it out, and I started to howl. It came upon me that Hegel was a fascist—a goddamned fascist—coming up with masters and slaves. And if Marx liked Hegel, even if he turned him on his head, there had to be something screwy about Marx. I had tasted Hegel's dialectic, and I felt like I was going to puke.

"I need to explain," I said, apologetically. "We were taking a lot of LSD and mescaline at that time. I may have been . . . maybe I was hallucinating . . . Who knows: At that moment, I may have *been* Hegel."

"Is that so?" she went on, nonplussed. "Yet if I had a classroom filled with students like you, if everyone had been as engaged as you were, I would never have been able to teach. You were so serious, so driven. *You were the student who felt too much.*"

This produced a jolt of mixed emotions. I did feel too much—each thinker would plunge deeply into my soul—but I may also have been playing, simply tripping out that day in Hegel's world.

I stammered an apology, but she dismissed it with a wave of her hand. It was a teacher's memory, a moment of pleasure and terror. That was all. And we went on to talk about Stanford and what I was doing now, teaching and writing, and how times had changed.

"You know, we had another encounter," she suddenly interjected. An overpowering feeling of dread filled me. "It was during the strike in '68." She lifted her eyebrow. "You *spit* at me."

"I did? I spit at you?" I stammered in shock. "I don't remember! When did it happen? What was the reason? A lot was going on. I believe you, and I'm sorry—but I can't remember the incident. Can you tell me?"

She waved her hand again.

For decades she harbored this memory; it was a persistent intellectual puzzle that intrigued her: the student who had felt too much who had come to betray her. And through all that time I had not remembered it—the incident may not have even registered in my memory in the first place—and she was not going to ease my remorse by recounting the offense.

"Whatever it was, I—I believe you—I must have done it—and I apologize."

It didn't matter. She had been offended, and I had lived free of any guilt. For decades, I had felt no punishment. While she puzzled over my crime, I was oblivious.

It was as if I had spit in her face once again.

She spoke of walking around the campus during the protests with Otto Kirchheimer, a fellow political science professor, a refugee from Germany and a Marxist, and of how both of them were amazed at the students. Clearly, the conditions for revolutionary insurrection were not present, and yet the students acted as if the Revolution had begun. They thought we were deluded, outright crazy.

"What were you students thinking?" she asked.

There was nothing I could say. After so many years, I could feel that the famous "generation gap" still yawned between us.

What were you students thinking?

COLUMBIA REVOLT

From Eisenhower to Grayson Kirk
Columbia lurches from jerk to jerk

When I got back to Hamilton Hall, the main classroom building for the college, early that Wednesday morning at the end of April, I discovered that the black students had asked SDS to leave. Hamilton Hall was theirs, the doors barricaded, Dean Coleman their hostage now, and there they would make their stand, alone.

"Take your own building," Cicero Wilson or one of the other black students had yelled, which was exactly what the white students had done in the early dawn. "They went to Low," was the word I got, so I went too, easily scaling the thick bars over the first-floor window onto the ledge of Low Library, the former library with its iconic rotunda, then through the open window into President Grayson Kirk's inner sanctum.

Except for a brief excursion to change my clothes and make some phone calls, I stayed in Kirk's office throughout the entire occupation.

When I hopped over the sill, I had no intention of remaining, but when the cops came in that first time early Wednesday morning, I didn't dive out the window with Mark Rudd and the rest.

I don't know why.

I just sat on the floor and waited, fully expecting to get hauled away. Maybe I stayed because everyone believed that the black students had guns in Hamilton, that they were willing to die. They were making their stand, and so would I. Even if getting busted for trespassing in the president's office was not quite the same thing as shooting it out with the cops, I just sat down.

Rap Brown had told people in Harlem about the gym that Columbia planned to build in Morningside Park, the gym that the university was so gracious as to allow the community limited use of, just as long as the colored folks used the back door—the gym that stank of Jim Crow: "If they build the first story, blow it up," Rap declared. "If they sneak back at night and build three stories, burn it down. And if they get nine stories built, it's yours. Take it over, and maybe we'll let them in on the weekends." I hadn't thought it out, I hadn't planned it, and I had no blueprint: I just knew that the time had come to do what Rap had said: Take it over.

It's hard even to tell when it all began. On Monday a leaflet had circulated around the campus: "Can democracy survive at Columbia University? Will Mark Rudd be our next dean?" Signed by "Students for a Free Campus," the flyer called for a counter-demonstration against Students for a Democratic Society's usual noon rally at the Sundial in the center of the campus the next day. But most ominously, it ended with a cryptic note: "Be there on the 23rd—Prepared." We could only assume that "Prepared" meant that the right-wing jocks would pick a fight, so everyone had to come to the next day's noon rally at the Sundial to back up Students for a Democratic Society. Most of us didn't think of ourselves as especially political, and we thought SDS was pretty ineffective. We were "freaks," stoned out and seeking cosmic inklings, poets and artists, but the jocks regarded both SDS and us as "pukes," and like them we hated the war and the racist bullshit, so we came to the defense of SDS.

But of course it had begun long before that. There was the campus memorial service after Martin Luther King was killed during which Rudd, as the head of SDS, got up and grabbed the mike, denounced Columbia for hypocrisy, and then led a stream of students out the door of St. Paul's Chapel to boycott the official claptrap. Then there was President Kirk's speech charging that students "have taken refuge in a turbulent and inchoate nihilism whose sole objectives are destruction." We contemplated the idea of an "inchoate nihilism"—what did that mean?—did we only want destruction? Mark Rudd answered with surprising eloquence: "If we win, we will take control of your world, your corporation, your University and attempt to mold a world in which we and other people can live as human beings." Rudd's letter concluded with the cry that ended up being heard round the world: "There is only one thing left to say. It may sound nihilistic to you, since it is the opening shot in a war of liberation. I'll use the words of LeRoi Jones, whom I'm sure you don't like a whole lot: '*Up against the wall, motherfucker, this is a stick up.*'"

Even before all this, there were the demos against the university being involved in counterinsurgency research for the Institute for Defense Analysis, or IDA, demos against the university's complicity in Vietnam, demos against the construction of the apartheid gym in Morningside Park, demos about the ban on indoor demos after students got disciplinary charges for previous demos under Low's rotunda.

Demos about demos about demos . . .

Every spring there had been protests—against the Navy ROTC, against Dow Chemical, against CIA recruiting. Every year the "Spring Offensive" got heavier, although it never really amounted to much, and even though there had been the stunning Tet Offensive only a couple of months before, we really hadn't hatched a plot to raise the Viet Cong flag over the Math building.

But I count the real beginning as when LBJ announced he wouldn't run for president again. It's not that anything actually happened right then; certainly not much did on campus. But it was that brief week or so after his abdication speech, those few days at the end of March, when we felt that maybe, just maybe, the war would end and the country would dig itself out from under its mountain of shit. It was that brief flicker, that moment when even the inconceivable took wing.

And when King was gunned down soon after, when city after city exploded into flames, the bitterness was worse than ever before.

That was when it all started: when we got a whiff of the possible.

Expecting a rumble, we gathered around the Sundial that Tuesday, along with about a hundred jocks holding signs like "Send Rudd Back to Cuba" and a crowd of professors trying to keep the two sides apart.

"There may not *be* a Columbia University after this summer," Cicero Wilson, speaking for the black students, warned, and in response a dean offered to hold a meeting with students.

Then Tom Hurwitz from SDS jumped up and yelled, "Did we come here to talk, or did we come here to go to Low?" The crowd roared, and chanting "*I-D-A must go!*" they pushed across Campus Walk to the side door of Low, which was locked, of course. Rudd stood on an overturned garbage can trying to hold a meeting about what to do next when someone else shouted, "Let's head to the gym, let's go to the gym site!" and the crowd bolted.

It looked like one more aimless, ineffectual outburst, so I stayed behind, hanging out with Les Gottesman and Alan Senauke, my friends from the college literary magazine, on South Lawn. After a while, people who had remained at the Sundial to hear more speeches also headed for the gym site, only to collide with the first contingent marching back. It turned out that when they had stormed into the gym site, they stomped down the cyclone fence around the construction work in their fury, the cops jumped in, and a student was arrested. No one knew who this student was, but the idea that the cops were arresting students made everything suddenly seem very different and much uglier.

Bill Sales, from the Student Afro-American Society, got up on the Sundial and gave a speech on how there was one oppressor—in the White House, in Low Library, in Albany. "You strike a blow at the gym, you strike a blow for the Vietnamese people. You strike a blow at Low Library and you strike a blow for the freedom fighters in Angola, Mozambique, South Africa." But then he criticized white students for being an incoherent mob. "We have to get more sophisticated," he ended. "Now, need I say more? *I don't want to get arrested for sedition.*"

At this point the crowd was ready for anything when Rudd got up and spoke in his offhand, lanky manner: "We don't have an incoherent mob; it just looks that way." I-D-A must go, he yelled, the gym must be stopped, and that student who no one ever heard of before must get "un-busted." Rudd went on some more, but then he ended with a surprise. He said there was only one thing left to do, and then he yelled, "We'll start by holding a hostage!"

Later, Rudd told me that what he really meant was that we should take a *building* hostage and not an actual person, but it didn't matter. "Seize Hamilton!" someone screamed, and almost a thousand students did just that. That's when Dean Coleman barricaded himself inside his office, and suddenly we really did have a hostage.

Some big jocks stood guard in front of the door, glaring at us, but we filled the lobby around them. Posters of Stokely Carmichael and Malcolm X went up. Che's face dangled crookedly over the dean's door. Coleman never did try to leave, even when the jocks offered to run a block for him, and we stood around listening to speech after speech. A steering committee of black and white students was formed, six demands were hammered out—including stopping the gym, cutting all ties to the Institute for Defense Analysis, amnesty for the student rebels, and more—and Soul Syndicate set up their amps in the lobby to begin blasting away with rock-and-roll. We didn't block the doors—students passed in and out going to classes—and Coleman remained safe behind his big mahogany door.

It was hard to tell where all this would lead. As the occupation of Hamilton Hall dragged on into the night, a phalanx of burly black men suddenly appeared and whisked the jocks from Coleman's door before anyone could bat an eye, taking up the guard positions in their place. More and more, Harlem's presence began to be felt, a seething angry presence.

Sometime after midnight I had had enough of the circus and went back to my apartment at 110th Street. I figured they would just stay up all night and then split. Bill Sales was right: It was pretty much an incoherent mob.

Only when I came back early the next morning did I realize that things had taken a much more serious turn than I had expected. Hamilton was barricaded, no one allowed in. Bill Sales, Cicero Wilson, and the rest of the black students had been joined by Harlem militants, and they had announced their stand, asking the white students "to do their own thing."

When I climbed onto the wide ledge of the window and stepped into Kirk's office, I could see a swirl of activity. In one room some SDS people were going through Kirk's files, yanking each folder out to photocopy and then carefully placing it back. Eventually, they dug out details on the university's secret plans to make Morningside Heights an all-white enclave; they found the scheme on how Columbia was going to pull out of the Institute for Defense Analysis officially, only to let President Kirk and others sit on its board of trustees as individuals so as to let the murderous counterinsurgency work continue; they got the goods on the university's easy compliance as a tool of the CIA; and the files were printed in an East Village underground newspaper.

Students took turns sitting behind Kirk's desk, sniffing his brandy, chewing his cigars. David Shapiro, child-poet prodigy and now college literary star, stuck a cigar in his mouth and lofted his feet up high on the juggernaut desk, his hands behind his head. With his brushy moustache he looked a lot like a young Groucho, and Tom Hurwitz promptly took his photo. *Life* ran it, and David's image—cocky, contemptuous—was wired around the world as the Symbol of the Scruffy Student Radical. David soon jumped out the window, never to return, but the die had been cast, and that image would come to haunt him the rest of his days.

Rumor had it that someone had found Kirk's Trojans, although I never did see them. I suspect it was just a rumor, but it was a good one, a sizable one, a rumor worth spreading, so we did, elongating it, so to speak. We literally sat in the forbidden seat of power—no student was ever allowed there, not even the tweediest of tweeds—and we were dead set on exposing the hairy truth: Grayson Kirk had a private toilet, a real throne—and he even had a dick.

When the cops finally did file through, all they did was whisk out Kirk's Rembrandt—I hadn't even noticed it—along with a few other precious artifacts. Then, mysteriously, they left us alone. We were glad they took the painting. None of us wanted to be responsible for preserving Western civilization.

It was peculiar why the cops didn't bust us then. Only later did we learn that the administration had truly licked their chops to bust us, but they also wanted to leave the blacks in Hamilton alone for fear of provoking Harlem's rage. No dice, the cops told them, they weren't going to play favorites, especially since they lusted for black blood and had no cause to go easy on them. Hence, the cops' perverse sense of equality: Everyone gets busted or no one. So Grayson Kirk and his recently appointed vice president, David Truman, faced with this dilemma, backed off. We didn't know this until after the big bust, of course, but it was clear to us even then that, while our stubbornness, our "inchoate nihilism," was our strength, the very real fear of Harlem's rage was our leverage, our deterrence, our atom bomb.

We sat around the floor talking about what to do when suddenly Orest Ranum, the French history professor, vaulted through the window. Ranum always strode across campus in flowing academic robes, so as he flew over the ledge we gasped. With his black cape billowing around him, he was a stunning, tripped-out sight, and we all turned to each other in wonderment as we sat on the floor, eyes wide, each of us with the very same silent thought: *"It's Batman!"*

Professor Ranum told us that we had already made our point and we were only going to foment a right-wing backlash, the faculty would take over and negotiate, so we should leave. We listened, we refused to leave, and in an instant he flew back out. But the idea that Batman had suddenly materialized, had actually come to speak with us, became a mystic talisman, an acid flashback that no one, in all the jumble of events that followed, would ever forget.

The police stood out in front of the windows now, blocking people from climbing up the grates, although it was easy to get up on the ledge from the rear of the building, then walk over to one of the windows. Once on the ledge, you were home free, and the cops would leave you alone. Climbing back in that way, Rudd read us a note of support from Rap Brown, told us that black groups like CORE and SNCC and the Mau Maus were reinforcing Hamilton, and then went back out to organize Strike Central. So we met about what we would do, trying to decide whether or not to barricade the doors.

The meeting went on for hours. JJ suggested putting the huge precious Ming vases that Kirk kept in the office in front of the doors to keep the cops from breaking them down. We didn't want to take responsibility for protecting Eastern civilization either, so that was turned down. Discussion went around and around in that endless, tedious fashion of participatory democracy. Everyone had to be heard, and we had to reach a reasoned consensus. We were tense but in no hurry, we had nowhere to go, and we knew that if we were really going to put ourselves on the line, everything had to be talked out, everything agreed upon.

In the middle of the meeting, Stephen Spender strode through the window. Someone whispered who he was, but I had already recognized him from the time in high school when I saw him read his poems at the 92nd Street Y. Tall, graying, dignified, he was the very image of the thoughtful, cultured poet—not an exploding, hairy galaxy like Allen Ginsberg, but a calm, tough nucleus. Several of us gathered around him. He asked us about the issues, our tactics, but when we asked him to join us, he only offered a tight grin and soon left. Clearly, this was our Spain, not his.

We still hadn't decided to barricade, and we could walk by the cops posted outside the door and stroll into the rotunda. That night, the composer Otto Luening, almost ninety, came to play piano for us, jovial, smiling, wanting to know what agitated the young so much. "Being old is the same as being young," he told us. "You want the same things, but you don't have the energy—so you have to be *sly*." We smiled back and listened to his music echo in the cavernous rotunda, although I don't think he ever did figure out what we were doing. Still, professors, poets, big shots who had never even talked with us before were now suddenly sitting at our feet, begging to know why students were doing such crazy things.

In the afternoon, the blacks in Hamilton let Dean Coleman go— probably a good public relations move—and the militants from Harlem split, leaving the building entirely in the hands of the Student Afro-American Society. The architecture and city-planning students took over the School of Architecture in Avery Hall, signing up with the six demands, plus tacking on some of their own about the gym, particularly how wrongheaded and even ugly the design was. A university strike was declared, and a strike committee was formed with representatives from each of the buildings.

Some Barnard girls set up a makeshift kitchen in Kirk's pantry; another girl vacuumed the floor, and we all took turns keeping the place clean. (It would be months before the women's movement exploded, and it hadn't dawned on us to overturn all the standard gender roles.) The administration was already tooting that we had vandalized the place, but we were actually very careful not to wreck anything, considering what kind of mess a hundred or so people can make cramped up in three small rooms with one small bathroom.

At a rally at Broadway and 116th Street the next day, Charles 37X Kenyatta from the Mau Maus warned Kirk that Harlem would burn

Columbia down if he didn't stop the gym. Then the crowd tried to march across Campus Walk to Amsterdam Avenue. We couldn't see the jocks trying to block the Mau Maus, but we could hear the yelling. All of a sudden the cops pushed the jocks back and formed a corridor, and from Kirk's window we could see the chanting blacks march across the campus. How strange, the cops providing a royal escort for the Mau Maus—another weird sign of imminent apocalypse.

We started to hear about all sorts of meetings. The jocks, howling in their old gym about the niggers and the pukes, formed their Majority Coalition, and Dean Coleman soothed the savage beasts with a promise of "definitive action" that very night. The faculty formed their Ad Hoc Committee, trying to be go-betweens to negotiate, declaring their silly "Doctrine of Interposition" like they were the United Nations or something. This doctrine meant they would stick themselves in the middle, trying to block the inevitable brawl between jocks and pukes, while offering half-assed ideas to the administration for compromise.

That day another building, Fayerweather Hall, was taken over by graduate students, and very late that night, while I dozed on the floor, I could see JJ and a squad from Low jump out the windows and run right across the lawn to join Tom Hayden and other commandos from Fayerweather to occupy the Math building. In the end, five buildings were occupied, and after the administration announced they were shutting down the university, the General Studies students voted to keep Lewisohn Hall open in defiance of the order, a kind of anti-lockout strike.

But "definitive action" had been in the air that night, and we kept on meeting to determine how to respond to what seemed to be the increasingly inevitable bust. JJ had wanted to push the Ming vases off the ledges onto the cops, but he was overruled again. Not only did we not want to damage the vases, but we also wanted to remain nonviolent. So JJ next proposed that we push the cops off the ledges — "nonviolently."

JJ always went for the most militant action, and he was joined by the Motherfuckers, anarchist digger freaks from Tompkins Square, who sported motorcycle helmets and terrific floppy leather cowboy hats over their straggly long hair. The Motherfuckers loved nothing more than fighting cops, and they certainly jacked up our spirits to resist. I liked JJ, and I thought the Motherfuckers were a trip, although I suspected they could get us all killed. I was relieved when they went to mount the guerrilla assault on Math.

An hour or so after their takeover of what they quickly renamed Liberated Zone Number Five, word came that cops were pouring into the other side of Low: The bust was on. We finally resolved to barricade, closing up the doors, tying ropes around them, piling up chairs and desks, and we got ready for passive, nonviolent resistance.

The more radical faculty lined up on the lawn outside, standing between the windows and doors of Low and whatever phalanx of cops would appear. Crowds of crazed jocks and pukes sprawled in front, yelling and chanting at each other. Suddenly, plainclothes cops in the darkness pulled out clubs and charged into the line, cracking some French professor's skull open. "*KIRK MUST GO!*" people screamed, and the faculty line held despite the blood. Kirk and Truman were in offices just on the other side of the rotunda, and after frantic faculty members pleaded with them, they backed off. The administration canceled the bust, announcing that the university would remain closed until Monday.

The next day, black high school kids paraded through the campus chanting, "Hell, no! We won't go!" and "Get your gun! Get whitey!" We heard that Rap Brown and Stokely Carmichael had visited Hamilton—now named Nat Turner Hall of Malcolm X University—and came out to give full support to the brothers at a press conference in front. All of black America—the whole world, in fact—turned to Columbia to see what would happen.

Also that day, the faculty set up a permanent cordon around Low, declaring that they would keep the warring factions apart. With their line of suits and ties and white armbands, access to Low was cut off. They even blocked Robbie Roth, our rep on the Strike Coordinating Committee, from getting back in. From that point on, we were cooped up until the bust, and we thought the professors, in all their vaunted neutrality, were actually doing the job of cops.

"What are you doing? Hilton, I *taught* you Marx. *What are you doing?*" Dr. Ross, my Government instructor, shrieked at me from his post behind the hedge. "*I TAUGHT YOU MARX!* Come out! This isn't going to work!"

He had in fact taught me Marx. I had written a paper for him on the division of labor in the sexual act based on *The German Ideology* and the 1844 manuscripts, which reached the inevitable conclusion that full-blown communism meant nothing less than one endless, nonstop orgasm. It was a convoluted Talmudic argument that the universe was simply a giant Reichian orgone box, and history was waiting for us to enter it. Ross liked the paper despite my conclusion, which, ludicrous as it may seem, made complete sense according to the texts' internal logic, and he gave me an A, the only unmitigated A that I ever received at Columbia. I had liked him, too. He took students seriously, and we did read Marx and Lenin and Sorel and Kropotkin and all the rest. But now he stood on the lawn, and I looked down upon him from the ledge in sad silence as he shrieked up at me and the rest of Low: "*I TAUGHT YOU MARX!!*"

Maybe he did feel that what we were doing wouldn't work, but what I felt was that he couldn't *live* revolution; couldn't put his life, his career, on the line. All I could feel was sorrow at how ineffectual, how pathetic, how confused he appeared as he wailed at us from the little lawn between Low and the hedge. I just stared down at him without saying a word, and even now I can still feel the sadness of my disappointment, my loss of respect. A huge gulf right then widened between us.

Later that day, Kenneth Koch did his stint on the faculty cordon. The poet smiled in his affable way, didn't preach or wail or gnash his teeth; and he offered a friendly wave at me and the other editors of the literary magazine, Les and Alan. He couldn't keep from enjoying himself, couldn't take things too seriously, which was in its own way very unnerving. But it was good to see the poet, in all his goofiness, and we waved back. He had thrown his lot in with the rest of the feeble faculty, which saddened us, although we couldn't be mad at him. His humor lent him some transcendent grace.

"Did you write any poems?" he chuckled up at us.

No, we hadn't. We set right off to punch out a bunch of spontaneous three-way-collaboration poems, each of us taking a turn on the typewriter we had liberated from President Kirk's secretary.

So terrible, so embarrassingly idiotic were these poems that we threw them away almost immediately. The muse of André Breton and Tristan Tzara and Frank O'Hara had failed us, and moment-to-moment rhapsodic bop would sound only like Allen Ginsberg, and there was only one Allen Ginsberg. We couldn't bear to write tedious Fight-Team-Fight anthems or lugubrious, boring manifestos. All we could knock out was intense, manic gibberish, when what was needed was something entirely new, written in a language no one had yet invented.

Still, I marveled at Koch's sweetness, his unwillingness to change his peaceable demeanor in the face of chaos and violence, his chuckle, and his question: "Did you write any poems?"

All the newspapers—and many of the faculty—thought we were simply in it for "the kicks," college pranksters out on an overblown panty raid, or we were drug-crazed hippies simply tripped out of our minds. Above all, especially to the Daily News, we were the Ivy League, we were elite spoiled brats who were intent on soiling our own sheets, pampered kids, Human Be-In monsters of permissive Dr. Spock.

Although we laughed all the time, we were totally serious. We met and talked nonstop, weighing every twist and turn in the negotiations. Sundial rally after Sundial rally we had heard Dave Gilbert and Paul Rockwell and Mike Clare and others patiently, eloquently explain the ways the university was a corporate leviathan and not the exalted acropolis of learning we had all come there expecting it to be. Exactingly, they detailed which Columbia trustee was on the board of which corporation, how one interest scratched the back of another.

We had learned that almost ten thousand people in the neighborhood had been evicted or otherwise forced to move in the last eight years—poor folks, black people, the elderly, like my grandmother who had lived in the 110th Street apartment I had taken over after she died two years before—and the university was slated to push out ten thousand more in their plans to create their all-white, middle-class enclave. We knew all the lies, all the university's stupid moneymaking schemes, like their plan to market a cigarette filter commercially, promoting it with the bullshit "science" of low nicotine as their excuse—until they were exposed and laughed at as fools. We knew all their lies, the same as we knew with such bitterness and sense of betrayal all the lies about Vietnam—all the phony body counts, the cold-blooded kill ratios, the cooked-up Gulf of Tonkin incident; all the tumbling dominoes.

We laughed and played, but we were on no panty raid.

Right at the start, we decided on a policy of no grass and no beer, just so the administration couldn't dismiss us with a cheap drug bust—although some people objected that life without a joint was just another way of caving in to the straight Establishment.

But really, Low Commune was already an incredible high. For the first time, students were working together instead of trying to cut each other's throats in class. No more competitive, masculine, intellectual one-upmanship pushed by professors. For the first time, we had a real feeling of mutual aid, of group yearning and learning, of one-mind determination and compassion. We were bound together, girls and boys, no longer isolated in girls' or boys' schools, alienated, stuffed into narrow dorm rooms or dark apartments by ourselves. Now we were a group of intersecting obligations to each other and to the world, sharing blankets and peanut butter, and we were set to overturn the System; and the discovery of that power kept us cool, kept us deliberate, filled us with joy.

Early on, we had felt that high, but after the bust scare Thursday night it became a palpable, overarching, living thing. Once we had decided that we would barricade, that we would allow ourselves to be arrested, that we would offer nonviolent resistance in the face of cop terror, we knew we had crossed some kind of Rubicon.

Having made that choice, it was as if we were already busted, as if we were living knowing that we were already dead, so the fear of death could not sway us. Faculty, liberals, administrators, everyone was hollering at us that we were ruining our academic careers, wrecking our lives. And they were right, we were. But we knew that our old lives didn't matter anymore. None of us would take our expected place in the corporate war machine; none of us would allow ourselves to be used again, even though it would have been "for our own benefit," no less.

The most horrible genocide was being committed right before our very eyes, and none of us would be Good Germans; a whole generation said "No," no matter what the consequences.

Afterward, I realized it was that sensibility—that terrible concentration camp feeling—that drove me to my "already-dead" sensibility. Sure, this time it wasn't the Jews, my entire family, being slaughtered, but it was the same thing. But, unlike what happened in Germany, our great *HELL, NO, WE WON'T GO!* would in fact gum up the works. Our spoiled-brat, "nihilist" refusal, that was life, real life, and we knew we were catching a peek of another universe, and that glimpse would keep us solid, whole, honest—and that vision turned us into a commune.

It's not as if I really got to know anyone in the usual sense of collecting details about someone's past, what they majored in, where they came from. I don't even remember a lot of people's names. We were so busy meeting over one negotiating ploy after another, deciding how to resist, fending off attacks, that anyone's individual ambitions or past didn't seem to matter much anymore.

During breaks in meetings or after the danger of busts or assaults by jocks had subsided, I would merely doze or hang out with Les and Alan and our other friends. We were talked out, emptied, and could only feel dazed and oddly bored because of the excess of tension.

At the same time, I realized that I was being held captive. Of course, I could step out onto the ledge and climb down anytime. No one would stop me, and the faculty would welcome me in their arms. Yet, while I knew I was staying put by choice, I also knew I was being kept in by some inexorable force, like one of the bourgeois dinner-party guests in Buñuel's *Exterminating Angel*.

Some politicians tried to make out that we were manipulated by Communists, saying that we were brainwashed or coerced into staying, which only made us laugh. After all the lies, no one could manipulate us. Robbie Roth chaired one meeting (before the faculty cops prevented him from getting back in), and when he hadn't called on everyone who had their hands up, we went up to him afterward and told him he couldn't pass over people like that, and he reconvened the meeting. After that, nothing was decided, no action taken, until everyone got their chance to speak.

Later, Tony Papert would chair the meetings. Tony was from the Maoist Progressive Labor Party, but he scrupulously encouraged every point of view, never quashing or silencing anyone, always in his soft voice reasoning everything out. Maybe it was our insistence on participatory democracy—that those who act must decide, and those who decide must act—which made him fair-minded. He respected us, no matter his dogmatic Maoist bent. No, the invisible force that held me captive was something too powerful to be wielded by one guy.

Mark Rudd was the leader of the strike, and he became "The Student Radical," a certified "Star," in the eyes of *Time* and David Susskind and Walter Cronkite, which we found nothing but wickedly amusing: No one occupying Kirk's office in Low Library made Rudd out to be anything too special because he was only a schlemiel like the rest of us, and he knew it, and all his friends knew it, no matter how much Day-Glo the media might drip on his aura. Still, he had a way, a manner, a style of low-key, participatory, anti-uptight goofiness that made him not just "represent" us but "be" us, and I suppose that meant real leadership qualities—just so long as he wouldn't try to be "a leader" in the traditional sense of the word.

"Kirk is a jerk!" became a favorite chant in front of the windows of

Low, and as negotiations about the IDA and the gym dragged on, it became patently clear how true. He and the rest of the administrators were the real manipulators—except they couldn't get away with it, not anymore. When confronted at a demo before the strike, Kirk or some other administrator had rejected student demands with the remark that we were nothing more than "transitory birds." Students migrated a mere four years across his realm, so we could have no say over how such a lofty institution could make its decisions.

Now those birds had perched in his office, crapping all over his cigars and condoms.

True to form, Kirk at first refused to budge, insisting that the gym could never be stopped; then that only the trustees could decide, and he could only put it on the agenda of their next meeting, weeks away. Finally, he announced that he would temporarily suspend (merely suspend) construction—but only as a courtesy to honor Mayor Lindsay's personal request. While the faculty clamored that that was the most we could ever hope to accomplish, we knew we had only just begun.

After a few days it became clear that no matter what Grayson Kirk said, the gym was dead, and he and his cohorts would even have to disentangle from their Pentagon deals. So, out of our six demands, the one demanding amnesty for those in the buildings became the crux of the struggle. The administration adamantly refused, declaring, in their own game of falling dominoes, that if Columbia students went unpunished, then campuses all across the country would capitulate to the forces of darkness. Like McNamara facing down Communist bogeymen in Vietnam so that he wouldn't have to battle the Red Menace in Honolulu, Kirk had to stand his ground at Columbia, or else Harvard, Yale, and Oneonta State College would likewise fall.

Giving in on amnesty was never a question for Low Commune.

How could we allow ourselves to be expelled or otherwise punished—by an arrogant administration that held its own students in contempt, no less—for doing what was right? Sure, they could call in the cops, they could even expel us, but why the fuck would we agree to *let* them? Liberals thought giving in made sense: We broke the rules, so we had to pay, even if we had just faced down imperialist genocide and racism. After all, that was all part of fair play: The faculty would pat us on the back and then sell us down the river.

"*Bullshit!*" was our response, which was exactly what Rudd said, thus freaking out the faculty at their meeting Friday night, but we knew he was right. Some buildings wavered, especially Fayerweather, our Fair Weather friends, we called them. Filled with a mixed bag of ambivalent graduate students and instructors, Fayerweather never ceased agonizing and waffling, at least in our eyes. Meanwhile, the black students in Hamilton remained stone-faced, hardly uttering a word after assuring SDS that they would stick by us and not make a separate deal, no matter what.

Maybe because we had that life-after-death feeling, Low just sat serenely, never budging for an instant. Intractable, we developed a reputation for being militant, although we were never the banner-waving guerrilla types like those who occupied Math. We considered every deal carefully, every proposal that was floated to us; we rejected each one point by point and then just stayed put, watching all hell break loose from the windows of Kirk's cockpit.

It gets harder and harder trying to recall events after Saturday, especially as cordons and blockades and brawls broke out one after another. That evening, Rudd spoke from the Law Bridge over Amsterdam Avenue to a contingent from the huge peace march in Central Park. He called the faculty worse than cops. This outraged a lot of people, but when we learned what he said, we knew exactly what he had meant: We had been betrayed by our teachers, and that felt a lot worse than the expected brutality of the NYPD.

Around midnight, nearly a hundred supporters tried to break through the faculty blockade, storming up the window grates to the ledge. The professors pulled them down, grabbed them by the legs, and hauled them off, while we tried to yank them in. We pulled and screamed from above, a jumble of arms and legs in the darkness, and in the tumult and rage all that several of us could do was spit at the "neutral" faculty. (*Was Elisabeth Hansot in that melee? I don't remember seeing her, but perhaps that was the time I spit on her.*) About half a dozen students made it through the window, while the rest were yanked off and shoved back.

Around five the next evening, the jocks set up their own blockade on the other side of the hedge from the faculty, declaring that nothing other than medical supplies would pass through. By now, everyone was marked by an armband: white for the faculty, red for our supporters, blue for the jocks, and even green for those liberals who supported amnesty even though they didn't really like us.

When a group of red armbands who tried to push through with a box of food were shoved back, Robbie Roth made a break around the side for the ledge. Blue armbands charged after him, and white armbands after the blue. All hell broke loose, but Robbie didn't make it up to the window, and the faculty quickly ruled that they would enforce the jocks' embargo, allowing in only medical supplies (which meant, at least, that we got Vaseline for protection against the anticipated teargas attack).

Late that night we learned that there was a wedding at Fayerweather officiated by the radical campus chaplain Reverend Bill Starr—"I pronounce you Children of the New Age"—and soon after we could peer out Kirk's window as the bride and groom—he wore a green Nehru jacket—led a procession around the Sundial. We thought it was a giddy trip, another way to swat at the straight world, although we also snickered at how flighty the people occupying Fayerweather could be while we sat besieged in Kirk's office.

Soon after the procession, the mood shifted again as JJ tried to lead another contingent though the jock blockade, and nearly a thousand green armbands camped out all night at the Sundial in a peace vigil against a bust.

But a bust was becoming inevitable.

On Monday, the university stayed shut while the faculty tried to negotiate one last deal. Meanwhile, JJ and others kept trying to run the blockade. I stood on the ledge—we each took turns at the post to ward off jock attacks, to help anyone who made it through, and to show that we were the ones who had command of the heights.

Barry Willdorf, the law student who led Low's security committee, pointed at the fat, heavy books with uncut pages that Kirk never read but kept around to show off his phony intellect. He suggested that we hurl them down at the jocks if they tried to charge through the faculty cordon. But we rejected that idea: Our war wasn't with books, and heaving them down like a bunch of Quasimodos seemed only to play into the media's nihilism fantasies. Besides, I had kissed my *siddur* whenever I dropped it on the floor in Hebrew school, so the thought of tossing books like grenades made my heart ache. Barry was only looking for some way to ward off the expected assault, and he muttered that it was a good thing the jocks didn't know we wouldn't defend ourselves, or else we would really be up shit creek when they did storm the windows.

Demonstration at Low Library,
Columbia University, April 1968.
The author stands before
second window from right.
Photograph with permission
of the University Archives,
Columbia University
in the City of New York.

Instead of throwing books, we decided to wield the long poles with small metal hooks used for opening the window tops to push back any jocks who might try to climb up the ledge, although we mostly kept the poles hidden, not wanting to provoke an unwarranted escalation. So when it came time to stand on the ledge, I had only my hands to ward off whatever Coke bottle or spit or giant linebacker would come my way.

About a hundred of our friends marched around Low with boxes of food. Around and around they paraded, chanting, *"Food! Food!"* Suddenly the crowd veered toward Low and charged into the jock line. Fists flew, our people sprayed ammonia, I saw a jock with a knife glinting in the sun, a soda bottle swung up high above the boiling heads then dashed down, and I hollered from my position on the ledge. The professors broke up the melee, no one seriously injured, and our contingent backed up, unloading the goods in the boxes to throw their contents piece by piece to those of us doing guard duty on the ledges.

I teetered, I lunged, and I even caught a few grapefruits as they flew over the heads of the blue and white armbands. Strikers cheered as each sardine can or loaf of bread was caught. Jocks jeered when salamis or oranges went wild or fell short, or when I, the puke poet, bobbled and dropped them. Soon the jocks were waving blankets and frying pans trying to block each flight, then began flinging eggs and grapefruits and rocks at us, and I had to dodge or try to catch each missile or simply allow myself to be hit as I focused on catching the goods.

Friends told me I looked very grim on that ledge. I know I didn't smile as I concentrated intently at the fierce barrage coming at me. By the time it was all over, I had avoided most of the eggs, and I had even managed to haul in a decent catch of groceries. But I had never felt closer to war than during my stint on the ledge, and I was certain that the next battle could only end in bloodshed.

In response to that brawl, Kirk and Truman sent a squad of cops to form yet one more line, this time in front of the jocks, to keep the warring sides apart. Now we had three cordons around us, and while still we held the heights on the ledge, we could only wonder how long this danse macabre could go on.

Not long, as it turned out.

That night, Low voted unanimously to reject the faculty's last deal, what they called their "bitter pill," the compromise that would be hard for all sides to swallow.

Now the bust would surely come.

We met for hours deciding how we would make our last stand. One suggestion even floated around that we should all strip and resist nonviolently while stark-naked. This tactic had its charms, but it was dismissed as too dangerous—who knew how the cops might react to a bunch of girls and boys in the buff?

Bobby Plower argued passionately yet calmly for fighting the cops. If the blacks were willing to defend themselves with guns, we could at the very least use our fists. Discussion went on and on, but finally we voted in favor of nonviolent passive resistance, clothes on. Some would go limp, while others would allow themselves to be taken.

"Then let me barricade myself in a separate room so *I* can fight the cops," Bobby pleaded, tears in his eyes.

No, that would only court disaster. Bobby was a Navy Vietnam vet, a munitions expert, and despite his quiet, sincere demeanor, some thought he could have been a provocateur.

No, we had to stick together, our obstinate unity the one thing going for us, and a lone warrior could bring down a hail of bullets.

A crew went off to reinforce the barricades.

"You know I respect the Commune's decision, no matter what,"

Bobby softly responded, "so I'll leave. I'm going to Hamilton. At least black people are willing to fight, and the time has come to fight."

Bobby was no grandstander, no loudmouthed braggart. He was serious, ready to make the sacrifice. The war had etched a deeper, more sorrowful scar in his soul. But it was still an odd, lonesome feeling watching him climb out the window. He raised his fist in one last salute, then plunged into the night and the chanting crowds to make his way to Hamilton and possible death. A year or so later, he was arrested for setting off bombs at recruiting stations; he was convicted, sent to Attica, took part in the uprising there, yet managed to survive the onslaught by the police.

At 2 a.m. the water was shut off, while word came over the walkie-talkie that cops were massing on Amsterdam Avenue.

This was it — no more false alarms, the bust was on.

Crowded into the largest room of the suite, we stood with our arms linked in a series of concentric circles, singing "We Shall Not Be Moved" and other civil rights songs. Axes and hatchets began chopping through the barricade of desks and bookcases and nailed-up boards, the rhythmic thuds playing counterpoint to our hymns.

Suddenly, a swath of blue uniform could be seen through the rubble, then a blue arm. A girl screamed, and we sang even louder to drown out the fear.

By chance, the literary crowd from the *Columbia Review* had formed the smallest orbit in the very center of Low's concentric circles. I clutched Alan Senauke's arm tighter when the cops broke through; I looked at Les Gottesman's bulging eyes, at Kathy Knowles's and Nancy Werner's pale faces; and we howled "We Shall Overcome," knowing our time had really come when the first cop stepped through the hole.

That's when I noticed David Somerset.

David stood by himself in the very core of our innermost circle.

There, in the heart of Low Commune, was David, an open paper-back in his hands. Arms linked to no one else's, he clutched his book, his eyes steadily moving along the type.

I did a double take, but there he stood, reading with unaccountable serenity, his glasses teetering on his nose.

So intent on finishing the book, invisible in his wry, unassuming manner, he wasn't noticed by anyone else. Despite the rising panic, de-spite the smell of violence, despite our straining voices, he kept on read-ing, unperturbed.

I gaped at him as he turned the last page, catching his eye as he looked up.

"Gotta finish the book, you know," he answered my astonished look with a wisp of a smile. He tilted it up to show the cover—Raymond Chandler's *The Big Sleep*—as if that were explanation enough, then he stuffed it into his back pocket.

How could he read a book, even a Chandler book, at a time like this? David simply offered his wry smile.

All the cops—dozens—shoved their way through the cleared barri-cade to take their positions, the final, blue concentric circle surround-ing ours. Some officer blared through a megaphone—probably the of-ficial announcement that we were trespassing, would be arrested, et cetera—although exactly what he said was unintelligible above the din of our chorus.

Then one cop, anonymous in his helmet, sauntered up to a girl in the outermost circle—he seemed casual, almost nonchalant, a slight, fixed grin pasted to his lips.

He grabbed her shoulder with one hand; then, with his other, he raised one of those extra-long, aluminum utility flashlights high up over her head.

For a moment, time stood still, the silvery flashlight suspended above her head.

I stared at the frozen glitter of light on the long metallic tube, and even now I can see it glinting, forever poised above her head.

Then, in a slow, heavy arc, the cop brought the flashlight down on her skull.

Raising it up and swinging it down. Up and down, again, then again, repeatedly he pounded the girl's head, methodically clobbering her, the ghastly grin never leaving his lips.

She shrieked in pain and fell to the floor, yet he still kept swinging.

We howled in horror and rage, clutching each other more tightly, singing even more loudly.

Maybe they had drawn straws, and he would be first. Once that cop began battering the girl with his silvery flashlight, the rest of the horde as if on cue descended upon us from all sides. Yanking each circle of arms apart, they beat us wildly with their fists, their clubs, their flashlights.

Long talks on whether to accept arrest or go limp had meant nothing: The cops had made up their minds to beat the shit out of all of us, no matter what we did.

One by one, our concentric circles were pulled apart and battered. I had hoped they would have shot their load before reaching us at the very core, but their fury raged unabated.

Out of the corner of my eye I could see one cop crack Nancy's skull open, blood gushing over her eyes.

Alan yelled, *"Hey, don'—"* but before he could finish, he was thrown down on top of one of the desks, a half-dozen cops working him over, fists and clubs pumping like high-speed pistons.

When I turned back, David Somerset had disappeared, swallowed up; only his book had been left behind, torn and tossed on the floor.

I stood by myself then. Trying to be very small, very quiet, I inched my way toward the other rooms and the door to the rotunda.

Suddenly I was hit from behind and shoved through a gauntlet of cops.

Wallops, blows, jabs, a swirl of fists—I tried to keep my eyes open wide, watching the nightstick as it formed a crescent slicing into my gut.

Then, oddly, the floor quickly thrust up to my nose, and all I could see were bits of rug and dirt and darkness.

Barricades
MAY 1968

After I was bailed out from the Tombs, I slept for a day, smoked a joint, nursed my bruises, and scarfed down a greasy burger in the West End while reading A. M. Rosenthal in the *New York Times* dish out hideous jumbo lies. To Rosenthal we were nothing but barbaric nihilists who took a shit on the very seat of civilization, which so happened to be Kirk's inner sanctum, although we had taken great pains not to wreck the place—and we had done a pretty good job, when you consider that more than a hundred people had camped out in the president's suite for a week. Naturally, there was some mess, and someone did smoke the creep's cigars, but the vases, the books, the equipment, the furniture, everything was kept as tidy as possible. Nonetheless, the photos, augmented by Rosenthal's mendacious bullshit, told otherwise: paint and ink splattered on walls, graffiti; everything torn up, shredded, wrecked. I suppose the police, wanting to smear us, had mauled the premises as hard as they had pounded our skulls, while Rosenthal glee-fully joined the melee with his wrecking-ball pen.

It was yet another Gulf of Tonkin frame-up, but I was not shocked, not even outraged, and I sat reading the *Times* in a kind of calm, come-down daze of worn-to-the-bone expanded consciousness. I no longer believed nor concerned myself with the pronouncements of bombas-tic A. M. Rosenthals. The owners of the *Times* were trustees of Co-lumbia, and I was certain as never before that the Establishment was held together by nothing but napalm, cops, and lies—and the lies were the more insidious and therefore more dangerous of the trio.

This, I thought, was my true Columbia education.

After the bust, the revolt raged on, of course. Now liberals teamed up with the radicals, and ideas about "restructuring" the university were bandied about, while the SDS crowd, keen to keep the radicaliza-tion mushrooming, just went on talking revolution. We elected Alan Senauke as our delegate to the Strike Committee, which now repre-sented five or six thousand students and even a large proportion of fac-ulty, all outraged at the brutality of the cops and the arrogance and stu-pidity of the administration. The pitiful faculty had finally realized that they did not hold even a modicum of real power before the autocrats of the administration, and the violent bust propelled all kinds of juicy notions for new legislative bodies: for a "Student Thing," for a "Faculty Thing," then finally for a "Joint Thing." It was like the Constitutional Convention, and no one had even invented the names yet.

Although the most radical of the restructuring students couched their reforms as creating a base to spur all of society toward revolution and not as ends in themselves, Rudd and SDS saw the "Things" as nothing but sops to smother a wildfire that threatened to spread across all of America—and in fact dozens and dozens of campuses did explode into sit-ins, occupations, and riots in the weeks following the bust. How could a university exist as a humane institution in a sick society, anyway? SDS had little interest in diverting energy toward restructuring an institution that had to collapse by the very weight of its own corruption, which is why during the occupation Rudd had simply asked David Truman for the keys to the bursar's office and left it at that.

Both the radicals and the reformers were right—and both wrong. We needed to reconstruct the university and build the Revolution at the same time—two equally necessary and equally impossible tasks—and Alan would come back from meeting after meeting torn apart, exhausted from all the maneuvering and manipulation on all sides. No longer was this the "already-dead" paradise of Low Commune, and I did not envy him.

Meanwhile, cops occupied the campus, classes were suspended, and when the administration finally announced that they would resume, no one crossed the picket lines to attend. Instead, the "liberated university" convened on lawns, in the West End Bar, in people's apartments. Classes unimaginable before the uprising were concocted, ranging from the heavy-duty ("The Secret History of the War," "Physics and Imperialism") to the seemingly trivial ("How to Belly Dance"), but even the more standard required courses ("Contemporary Civilization") could not be held unless the old teacher-student elitist crap was banned. No more force-feeding, no more passivity, no more pontification, no more cutthroat competition egged on by tweed jackets stuffed with straw, no more irrelevance, and all that ejection of bullshit just by itself constituted a revolution, an idea of education that meant a truly mutual quest, not a garnering of kudos and privileges and ego trips but an accountability to a broader need.

I thrilled at it all, even though I was too busy working with Alan and Les and other poets in the hastily formed Strike Cultural Committee to attend very many liberated classes. No, we were bent on blowing minds through art, putting on readings, concerts, instant be-ins, anything to trumpet the strike. I accompanied Jerry Jeff Walker to the steps of Low to sing at a rally, I sneaked Allen Ginsberg across police lines to chant Om and declaim poems, and when a group of female impersonators from the Village showed up, I paraded the drag queens through Ferris Booth Hall like royalty. The Stonewall Riots would be the next year, and this turned out to be a taste of things to come.

Our biggest triumph, however, was when some of Alan Senauke's friends hustled up some contacts and the Grateful Dead plugged in their amps in front of Ferris Booth Hall. We stood on the low roof overlooking the patio goofing down on them in ecstatic mind-fuck wonder as Jerry Garcia wailed out across the entire campus. We hooted with laughter on the rooftop above them, but our voices could not be heard above the thick, luscious rock-and-roll soaring out before us; and for one brief afternoon the Sundial, South Lawn, the steps of Low, the whole vast space filled up with otherworldly vibes. Nothing else could get done, no classes could be held inside Hamilton or on the lawn, the chugging, twanging chords, the high-flying harmonics, the squealing riffs blotting out all before them. That day, Columbia came closest in its entire history to collectively tripping out on acid, and what a good trip it was.

When a few days after the Dead concert the streets of Paris erupted, the newspapers printed a photo of a French student holding a placard with a new version of Che's slogan: *"Create Two, Three, Many Columbias!"* Yes, we were delighted, even awed. The spirit of our revolt had carried straight across the ocean to screw de Gaulle—and yet our strike ground on, with Kirk and Truman and the rest of the administration as intractable as ever. A couple of weeks later, tenants of a Columbia-owned apartment building on 114th Street barricaded their building to protest their eviction. Students massed out on the street to support them, which led to yet one more bust. Still, the administration would not budge on any of the issues, and it looked like the academic year would simply peter out with nothing much resolved.

Then the administration singled out Mark Rudd, Nick Freudenberg, Morris Grossner, and Ed Hyman, sending the four of them notices to see the dean for disciplinary charges. Clearly, Kirk and company thought that if they targeted "ringleaders," the whole horrible nightmare would vanish—an old divide-and-conquer routine that only enraged students more. SDS called for yet another Sundial rally on May 21. "We're not going in to see the dean—but everyone else is," Rudd announced slyly. "I've got that déjà vu feeling." The parents of the four and their lawyers—along with a thousand students—all poured into Hamilton once more, and after the delegation met with the dean, accomplishing nothing, no one felt like making an exit. The posters of Mao and Che went up again, and it looked like "Showdown No. 2," as the rally leaflet called it, was in the works.

The crowd debated the wisdom of the move. Rudd and others advised that those who had been busted earlier should consider withdrawing, since a second bust could entail far more serious consequences. I mulled that one over for a moment and decided to sit this occupation out, joined by several thousands who contented themselves with demonstrating across the campus.

Barricades went up inside Hamilton again. Barricades also went up across the Broadway and Amsterdam Avenue entrances of Campus Walk, no doubt inspired by the street battles of Paris. Huge flowerpots, construction lumber, garbage pails set on fire, even a metal ramp from the IRT station on 116th Street were hauled across the gates. Just after midnight, word came that the cops were moving through the tunnels, and soon people on the outside could see blue uniforms through the doors of Hamilton swoop down on our friends inside. Howls of rage swept through the crowds. Suddenly, as if on cue, fire danced out of the top floors of Hamilton, sirens wailed, and I felt certain that Columbia would really burn to the ground that night. Later we learned that someone had set fire to Orest Ranum's office, torching Batman's notes on, of all things, the history of Paris. This was sad, clearly the action of a provocateur or a nut, which afterward SDS denounced.

I'm not sure how to describe the strange feeling of that moment around two or so in the morning. Our collective mind seemed suddenly to snap, and the roaming mob flipped out with rage. Students began to dig up the huge bricks from Campus Drive and hurl them at the cops on Broadway. On Engineering Terrace overlooking Amsterdam Avenue, students rained down potted plants and garbage cans on the paddy wagons. Another fire broke out in Fayerweather, smoke and sirens spewing into the night. Then the cops tried to batter down the barricades, and bricks, cans, chairs flew down on them, a chorus of girls on the roof of Barnard shrieking "*Up against the wall, motherfucker!*" over and over again.

A phalanx of cops pushed their way from Amsterdam Avenue through the gates between Hartley and Livingston halls, and when they suddenly burst out into the Quad, what I beheld I still can't quite believe. At the opening between the two dorms, a seemingly random pack of unarmed students charged into the surprised cops, flailing, punching, kicking, beating them back. *Students fighting cops!* I was astonished beyond words—and they were winning, at least for the moment. But I knew that the next time, after the cops recovered from their shock and humiliation, they would come out with their nightsticks swinging—or worse. The smell of blood began to mix with the acrid smoke.

The cops finally succeeded in tearing down the barricades at Amsterdam Avenue, and they marched in military formation down Campus Walk. Students formed a line opposite them, chanting *"Cops off campus!"* with their arms linked as they headed straight into the jaws of the beast. A few plainclothes cops charged ahead with nightsticks, grabbing and beating students mercilessly, yet the freaked-out students still advanced. I joined others who kept farther back at the Sundial, and with cops now pouring in from Broadway as well, we backpedaled frantically in retreat. Clusters of us still stayed ahead of the approaching columns, jeering, chanting, screaming, *"Cops off campus!"* while the Barnard girls kept on screeching from their rooftop perches across Broadway, *"Up against the wall, motherfucker!"*

Suddenly the cops sprinted after us. One moment Ron Carver, the press secretary for the strike, was standing beside me; the next he was gone, bolting through the doors of Furnald Hall with a squad of plainclothes cops, guns drawn, charging after him. When I saw Ron two days later—he was already a veteran of some rough times as a Freedom Rider—his head was covered with an African skullcap to cover his wounds, and his face had become such a blob of lumps and welts with dozens of stitches crisscrossing his skull that I did not recognize him.

I could see that I was next. I dove for the large plate-glass doors of Ferris Booth Hall, which someone swiftly opened for me and then slammed shut just seconds before a beefy cop hurled himself against the glass. I turned and screamed at him, my face contorted by rage, separated only by that thin transparent pane, just inches from his snout. I would have killed the bastard that instant, as he stood there, pressing his large bulk against the glass door, waving his club, snickering, taunting, pointing at the piece of duct tape slapped over his badge to hide his number with arrogant snorts of laughter. I taunted back, "*PIG! PIG! PIG!*" until my voice contorted into a high-pitched shriek. Moments later a girl came running to the doors, pursued by a half-dozen cops, who slammed into her just as she reached them, the glass shattering to splinters. They shoved her through the jagged entry, cut and bleeding and howling in fear and pain, and the students pulled her through, slamming the inner doors shut.

I huddled in the *Columbia Review* office until about six in the morning, my teeth chattering, and then passed like a ghost through the police lines—they would let us out but not back in—to my apartment.

"*Are you crazy? Are you trying to get killed?*" my girlfriend, Amy, berated me, as I sat on the bed sobbing and heaving incoherently until I passed out. She had supported all the demands, but she had left the campus early that night, unconvinced that more confrontations would do any good. I had actually gone so insane with rage, had turned so bloody-minded, that I would have killed someone. I could have easily been one of those crazed students who had charged into the cops, flailing at them with no thought for my own safety; I could have hurled boulders down at their heads; I could have torn their hearts out—and I shuddered as wave after wave of adrenaline and hatred and fear and revulsion swept over me.

That day, May 22, was my twenty-first birthday.

"Meat!"

That was enough for me. I skipped the riots at the Democratic Convention in Chicago during the summer and took off for California, where I walked through teargas and police lines on Telegraph Avenue to sit zazen at the Berkeley Zen Center, trying to convince myself that war was just another form of attachment. When we returned to school in the fall, Grayson Kirk had finally resigned, replaced by the more conciliatory former diplomat Andrew Cordier; charges had been dropped against almost all of the students; more blather about restructuring was in the air—but none of it was sincere. Columbia was trying to paper over its sins, the war continued just as before, SDS tore itself to pieces in faction fights, and I dove back into writing poems and into my job churning out sex-crime stories for the tabloid *National Star Chronicle*.

Satori I would not achieve, but I did discover that the only way I could survive the pretensions of Columbia was by practicing the dharma of Dada. I would exorcise my bloody-mindedness while still exacting revenge on all the pigs through laughter that would explode on the sheets of *Janet Benderman*. Cut on mimeo stencils two times a week, *Janet Benderman* was a satirical broadside that Phil Lopate and Aaron Fogel and others on the *Review* had toyed with in the past—named after no one knew who, maybe a long-lost Barnard student or a character in a Lenny Bruce routine. But when Alan, Les, and I and others revived it for purposes of student revolt, it became a popular organ of inanity. The weather, no matter the date (September 1, 1939), was always "Sunny but Mild," and with such mildness we toiled at being as puerile, as obscene, as inflammatory, as slanderous, as scatological as possible. We tried to perfect the worst taste imaginable—and the silly, crudely mimeographed sheet we passed out touched the jaded masses in the student burger joint the Lions Den. Each issue was snatched from our hands by readers eager to laugh at mock revolutionary manifestos, ridiculously gross pornography, zany poems, and ludicrous character assassinations.

"Mass action is a bore nowadays, so, for the time being, all anarchist longhair bastard pricks should alter tactics and deal realistically (which means 'BALLS!') with the situation," I declared in the first of a series of communiqués of what we called *The Cordier Papers* in honor of our new university president. "Individual Revolutionary freak-out has to be the next step," and I proposed that students stalk professors and administrators, mimicking their every move. "President Cordier walks into his office and so do you. He sits at his desk and you likewise, right in his lap. 'Who are you!' he yells, and he freaks out, calling in campus security pigs. You answer, 'I am President Cordier!' Refuse to budge, insist repeatedly that YOU ARE CORDIER! . . . Remember our aim: To destroy this cocksucker place!" A goal that would be achieved by infinite replication of Cordiers and Lionel Trillings until all bounds of authority and ownership and even identity would dissolve.

"We can make art explode in their faces like a shitbomb," Alan declaimed, and since the pigs considered us barbarians, we would simply deliver the goods. I declared that I would burn all the books in the library, "and all the people in the stacks too, on March 27, 1969." David Somerset advised that "the Columbia central computer will melt if its air conditioner is turned off more than three minutes," along with the fact that "Andrew Cordier's office safe contains $5,000 cash at all times." Ron Padgett, Ira Stollack, David Lehman, Michael Steinlauf, and others wrote wacky obscene rants and nonsensical poems, and Nancy Werner scratched in the stick-figure pictures. When open enrollment became the demand of striking CCNY students to demolish the obstacles keeping Third World students from going to college, I cut a twisted editorial into the mimeo stencil:

Open Enrollment! A great idea! That way the Outside can finally seep into the Inside.

And isn't that the reason why we take LSD?

"But *academically* those Spics and Spades don't *deserve* to get in!"

Well, let me answer that by asking this: "Do you *deserve* to get out?"

Each of us has to do something *worthwhile* in order to achieve official membership Outside.

Me? Well, I done some. I admit right here, I'm the man who burned up Orest Ranum!

And what's more, there's more work to be done. Mr. Cordier, your life is in utmost danger. Some one—I'm not saying—aims to throw lit matches down the throat of diplomat liar you!

So, with a little help from friends, we can all graduate.

After graduation a few will discover they like to fuck amputees. Those will join the Army.

But the rest? Ah, love has its many charms. We start planting little bombs in the Bronx Botanical Gardens. A great flower will sprout and by that flower Macys will burst apart, Penn-Central tracks will be laid to rest, and Huey, Dewey, and Louie will be free!

The fact that we mocked "Free Huey!" along with Cordier only seemed to endear *Janet Benderman* even more to our readers. We printed letters by the crazy woman Hope Gordon that Les had found in a garbage heap—the Nazis were on the moon sending signals to control us—along with some sex-crime stories left over from my job ("NO SEX? 13-YEAR-OLD GIRL KILLS DAD") and random recipes, but above all we lavished heaps and heaps of genitalia. "Our topic is Brotherhood," Les expounded, "and I'm talking about my cock in your cunt while his cock is in my ass and her crotch is tickling my chin while her tongue is probing her asshole and her cunt being reamed by Hilton who's being fucked in the ass by Alan while his (Alan's) asshole is being licked by . . ."

The administration finally cracked when, after learning that David Truman would resign as vice president, we printed a letter signed by Michael Steinlauf:

> It is with a sense of indescribable satisfaction that I learn of your imminent departure. For many years now, the very sight of you has filled me with loathing. You remind me of a festering hunk of meat. I tremble with rage at the thought of the numerous times I have looked at your bovine face only to notice tiny transparent worms crawling between the yellowing stumps of your teeth. O you dapper little man! You are a perfumed toad; each morning you bathe away the pus with lavender soap . . . Do you know that you are a walking prick? David, you must understand that there is nothing gratuitous about this metaphor . . .

The farewell letter went on and on, adding one gross, metaphoric insult after another; then we affixed a fake quote from Boccaccio at the bottom: "Poets are not liars." Considering our hyperbolic threats of arson and murder, such an epistle was simply a lively exercise in high-toned gutter eloquence, and we didn't think much of it. But the administration did. Perhaps to them it was salt thrown at Truman's wounds, a last straw. In any case, Michael, who was a graduate student, was called into the dean's office and given an ultimatum: His fellowship would be yanked if he didn't grovel at their feet with a public apology.

Poor Michael! He hadn't even intended publishing the damned joke in the first place—we took the liberty of publishing anything or signing anyone's name we wished—and now he would have to take the rap, since it was unthinkable to give in to the creeps. We felt pretty bad, of course, and came up with a plan. Michael would write a complete, total, abject retraction with the explanation that "the realm of poetry and the realm of life are a priori opposed and absolutely distinct . . . . The poem does not, so to speak, 'mean' the things it says," which meant that "the piece of writing in question, erroneously labeled 'Letter,' ought to have borne the title 'Poem,'" explicating further "that, therefore, problems arising out of an unfortunate misreading of the writing in question, viz., of clandestine relations between President Kirk and Dean Truman, of the latter's actual resemblance to the male member, of Dean Truman's tacit consent to Dean Coleman's strange request, are, with the context heretofore elaborated, meaningless." Then he concluded his over-intellectualized flatulence with the statement, "I hereby entirely renounce and disown the statement 'Poets are not liars' attributed to Boccaccio and appended, without my knowledge, to the end of the piece of writing in question." Not bad.

But just to make sure, David Somerset followed Michael's so-called "Retraction" with a "Comment" that "the idea of a retraction is to take back something you've said. This can always be done in one sentence: 'The things I said about Andrew Cordier really weren't true.' If you use more than one sentence to retract something, either you don't know what you're doing or you don't mean it. Michael Steinlauf's retraction is more than one sentence long, so, does he mean it? Why should he?

People generally take things back because they're threatened with greater power or bad taste. This is the case with Michael," and David's "Comment" soon devolved into an obscene, mad rant about "the black insects that come out of the mouths of the faculty . . . . They want to eat his dick," etc. Not bad at all. In any case, the administrators, realizing that they were not going to get anywhere with such games, simply forgot the whole thing, and Michael's flow of money remained safe.

Yes, *Janet Benderman* was a wonderful vehicle for venting ourselves, but I wanted more. I would not burn the library or throw matches down Cordier's throat—not really—but I did keep crossing from the realm of poetry to that of life. Once I went to the Museum of Modern Art with Paul Auster to hear Pauline Kael lecture about Godard's films. She was OK, but it seemed as if she did not really capture the French filmmaker's strange, splintered vision, and we squirmed in our seats, mumbling our own fantastic commentary of raunchy jokes. Auster suddenly dared me to ask Miss Kael to dance. I took the bait, and in an instant I jumped up, denounced the critic for being an empty windbag, and proposed that she prove otherwise by joining me in a dance. Then I leaped onto the stage, grabbed her by the hand, attempted a quick foxtrot, she laughed, and then I hopped off before security could nab me.

Most of all, I launched my meat campaign. I would pick up some particularly bloody mess of raw stew meat or shank bone from a butcher shop. Then, randomly selecting a classroom in Hamilton abuzz with some professor's profundities, I would quickly throw open the door and, pushed against the wall to one side, toss the hunk of bloody flesh into the room while howling, "*MEAT!*" I could argue that some real flesh, some real blood had to enter the groves of this particular academe, that I had a mission to jolt the soporific bastards into the horrors of the moment. "Get out of Plato's cave!" each bloody bone declared:

"There is no cave! No Plato! Just meat!" That sounds good, if you wish, but I don't really know why I began lobbing raw flesh into classrooms like hand grenades—only that I felt a deep satisfaction doing it. In George Stade's seminar I gave my presentation on the masquerade of Jesus-as-Devil (or was it Devil-as-Jesus?) in Melville's *Confidence-Man* by first slapping a lamb chop down on the table. Professor Stade took it in stride, and pretty soon every class I attended had a chunk of raw flesh or entrails on the table before me or on the chair beside me. I felt soothed by the presence of gore.

I was not alone in such endeavors. Mitch Sisskind came up with a scheme to inflict the biblical ten plagues on Columbia, calling together a clandestine crew of Dada disciples—including Alan Senauke, Les Gottesman, David Somerset, Paul Auster, and me—to carry out his deliciously diabolical plan. First came blood—red dye—in the fountains in front of Low. This was the first plague—and it hardly caused a stir. Then we moved on to larger schemes: Mitch knew of a company that sold frogs to labs and schools in lots of 12 each in Chicago. We pooled our money to order 144 frogs, and then Mitch took a flight in a disguise and picked up the amphibians in a carefully orchestrated clandestine operation. Boxes in hand, we stationed ourselves on the second floor of Hamilton and, our watches coordinated, dumped the frogs out onto the floor seconds before classes changed. Several of us, barely suppressing our glee, handed out leaflets denouncing Columbia's sins, declaring that today the ten plagues had descended upon the head of the unrepentant institution.

But to our dismay the frogs went virtually unnoticed. They were merely a brief distraction as students and faculty clumped around the hopping, slimy creatures on their way to class, completely unfazed. The frogs were swiftly scooped up and dumped at the biology department to be used for dissections with not even a small article appearing in the student newspaper. After occupation and riots and mayhem, perhaps the ten plagues seemed tame. Our plan had so backfired that we had actually, of all things, assisted the university, saving them money by providing victims for biology student dissections. The frogs were the last of our plagues.

Eventually, no matter the bounds of art and life, my last year stumbled to a close.

Surely I had done enough to deserve to get "out."

I had no more need for the company of raw meat.

THIRD SUITE

LOST THINGS

The Scholars Consider Lost Things

There was King Philip's crippled hand. For a long time it was passed around in bars in New England, pickled in a jar of brandy, and then it was gone. Also, Cotton Mather reached up and pulled off King Philip's jawbone from his skull as it rotted on a pole in Salem, and that too is lost.

Nat Turner's scrotum was made into a coin purse. In the South, before the Civil War, it was passed around for people to inspect, and no one can locate that either.

Phyllis Wheatley wrote a second book of poems, but no one can find it.

I hope it is not amiss to note the disappearance of the golden tablets on which Joseph Smith says the Book of Mormon was written.

Has anyone ever found Tom Paine's bones?

And then Henry David Thoreau: "I once lost a hound, a bay horse, and a turtle-dove."

There is "The Lost Colony" of Roanoke, and there's also "The Lost Generation" of Paris.

A New Age guru told his audience in Santa Monica: "GET LOST!"

The 307th and 308th Infantry Battalions and the 306th Machine Gun Battalion, "The Lost Battalion," were cut off from the rest of the 77th Infantry Division during the Battle of the Argonne in 1918.

I have been known to lose my glasses.

The manuscript of the novel *The Isle of the Cross*, by Herman Melville, remains lost.

Amelia Earhart's plane—somewhere in the Pacific.

Genghis Khan's grave—somewhere in the steppes.

Lost Kidneys

2003

Dear Hilton,

I was writing a thesis on the ethics of kidney sales and I had an idea: I would actually talk with people who sold their kidneys to find out what drove them to do it. I would not untangle the logic of Kant and Rawls in the absence of lived experience, and I would not look down upon those people forced to such a terrible decision. Ethics would have to be determined without condescension, and I was thrilled at the prospect.

So I traveled far away to India, to the slums of Chennai, Bangalore, and Kerala, to find them. I would talk to donors in the sweltering heat of their shacks. For each interview I brought a small sack of rice as a gift, and as I entered and offered my gift, some interviewees were so hungry that they tore open the bag to chew a handful of hard, uncooked rice before answering any questions. I had never seen anyone so hungry, and I was astonished at their desperation. The kidney donors were almost all women, and they all spoke frankly.

After a while the interviews began to sound the same, and I came to know it all as one story looping over and over, a litany of sorrow:

I have a debt the moneylender says pay the debt or I will kill your husband we have no money no income I have no choice I am scared of surgery and if I could have done otherwise I would have and the doctor said there might be some risk but I said I have so many problems with the debt that the risk was OK the debt was too big and if I could not have donated I would have committed suicide I would have drowned myself if I could not have been able to sell my kidney it's illegal but I didn't care we borrowed the money at 400 percent at 1,000 percent interest because we needed it for our son in the hospital our daughter was getting married no food no place to go nowhere to work and I never even heard of a kidney before and what it did and besides they told me I have another so I was able to get the money and pay off the debt and we were alive and we saved someone else's life too I never felt any difference after the surgery I have a debt the money lender says pay the debt or I will kill your entire family . . .

It was overwhelming: the agony, the ignorance, the exploitation. If such abject poverty didn't exist, no one would be forced to sell their body parts, but the horror does exist, the poverty will not disappear, at least not right away, and what will we do in the meantime?

Should kidney sales be legalized and therefore regulated so that the seller receives adequate treatment and fair payment? Or should it be kept illegal because selling irreplaceable body parts is noxious, a violation of human autonomy and sanctity? But if you make it illegal, all you do is drive the sales underground and leave the sellers unprotected; if you make it legal, you slide down a slippery slope of other, even more noxious markets, and body parts are turned into commodities with even more hideous results. What mother would not sell her liver or her heart for transplant even if it killed her, just so that her children might live?

But when I watched a mother so hungry that she tore open the small bag of rice and threw a handful into her mouth, when I heard the uncooked rice crunch and saw her eyes film over in contentment, something snapped in me. No matter how well I could parse values and determine correct choices according to philosophy's thought experiments, actual horror comes in the flesh. Horror would make the choice for the women, no matter what I said. They had no escape.

That's when I had one of those realizations you're looking for, Professor Obenzinger, although I don't know if I can express it properly. It was simple but dug down deep inside me. I realized that these poor people who crunched frantically on uncooked rice had no escape—
AND THAT I HAD NO ESCAPE, EITHER!

How's that for a sudden realization?

Sincerely,
Joseph _____

American Myth
2003

Dear Professor Obenzinger,

I'm not sure that this is what you wanted when you talked in class about collecting stories of people hearing divine quacks like the one you heard, but I do have something to share. It's something that sort of irritates me, although it's not about your class, which I think is great. I do like William Burroughs, gross as he is, but I admit I can't stand Gertrude Stein. I firmly believe she abuses her readers, and I think you're surprised by that, and I apologize.

In any case, I'm doing an honors thesis in Humanities, and I decided to find out about Horatio Alger because people have always yammered at me about the Horatio Alger story, and how I too was able to rise up and go to Stanford. You know I have a pretty hard-luck story myself: Dad dies and Mom gets strung out on pain pills and goes to prison for phony prescriptions; homeless girl raises her brother, works full time, yet gets straight A's in high school. So I read a few Horatio Alger books, and they're interesting; they're not "rags to riches" as people think, but they're about boys (sorry, no girls) who, with "luck and pluck," make it from rags to respectability—something a little bit different from the myth that began to be promoted in the 1920s by fans of Alger's books who wanted a way to feel good about their own greed (this is my own editorial remark).

Then I read about Alger's life—and that's where things began to disturb me. It turns out that Horatio Alger graduated from Harvard and became a Unitarian minister somewhere in Massachusetts. But after a year or so he was accused of "a most heinous crime," and this turned out to be "the abominable and revolting crime of unnatural familiarity with *boys*." He resigned immediately and fled the very next day—ahead of a lynch mob. This is shocking, but it gets stranger, at least in my opinion. After a while, Alger recovers from his shame and decides to dedicate himself to a "literary ministry," which means he ends up writing books for young people, eventually developing his famous series of stories about boys who are naturally moral and decent and who with luck and the help of a grown-up patron make it out of the muck and grime: always, an aspiring boy with an older man.

Over and over he wrote the same story, basically—set in the city, in the country, wherever—over and over the way you repeat prayers. Or maybe over and over the way pornography goes through the same motions, more or less, until there's some kind of climax. OK, don't get surprised I know about porn—I did live on the streets, plus I'm a child of the Internet. In any case, maybe I'm getting carried away, but all of a sudden I started to read his stories as covert sexual fantasies of sorts.

All of this is fine—a little weird but harmless, loose interpretation on my part. But, you see, Horatio Alger surrounded himself with boys, especially homeless boys, those urchins they called "street Arabs," who suffered from the utmost neglect and violence and sexual attacks. They would swarm all over his rooms in his boarding house—and for a while he even took a room in the Newsboys Lodging House, a shelter for those homeless boys who would often work selling the daily papers in New York City. For his "literary ministry," Alger vowed to make up for molesting boys by dedicating his life to bettering the lives of these "street Arabs."

So, imagine this: Horatio Alger is surrounded by his deepest, darkest temptation—young, beautiful boys—and yet he had to keep himself from touching them. He would pull little Johnny onto his lap, wrestle with spry Freddy, trying to keep it all innocent, but he was actually circling around like a moth attracted to a flame . I realized that the really incredible thing about Horatio Alger wasn't his stories, but the fact that he repressed all this sexual energy and turned it into fantasies of uplift. What agony he must have suffered being tempted so deeply and so constantly, all the while keeping his hands to himself. The real myth is not "rags to riches" or "rags to respectability," but "arousal to repression." Every night he must have retired to his little room in the Newsboys Lodging House only to masturbate like a demon.

But then I began to wonder. Upon his death he left orders for his family to destroy all his diaries and letters and other personal writings, which they did with enthusiasm. They even slipped out some document about his time as a minister from the Unitarian archives and burned it. Horatio Alger was disappeared, so to speak, and when some joker wrote his biography in 1928, he wrote it as a hoax, making up a parody of a typical Horatio Alger story as a stand-in for a real biography, since he had almost nothing to base it on. Of course, everyone believed the hoax was the real thing. But why did Alger want everything destroyed? Was it because he was not entirely successful in sublimating his lust? Did he keep an account of his "failures" in his diary? Was he actually a serial pedophile? Did he squeeze little Johnny onto his lap with less innocence than may be supposed? Did he display his raw desire?

This is not a moment of revelation when everything gets clear — this is a moment when everything gets murkier. No evidence exists to say that Horatio Alger was a sexual predator — and I can assume the nicer version, the author of saintly repression, is just as valid, if not more, and that accomplishment is astonishing enough. But the worm of doubt has crawled into my brain. I've learned how conniving and self-serving and outright sick people can be, even those who say they want to help you, and I've had to subject myself to the gross desires of Good Samaritans. So, I can't help but be suspicious. I can't stop thinking about it: The creator of the myth of American success was actually a child molester.

So, now I have this thing eating away at me. Maybe it's that cynical hurt feeling I remember from living on the streets, or maybe it's hard experience telling me that something is terribly, horribly wrong. Again, I'm not sure if a queasy suspicion fits your list of realizations, but you can take this story—the Great American Myth of the pedophile—and you can tell me what I can do to have it stop bugging me.

Best wishes,
Alice _____

The Author Meets Hilton Obenzinger
2005

Through some deft work on Google, I located Robin Dissin, now Dissin-Aufses, who was the faculty adviser for *Hilton Obenzinger* at Schreiber High School. Now a veteran teacher, the head of the English department at JFK High on Long Island, she remembered the escapade very well. It turned out that Josh Berman, the student who founded the magazine, was at the New York Psychiatric Institute—not a patient but a psychiatrist doing research on medications to treat psychosis. Robin's father-in-law was the head surgeon at Mount Sinai, and Josh Berman's bio said he had gone to medical school there. Robin's mother-in-law was a retired librarian, and she was eager to do her stuff, so she tracked down some phone numbers for him.

This was it: Josh Berman was cornered, and I dialed his office number.

"Josh Berman?"

"Yes?"

I told him that the voice on the other side was Hilton Obenzinger. There was a brief pause, and he replied, "I've been waiting for this phone call for years."

I assured him there would be no lawsuit. I only wanted to find answers to my questions. Why my name? Why "legendary Columbia student?"

It turned out that Josh's father had gone to Columbia (Class of '51), and he had read one of his alumni magazines in 1981. It was about *Janet Benderman*, and it had some story about me. I vaguely remembered someone from the magazine talking to me over the phone twenty-five years before, but I had paid little heed to it at the time.

"That was my inspiration," Josh said. He was so moved by the account of my wacky Dada exploits that he decided to name the magazine after me.

So the mystery was solved. The circle had closed, and other former members of the high school magazine contacted me.

Weeks later I went to New York to give a reading of a new book at the St. Mark's Poetry Project, and I went to the archives at Columbia to find the article. I brought a set of *Janet Bendermans* to donate to their treasure trove, passed the bronze bust of Grayson Kirk, patted his sad forehead, and entered the sweet air-conditioned wood-paneled room in Low Library. The archivist told me there was no unity on what to call the events of 1968, since some regarded the revolt as an abomination (I reckon the Republican senator from my class would be in that camp), so they called it, with some ambivalence and studied ambiguity, "The Troubles," like the conflict in Ireland. Ten years before, I had wanted to go to the archives to research "The Troubles," and I had made an appointment to dig through their extensive pile of 1968 stuff. But I just sat on the steps by the statue of Alma Mater, paralyzed. I couldn't get myself to enter Low Library. I overheard the students chat about classes and dates, the sun was shining, the students laughing, the blank windows of the president's office staring right back at me, and I saw myself standing on the ledge. Eventually I walked off in a daze.

Ten years before, it was impossible to pass through those doors—the weight of memory was too great. This time I lunged forward, swallowing my spit and tears.

The archive was richly paneled and filled with portraits of early America—John Jay, Alexander Hamilton, and all the others Columbia can claim as its own. We carried out the prisoner exchange: I passed over the crude broadsides to the librarian, while she handed me the bound volumes of *Columbia College Today*, unaware of my inner turmoil.

The article was remarkably accurate, describing the broadside that "elevated ridicule to a new plateau" and "drew much of its inspiration from the Dada tradition." There was the publicity photo of Leslie Gottesman, Alan Senauke, and me used for *A Cinch*, the literary anthology we edited for Columbia University Press, young and hip with baby faces, and a reminiscence of me:

> David Lehman remembers Obenzinger as the quintessential *Janet Benderman* character. "The unexpected was always upon us when Hilton Obenzinger entered the room," he says.
>
> One day Lehman ran into Obenzinger at the Cathedral Market, where the latter had just purchased a brown paper bag full of chopped sirloin steak. Always one with a nose for good food, Lehman asked him where he was going.
>
> "Hamilton Hall. Why don't you walk me?" Obenzinger replied.
>
> So they went to Hamilton, and up to the 5th floor, where a class on

Plato was being taught. Obenzinger then opened the door halfway, took out a fistful of the chopped sirloin, hurled it into the classroom, and yelled one word at the top of his lungs:

"MEAT!!"

Today, Obenzinger avows that he would like to do it again, only on a grander scale. Something with national impact.

"I'm one of those people from '68 who haven't changed," he says. "I've just ripened."

I was very aware that I was reading this article in the cool depths of Low Library just steps away from the president's office that I had camped out in for six days, and I sighed a little awkwardly. Twenty-five years after this article, I felt a little bit overripe.

The mystery was gone. Josh had become inspired by my antics, and he decided he would receive the torch.

He didn't do too badly, as he explained. He had published an article, convinced that it was written by a devout Catholic considering the priesthood, which began: "Immaculate conception strikes again! Pope steps down to welcome new Messiah. Jerry Falwell puts fault on Sesame Street, while scientists blame saccharin . . ." As a result, he had to write a retraction and an apology to the local Catholic Church. I suspect that his real error was to confuse Mary's birth exempt from Original Sin with the virgin birth of Jesus—but why quibble when it comes to ridicule.

That evening I joined the reunion of *Hilton Obenzinger*. They gathered at the Second Avenue Deli, across the street from St. Mark's Church, to eat dinner before my reading. I was a bit apprehensive as I came in late and slid alongside them.

"Hi, I'm Hilton Obenzinger. I assume you're *Hilton Obenzinger.*" They were, like Vic, the graduate student who had contacted me at Stanford, normal, well-adjusted, successful professionals. Robin Dissin-Aufses was a master teacher—and it turned out her father-in-law knew my brother and his wife from Mount Sinai connections—and she brought her daughter Kate, a student at Kenyon College. Josh Berman, now a psychiatrist and amateur humorist on the Internet, brought his wife and baby daughter. The New York Psychiatric Institute is associated with Columbia, so the Lion was brought back into the circle. They were joined by Carol Blum, a computer person for a brokerage house, who ended up coming to the reading across the street.

They recalled their old high school days—the one loony student who seemed to have disappeared, the pranks and the pratfalls, their remarkable ability to sell ads for *Hilton Obenzinger* considering its absurd status, the fun. Robin Dissin-Aufses was aghast at all the madcap adventures, astonished that she had not been fired. Certainly, the "21 Gun Salute" with toilet paper rolls in the school cafeteria should have triggered a SWAT team lockdown in the post-Columbine era on the basis of its name alone.

I let it all sink in—my alternate life, the me that I was and the me that I wasn't, my double—and I felt blessed by the Duck who had quacked that day I had come out of the shower.

A week later, there was an email from Carol:

> I just wanted to say how nice it was to see everyone after so many years, and to meet the next generation. Hilton's reading was great. No offense intended, but ... it turns out God really is a duck! I saw Victor and his fiancée last weekend in San Fran and filled them in on our reunion, so I think we're all caught up. I hope we'll stay in touch now that we've reconnected.

Hilton—I have to say the resemblance between you and the magazine is uncanny! If someone had asked me to bring our high school magazine to life, you are exactly what I would have imagined. Wait—I'm having a revelation . . .

—Carol

A CINCH

HE MAKES VIOLENT SEX TO HIS WIFE—
BY THE CLOCK!

1969

I first started writing articles for the *National Star Chronicle* in my junior year, a couple of months before the Columbia revolt. I had run into Beatrice the night I went with Les Gottesman to see Janis Joplin and the Grateful Dead, and before the concert we stopped over at Lana's West Village apartment to smoke a joint. Both Lana and Beatrice were artists, both had gone to the High School of Music and Art, and all the while I was madly and stupidly in love with Lana during high school I got to know Beatrice pretty well. Beatrice took a hit and told us about her job at the *National Star Chronicle*. I thought the place sounded terrific, but when she told me that I could even get freelance work there, I was blown away: I could be writing sex and crime stories at last.

Later, at the Fillmore East, Janis Joplin growled from her gut with so much energy that she seemed to pop out of her dress; and like every other boy in the crowd, I wanted to fuck her. But I also felt different. I had been blessed by the God of Mickey Spillane and Iceberg Slim, and soon I would be writing real hard-boiled prose. I was so thrilled at my election that, when the Grateful Dead came on and blasted so loud, my brain turned to jelly and I passed out, simply fell asleep in a cocoon of decibels. In the dense loudness of the Dead's set I dreamed of wandering city streets in search of *Fleurs du Mal* and Janis Joplin's tits.

But I had to shelve my Baudelaire dreams for more mundane trash when I started at the job. All of the newspaper's articles were taken from other newspapers—mainly the English tabloids, but also French and Russian. Beatrice sat around reading French newspapers with a dictionary, fishing for live ones. My task was simply to rewrite them according to the *Chronicle*'s well-worn formula. I had signed up merely as a hack.

Still, I thought I had found true poetry, so strange in its delights:

HUBBY TIES NUDE WIFE TO BED—THEN HANGS HIMSELF.

THREE DAYS AFTER WIFE'S FUNERAL—HE TRIES TO SEDUCE
THEIR DAUGHTERS.

QUEEN VICTORIA WAS A LESBIAN!

Sex-crime stories followed a strict template, especially in their intros: Each had to have a one-two-POW-in-the-kisser opening, including third-line caps.

The day Roger Ruffaut's wife left him for another man, he swore he'd get revenge.

After several months, Roger hit upon a scheme police called "diabolical" to make good his vow.

THE BETRAYED HUBBY RAPED HIS NAKED WIFE, TIED HER TO
A BED ... THEN HANGED HIMSELF AS SHE LOOKED ON, HORRI-
FIED AND HELPLESS.

The freak stories and girlie captions, on the other hand, required looser strophes:

> Knowing shapely Eleanor Bradley as a swinging gal, we were not surprised when she admitted to us that she's actually, of all things, a real lazybones.
>
> "Offhand," she confided during an interview, "I'd say that cat-napping and lolling around, doing nothing, are my favorite pastimes.
>
> "Early to bed and late to rise—that's the way I am."

It was fun, it was money, and—except for the time I occupied Low Library—I kept producing a small but steady flow of nutty articles.

I described the photo of "22-year-old Hollywood starlet Tandy Cronyn coming to the elegant Royal Ascot Races in a topless dress adorned with real chrysanthemums, roses and carnations. And just to make sure her outfit wouldn't wilt in the June heat, her escort—dressed in top-hat and tails—carried a watering-can!"

I hammered out how "33-year-old Keith Walters tore off a 16-year-old girl's panties then raped her three times before driving the teenage victim to a nearby hospital. When she entered in ripped clothing, almost incoherent with fear and revulsion, hospital attendants became suspicious and jotted down Walter's license number, leading to the arrest of 'The Good Samaritan Rapist.'"

And I told the tale of "a tourist from Alabama in a Rome, Italy restaurant who punched President Johnson in the jaw while yelling, 'Nigger lover!' at the former chief executive. Actually, the tourist had slugged Herbert Marboutis, the owner of a hotel back in the USA and a dead ringer for LBJ. Marboutis was in Rome for his role in a film called 'Coup d'Etat,' in which he plays the part of President Johnson. 'Marboutis plays his part very well,' a film company executive said. 'He's a walking target—I mean advertisement—for the picture.'"

Barry, the editor, a quiet Jewish intellectual, pored over the copy as if it were great art, tweaking and revising and editing, but for the most part keeping true to the clippings that Beatrice fished out. Alex, the publisher, kept out of his way and fiddled with creditors and distributors.

The obscenity arrest of the editors of *Screw* and the other outrageous sex magazines had been much in the news, and Barry leaned back in his easy chair with his hands in a tepee to meditate upon their fate and ours. "That crowd went in for cocks and cunts, so they paid the price," he moralized. "We, however, are mere peddlers of lurid tales and legitimate cheesecake, so I expect no problems. Quite the contrary," his mouth widened into a grin. "The *Screw* scandal makes for good copy and will probably do much to boost sales."

The porn was soft, and the articles did resemble the truth, although once Barry did get carried away, completely fabricating a devilish medical experiment carried out on black men in Mississippi, something like the Tuskeegee syphilis atrocity. To his surprise, the State of Mississippi threatened to sue unless the *National Star Chronicle* wrote a retraction. Alex went into a panic. He had no idea that anyone in Mississippi even read the rag, which mainly circulated through New York subways, or much less cared. The threat was, in some ways, a compliment, but one the duo sought to escape. They immediately wrote a groveling apology, quaking at the thought of a lawsuit that could bankrupt them or even land them in jail.

One day after graduation, I took a break from writing, and I went to the West End ahead of my appointment with the artist doing the cover of the anthology I was helping to edit. I wanted to fill up my head with a pitcher of beer and cigarettes. The West End was always more fun during the daytime than late at night, its dank cavernous space so alien when not jammed shoulder to shoulder. As you pushed through the door and passed into that thick, dark void, you would get an enormous rush. You had suddenly tumbled into the stomach of the whale with "Mr. Tambourine Man" belching out, and that elongated oval wooden bar curling you in like a giant smoky tongue. In a flash, daylight not only disappeared but became impossible, the digestive darkness impenetrable.

I spotted Paul Spike sitting in one of the booths against the wall washing down a greasy burger with a beer. I wouldn't exactly say that Spike—along with his roommate, Bloom—lived at the West End, but the place was a sort of headquarters for both of them. Bloom even got a job tending drinks behind the huge oval bar, while Spike provided a lot of his business. Everyone you would ever want to know would eventually be swallowed up by the West End, and Spike seemed intent on meeting all of them, one beer at a time, as each was sucked through the gorge.

I liked Spike, even though we weren't all that close. I liked his stories—one would be in the anthology—and I liked his sarcasm and the way he always sported the look of a demented prep school dropout. But I also knew Spike was torn and bitter, driven to boozy wisecracks by the murder of his father.

I didn't know anything about it, really, except what other people told me. Spike's dad had been a minister in the National Council of Churches, the God Box on Riverside Drive. Not just any minister, he was in charge of civil rights for all the Protestants. He was the one who got the white ministers down to Selma to march with King. Reverend

Spike knew everybody—Martin Luther King, JFK, Bobby Kennedy—and he was on the inside track of all the big events.

But in 1967 he ran afoul of LBJ. Johnson had tried to get Dixiecrat senators to support his miserable war in exchange for his shutting down some civil rights programs. Reverend Spike got wind of the deal and was ready to blow the whistle, but before he could expose the whole vile sellout, he was found bludgeoned to death in a motel room in Ohio. No evidence, no witnesses, but plenty of tales of homosexual liaisons—all smelling like shit. Spike's dad had been assassinated, even his character was assassinated, and Spike knew it; even Martin Luther King knew it, and said so in a letter to Spike's family. But King himself was blown away just months later, and the government could very well have been behind that one too. Spike was filled with grief and rage, yet his father's murder filled the vast dark gut of the West End without his having to say a word. He kept it to himself, and I never asked.

"Hear the good news, Hilton?"

"What good news?"

"Yeah, the war's over. Nixon pulled out twenty-five thousand troops. It's over." He laughed.

"This is 'the secret plan' to end the war?"

"You bet. Pull out a few GIs, bomb the shit out of the Vietnamese—rivers of napalm pissing from the skies—and free movies on the moon. That's the plan. Pretty smart, huh?" And he laughed again, a short sarcastic "*HANH!*"

"Yeah, a terrific plan," I joined his sarcastic assault.

"Don't worry. SDS will save our asses." I could tell he was ready to mount another sarcastic assault. "The Revolution is on—pick up the gun! That's the word. They think it's time for guerrilla war." He detonated another laugh.

"What if they're right?"

"It's bullshit, believe me, no matter what Mark Rudd or Bernardine Dohrn says. They don't know what the fuck they're doing."

Spike had a manuscript spread out beside him, and I nodded at it. "What the fuck are *you* doing?"

"I'm working on a novel."

"What's a novel?"

"*Yo' mama!*" he cracked back.

I had one of the stories for the *National Star Chronicle* in my book bag: "HE MAKES VIOLENT SEX TO HIS WIFE—BY THE CLOCK!" The story had gotten under my skin, and I was bursting with the perversity of it. It was like a picture of things to come: too ominous, too horrible—and too funny. I knew Spike would never show me his manuscript—he was not one to share his work until he thought it was polished and ready to publish—so I pulled out the file folder and tossed him the story.

"Wha'? 'Violent Sex by the Clock?'" The title triggered another explosive laugh. I watched his eyes drift down the page.

Suddenly we both felt a spectral presence glide silently to the mouth of the booth. There stood Brandon Watt. Dressed in his usual summer attire of white double-breasted suit, creamy bowtie, white summer fedora, and white kid gloves, he stood rigidly, one gloved hand held gently on his cane, the other held pensively aloft by the side of his face. Motionless, poised, he was a still white iceberg from the nineteenth century in the West End's oceanic blackness.

"Brandon! You're here! Come sit down, let's see the sketch!" I explained to Spike that we would both get a glimpse of the cover of *A Cinch* as the artist sat and carefully pulled the gloves off his hands to fold them elegantly into his hat. *A Cinch: Amazing Works from the Co-*

lumbia Review was the anthology of student writing that Columbia University Press, trying to mollify student rage, had invited Les and Alan and me to edit.

Of all my friends, I would say Brandon Watt was the one who really did live in a different world, one somewhat related to this planet but only by an odd tangent. Brandon was never shaken from his act, and he was not at all violent, yet he could freak somebody out simply by his undaunted presence. Once I went with him to a Grateful Dead concert where a bucket of acid was passing around. Whenever some stoned-out freak, arms flailing and jumping to the beat like a dervish, happened to notice the mannequin in the white double-breasted suit, white fedora, and white kid gloves who stood entirely motionless, absolutely frozen in the center of the writhing dance floor, one hand resting on his cane and his eyes beaming dead ahead at the band—well, that freak would come to a stop, gawk, and start to flip out. I posted myself nearby as a public service to reassure trippers whirling past that the motionless figure they were seeing was, in fact, real. "It's OK—he's *real*," I would casually tell each one just before a shriek would escape their lips. Brandon Watt was no hallucination.

"I trust you are well, and you too, Spike," he said in his cultured twang. He was a descendant of old America, maybe some Adams— Quincy or Frances, I'm not sure—crossed with Texas oil money. "I have come with a new map of the Nova, and I hope it will twist the cinch, as it were, quite tight enough. Tibetans have spent whole lifetimes studying the exit. I have only begun, but it is so much like space travel that I don't bother reading the newspapers anymore."

There wasn't anything anyone could say to that. "So, it's good?" I stalled.

He untied his thin artist portfolio to show the sketch. Brandon was capable of wild hieroglyphics—nuclear blasts, galaxies, high-kicking Rockettes at Radio City Music Hall, Osiris, men in suits and fedoras, mandalas, severed genitals, Aztec gods, crabs, insects, brains—all arrayed in indecipherable nonstop codes of paranoia.

In the mock-up, a cobralike snake flicked its tongue within a profile of a man's head, its hood raised up to the shaded brain like a question mark, which curled alongside a bright red disk, while a track of lines extended from the snake's eye directly through the man's to ricochet off the border around the page down a deep perspective parallel to a series of ever-receding green disks. On the back, an angel with wings was steering a star with both hands while kneeling on a cloud above yet another man's profile—this time without a snake—which, in a mirrorlike reflection against a line dropped by the angel, was doubled into a single face.

"Wow! This is terrific, Brandon." As it turned out, this was tame compared with some of his other works, and I was relieved, yet a little disappointed at the same time, although I quickly reasoned that a cover without disembodied cocks and tits revolving around an exploding sun might do just fine.

He smiled and bowed slightly.

"We speak with forked tongue—huh, Brandon?" Spike poked.

"The serpent is not my father's cold Teutonic mockery. It is a spinal column responsive to the rhythm of eons. I could say much about the betrayal of the simple faith, such as it is, of the American people, but this book is the last child in the Kingdom of the Dead. The snake makes you live."

"Brandon, have you ever been in a Henry James novel?" Now Spike was trying to go toe-to-toe with the visionary.

"At the party, the presence of William Boroughs was announced. Naturally, he wasn't there."

"Well, I like it," I interjected before Spike prompted Brandon to blast to the far reaches of the solar system. "We're all a bunch of snake-heads, angelic snake-head hipsters. It's a terrific cover."

"I'm no snake-head, Hilton. I don't smoke snake," Spike quipped back, but he nodded and smiled, unable to hide his admiration for Brandon's precision superrealism.

"Speaking of Henry James, I was just about to read a story Hilton wrote for the trashy tabloid rag he works for. Do you want to hear it?"

"Most certainly," Brandon replied, and he leaned back against the booth with his head cocked in studied attention.

The Byrds were doing "Turn! Turn! Turn!" on the jukebox as Spike declaimed the title, "HE MAKES VIOLENT SEX TO HIS WIFE — BY THE CLOCK!" He read the title not just once but three times, emphasizing first "violent," then "sex," then "clock" in succession. After this outburst, he hunched over the table, settling down to read the story in a flat, undramatic tone.

For years friends and neighbors liked and respected 31-year-old policeman Roger Volet.

But it was only recently that his wife revealed her husband's strange marital habits.

FOR SEVEN YEARS HE WOULD BE AWAKENED BY HIS ALARM CLOCK EVERY THREE HOURS AND FORCE HIS WIFE TO SUBMIT TO HIS DESIRES!

Seven years ago Roger courted Renee, the 24-year-old daughter of a wealthy farmer. The blonde and blue-eyed girl was so pious and sweet-natured that her family called her Angel Face.

Roger seemed as well-mannered and soft spoken as his bride-to-be. But on their wedding night the ex-paratrooper dropped his mask. The gentle lover became a monster.

As Renee rose on tiptoes to kiss him, he slapped her face twice. "That's to show you who's boss," he told her. "I've killed seven men in combat in Vietnam. I can finish you off with both my hands tied behind my back."

Then Volet put his combat dagger on his pillow. On the bedside table he placed his loaded pistol. And for seven years he kept both weapons within easy reach.

Every three hours the alarm clock went off, and every time Renee was forced to submit to what psychiatrists term Volet's "insatiable sexual appetite."

When they made love he would often squeeze her throat with his hands until she almost fainted. "When I refused," Renee told police, "he beat me until I was bruised all over."

Roger would never allow his pretty wife to sleep while he was still awake. "A good woman never sleeps while her husband is awake," he decreed on their wedding night.

Year after year Renee obliged her husband by the bells of the clock, while to their neighbors, the tall, broad-shouldered cop was always a "gentle giant."

But one night early this year Roger found himself alone in bed when the alarm went off. Renee could no longer tolerate her vicious husband, and with her 3-year-old daughter she fled to her father's farm.

The enraged husband drove to his father-in-law's farm. Wielding a butcher's knife, he ran into the kitchen, where he swiftly cut the throats of Renee's mother and uncle, with his wife cowering in terror. He left Renee untouched, then drove calmly to the police station to confess.

"I killed them both to make Renee suffer," he explained. "Many wives would have been happy in Renee's place that I made love so often."

Roger Volet goes to trial for murder in Lyons, France, next September.

"Jesus Christ!" Spike snapped at the end of his reading. "It's in *France! This motherfucker is in goddamn France, not America! All along I thought it was in America!*"

"It's an instructive tale," Brandon said softly. "My throat is already cut."

"Weird, huh?" I shoved the manuscript back into the book bag.

"Fucking by the clock, it's amazing," Spike mused. "Nixon's bringing home twenty-five thousand horny, fucked-up bastards. Do you think each one will get a bonus of a free GE alarm clock? Where do you get this stuff, anyway?"

I explained how the *National Star Chronicle* plumbed the world press for crud. Then I leaned back as Spike returned to setting off Brandon on one of his whacked-out explications of Nova. I didn't pay attention. I was still thinking about Roger Volet. He was a monster of the same Vietnam War, at least an earlier version of it, and everything he did made sense, at least to him. It's like he learned a language of death with a grammar all its own. He didn't even think he had really committed a crime.

Soon Brandon excused himself. He had yet another appointment to display his sketch, this time with Fred Seligman, our editor at Columbia University Press.

"I'm sure Seligman will think it's terrific, Brandon," I said as he methodically slipped his gloves back on and bowed farewell.

I downed my beer—and I could see Spike stare off into the dark. He was lost in memory for a long beat, his eyes glistening in the smoke, until he called himself back. Maybe he'd thought of his dad, I don't know.

"Well, we're all fucked," I said after I caught his eye, sliding out the booth.

"You said it," Spike chuckled, his odd mood quickly shaken off. "Don't trust anyone over the age of twelve, Hilton."

Everything's Under Control
1969

"Two krepla' and one beef lo mein?" the waiter repeated as he took our order.

Sam Wo's Restaurant stood in the crook where Mott Street bent to the left. It was the regular place that Dad brought his customers and contacts from Burlington and J. P. Stevens, and he was always tickled that he had gotten the Chinese waiters trained to recognize kreplach as won ton soup, although it was not as if he was the only Jew who walked over from the nearby textile district to eat in Chinatown.

"That's right—kreplach soup!" Dad laughed with delight. "He calls it kreplach soup! He's a Jew!"

After some customers had sealed their bargain—followed by some after-the-deal jokes and small talk, like cigarettes after sex—my father accompanied them to the door, the automatic doorbell offering its weak death rattle as they took their exit. Then we made our way to Chinatown.

"So? How'd everything go with your customers?" I asked in the restaurant.

"Everything's under control," he gave his stock answer.

The lunar module could crumble into a million pieces, Nixon could lynch the entire Democratic Party, but for my dad, everything would still be "under control." Like "God willing," it was a ritual invocation, more than a status report. In this case, however, it seemed to be accurate: He had, in fact, gotten his customers under his control, and he was buoyant, felt the exhilaration, the real zest of cutting a deal.

"And you? What have you been doing?"

"I'm writing for the newspaper."

"You call that a newspaper? Better you get yourself a real job."

Now would come the grilling, the pushing, the prodding. It was inevitable. He was worried, and with good reason, I guess.

"I'll get a job—somewhere—just so long as I can write."

"Why don't you go to graduate school? I'll pay for it. Be a professor. You get the summers off, and you can write all you want."

"I don't want to go to school anymore. Besides, my grades aren't so great, and after the strike and getting arrested I'm not so sure anyone will take me."

"But you've got to be practical. You can't live on poetry, on air—and I won't live forever to help."

"I don't expect you to pay for me. Anyway, I *am* being practical. Even if I got into a graduate school, there aren't any professor jobs available."

One thing for sure: I wasn't going to rot in a university while the whole world went up in flames around me, even if they were to let me in, which I sincerely doubted.

"So, what are you going to do? Dig ditches?"

"Actually, that doesn't sound too bad."

We went around and around, a conversation we had had several times in the course of my senior year, a conversation maybe a million other freaky middle-class kids were having at the very same moment.

Really, I didn't know what I would do, only that Amy and I would take off for someplace, cut through the shackles of New York, do something. This, I suppose, was the generation gap they all talked about: After the father reached the heights of the middle class and sent his youngest son to the Ivy League, all that the ungrateful jerk ended up wanting was to dig ditches, to live off the land, to hide out in some commune cut off from the flow of cash.

"I don't know. Maybe I'll write for an underground newspaper or something. Anyway, there's still the draft."

"But didn't your draft board burn down?"

"Yeah, someone set fire to it, but they got copies of everything. They'll catch up, and I'm not very far down in the lottery."

We silently shoveled the Chinese kreplach into our mouths while the restaurant roared with lunchtime chatter. On this we agreed: One way or another, I wasn't going to get killed for Nixon's war.

"I've got a proposal for you. Just listen. You don't have to say anything now, just think it over."

This was something different than harping on graduate school. He had that casual look on his face like when he was haggling and wanted to make a shrewd offer but didn't want to let on how crafty he really was.

"A proposal?" I was worried. I had no idea what was up his sleeve; only that no matter what it was, I would probably end up disappointing him.

"How about you come and work for me? You can start by doing the books. You can make money and do all the writing you want. Take time off and write. Write in the evenings. But come in and learn the ropes. I'm getting old, and this business is an opportunity anyone in their right mind would kill to get their hands on. I've got a million dollars owed to me. If anything should happen to me, it'll all go down the drain. You can get it."

"Work for you?" I was stunned.

"Just think it over. It's just the *shmata* business, I know, but it's nothing to be ashamed of. You can make good money, I can inch by inch step back, and you can have the whole thing, all yours."

"But what about Mark? He's the one who just got an MBA. He's the one who wants to go into business, not me."

"Mark is a Yankee. He wants to work for General Motors, the big corporations—he's a real Yankee, so he doesn't want it. He doesn't realize what it means to be your own boss, and he doesn't have that European feeling to get along with people. In this business you've got to get along with everybody, you've got to shmooze and kibbitz, and you've got to be straight. No matter how much I talk this or bargain that, I never finagle. Sure, in business you need a little touch of larceny, but I never cheat. Some customer needs a break, a loan, goods up front, I give it to him, and he comes back. Sometimes I lose, but most of the time I get them back because they know Nat Obenzinger is an honest fellow."

He went on, singing the praises of commerce. "One dollar after another—do you know how that feels, to get that dollar? To make money?" How he loved his business, to "make" money, his one solace in life, his joy, the sport of it—and I hated every minute of it.

I knew I could never work on Canal Street. Maybe I could glad-hand the way he said, but I could hardly picture myself buttering up the credit managers from J. P. Stevens or Burlington with won tons or bringing over the cases of whiskey to bribe the other goyim on whose good will his Jewish-middleman status depended. He would give gifts —whole cases of scotch, a new car—and he even sent a big mill's representative's son through college, actually paid his way. He had to grovel like any Merchant of Venice.

More important, I couldn't bargain worth a damn. I was the son of a merchant, but I always squirmed whenever I had to argue even over the bad addition on a restaurant check, much less a pound of flesh. I hated haggling. Even worse, I could not handle money if my life depended on it. I really was, as my father so often complained, too much like my mother, the suburban housewife artist wandering between the Art Students League and Macy's: I knew how to spend money, not how to make it. His business would go broke within a year with me at the helm.

"Me? You know I start gagging on the dust the minute I get to the place. How could you think I could do it? Mark's the businessman, not me."

"Just think about it, sleep on it. You'd be a fool to pass up this chance."

I had just been handed an invitation to join the fraternity of Jewish merchants, the ancient, honorable order of Buy Cheap Sell Dear, the real explorers who had linked the world with calculated risk while the goyim merely sailed the ships. His was not the hideous nightmare of Saran Wrap–napalm–DuPont–Dow, but I knew right off that I was exactly that fool to pass it up, that I even wanted to be a fool, a holy fool screaming at the sky.

But I felt, most of all, the dark hole in our lives left by Ronnie's death. Mark was a Yankee, too American—cynical, to be sure—but he was still thrilled enough to jump on the grand merry-go-round of capital. And I was the beatnik, too European—trying to be practical by dreaming the impossible, a goofball poet fumbling to pull the plug on the very same carousel. Only Ronnie, the eldest, was just the right blend of Old World and New, cunning yet compassionate, worldly yet wise, only to get struck down on his way to medical school. My father would never have asked Ronnie or any of us to take over his life's work. He wouldn't have felt compelled to, no matter how many accounts payable drifted in the void, because Ronnie the doctor would have made the extremes of his other two sons merely bookends to a dense, rich Talmud of "a doctor." We made sense, were made whole, only because of Ronnie; now we were just fragments, pieces of a jigsaw that never would fit together.

"OK, Dad, I'll think about. I promise," I lied. "I'll talk it over with Amy."

After lunch we headed back to his place, wending our way through the narrow back streets and alleys of Chinatown, past the Tombs.

"Remember this place?" he nudged me toward the prison.

"How can I forget?"

"I remember when your friend—what's his name?"

"Senauke, Alan Senauke."

"When your friend came in and said you were in the Tombs and needed bail."

"We'd collected all the cash we had to get him out—and you were right close by."

"*My son in jail!* I never would have imagined it."

"It doesn't bother me."

"What a meshuga! But now you can forget all that. You can't change the world, no matter how many times you get arrested."

"People can change the world, Dad."

"Don't even think of it. I'll break every bone in your body if you try."

"Don't worry—the cops would love to do it for you."

He just sighed as we shuffled past the huge penal monolith, the ache inside me pressing harder.

"Dad, I want to ask you something."

"What? You need money?"

"No, not that. I want to know . . . " I hesitated until I could find the courage. "Why didn't you tell me how sick Ronnie was?"

"What?"

"Why did you keep it a secret?"

He stopped by the ornately carved firehouse down from the Tombs. "Why do you want to know?"

"Because it's always bothered me—that I didn't know. Even the night he died, I didn't know until we walked into the hospital room."

"What was there to tell? You were a kid, you didn't need to know, you needed to pay attention to school, be a kid, play ball. What could you do?"

We both stood there before the gray cathedral-like building, gargoyles and delicate carvings obscuring the fact that a behemoth fire engine was hidden behind its facade. I looked down at my feet.

"Yeah, but I wish I'd have known, that's all."

Actually, I had plenty of chances to figure out what was going on, if I had really wanted to, but I had kept the secret as much as my parents had. It wasn't their fault. Yet I figured if they had told me, if I could not have hidden from the fact, if it were simply impossible, inescapable, if I had known, something would have been different.

We walked on in silence.

"I didn't even want to know, myself," he finally continued. "When they were operating, they told us to call up, and when I did, the nurse said there was some problem, that it was taking longer than they expected. That's when I knew. I knew it was the worst. We were driving to the Kozlows' house for a Seder—you remember the dentist and his wife?—and I couldn't even see the road, the breath was stolen right out of me. I couldn't even breathe. I had to pull over and cry. I knew then it was bad—no simple operation—they were cleaning the tumor out as much as they could, scraping it out. I told your mother, 'Don't say anything, make believe everything is all right. They don't need to know anything, and we don't need to ruin their Pesach.' So we went to their Seder, made believe everything was fine, and I was eating up inside of me, just eating up."

He abruptly stopped. He had never told me this before; he had never shared his pain. I waited, but I realized he would say no more.

"You were a kid. Be a kid, you should *live*, that's what I thought."

After he had talked with the shrink during my freshman freak-out, heard of my suicidal fantasy life, he said the same thing. He had taken me by the shoulder on the sidewalk on Broadway outside Furnald Hall, tears in his eyes, and he growled, "Live, goddamn it, *JUST LIVE!*"

The doorbell weakly rattled one more time as we entered the Hilton Textile Corporation. I stood at the doorway, fidgeting, ready to leave.

He reached for his wallet. Opening its mouth wide, he asked, "How much money do you need?"

FOURTH SUITE

NIXON'S SHOESHINE

Nixon's Shoeshine

First, Charlie found the photo in *Life*. It showed Richard Nixon, then vice president, sitting in the central square of Guatemala City, his foot propped up on a small wooden shoeshine box while getting his shoes shined by a small boy wearing a ragged Hopalong Cassidy–type hat. Nixon was on a "goodwill" visit one year after the 1954 U.S.-engineered coup overthrew the nationalist Arbenz government and installed the pro-American regime of Castillo Armas, and the photo seemed to represent the current relationship: little Guatemala at the feet of the huge, lumbering Yankee. In the background we saw a crowd of people from the waist down—the shoeshine was some kind of spectacle, maybe even a ritual of sorts. The vice president, in suit and tie, towered over the impoverished boy, attempting to be charming—they looked at each other, although the gaze between them was not mutual. It tumbled steeply down from Nixon on the park bench to the boy sitting below him in the bare dirt. Nixon's gaze was kindly enough, but the difference in status and power between the two was dramatic.

Then Charlie dug into the archives of *El Imparcial*, a Guatemalan newspaper, and he found another photo of the same scene. The caption told us that the shoeshine boy had a name—he was twelve-year-old Rodolfo Gonzalez. In this photo, the boy was standing, his ragged hat still on, but his box was slung over his shoulder. He was facing Nixon, who was also standing, but stooped over, one arm hanging long in front of him, his shoulder rounded in a sort of simian hunch. He stood in front of some garden steps and clearly had the look of an ape. The boy shined shoes, but we could see in this photo that he had no shoes himself. Yet he stood with dignity—while the lumbering Yankee seemed awkward, unacquainted with the basics of good posture. The picture was shot from a low angle, and the viewer was forced to look up at the boy, underscoring his dignity, even quiet defiance.

Charlie pulled out yet another unpublished photo from the dusty files of *El Imparcial*. In the background Nixon sat on the park bench, his leg up on the boy's box, and both the vice president and the little boy looked off to the left, with Nixon pointing. In the foreground was Alfred Eisenstaedt, the celebrated photographer for *Life*. He wore a suit, and he was crouching, his bag slung over one shoulder, his camera up to his eye, his bald spot prominent in the center of his scalp, as he took a photo of the scene. Charlie turned over the print, but there was no name, only the stamp of the newspaper on the back. He went through the rest of the files, and what he discovered by this anonymous photographer was an entire, parallel record of Nixon's visit, but one told with even greater irony than Eisenstaedt's prints. Of course, the story of these shots was couched in a careful, quiet code invisible to the clouded eye of the government censor: Nixon smiled and the people watched, all in appropriate frames, even when the grim colonels with dour looks gathered around his plane as he mounted the steps to wave farewell.

Charlie also discovered a series of photographs of Eisenstaedt, the great photographer himself, while working to capture the moments of Nixon's visit. What was printed in the newspaper were the photos of the visit—and what was filed away and left to gather dust was the study of Eisenstaedt at work. The anonymous photographer might have been curious, or perhaps it was a social commentary in itself—a view of the great artist as dutiful servant, as worker, as collaborator, or as independent chronicler. It was hard to tell. Eisenstaedt was treated with respect—never was he caught in an awkward or vulnerable position, even when he climbed trees to click the American politician from above.

"I learned something from this," Charlie told me. "I learned that there are stories within stories—and there are tellers within storytellers, hidden away, voices you never know are there, and unless you decide to find them, you never will. Except by accident, as I did."

High School Poet
1960–1965

I began writing poems in the seventh grade, several months before Ronnie died. The circumstances were accidental, even silly. I was in love with Franny Foxe, a tall, skinny beauty with a freckled pretty face framed by short brown hair. Most afternoons after school I spent at her house, listening to 45s in her bedroom—she was nuts about Jackie Wilson—flirting with her in the backyard, hanging out in the den; no matter where, always drooling for her, but not getting very far. Her parents didn't hover; they didn't need to. I never even got a chance to make out. Franny was very coy.

I don't know where I got the idea—probably it was some gush of romance from the myths of the Warsaw Jewish aristocracy I had ingested from my mother, something that flowed so irresistibly from the same Chopin waltz I would later practice over and over for the WQXR contest. In any case, I painstakingly drew an elaborate pencil portrait from her class photograph, my lessons at the Art Students League finally paying off.

I also wrote a poem, aching over every line: how an Angel had come to visit me at night and told me to go discover Beauty, so I went out "to discover what I would discover," and when I awoke, what I did discover was that the Angel was none other than Franny herself:

> Your eyes have the delightful freshness of a stream in the spring
> Flowing under a big old oak tree.
> I bow my head as if you are a supernal queen
> And I your humble servant.

On and on, I snapped out line after line of clichés and bad similes and awkward effusions—the lacerations lasting for more than six pages.

When I finally finished, I neatly wrote out the poem on onionskin paper, rolled up the drawing and tied it with a colored thread, bought flowers on Merrick Road, and knocked on Franny Foxe's door. I handed the pile of gifts to her, mumbled, and took off.

Later, she called on the phone to thank me, to say how lovely, beautiful, and all that. My heart fluttered. But the next day I slunk back into the long coatroom in our homeroom class as I watched her display the poem to a clutch of girls, all giggling and tittering at the whole notion

of a boy doing such a thing. Not only was I humiliated, but the love of-
ferings didn't even work. Franny kept on squealing as she listened to
her Jackie Wilson 45s—and I still lusted for her icy slender body.

But what did happen was a business success story. Other boys in JHS
59 asked me to write love letters for them—to use when slipping notes
back and forth during class and other occasions. They wanted "Your
lips are like red cherries," and all that, and I gave it to them, charging
twenty-five cents for each missive. I gained their attention, and I even
made some money. (It was not such a big jump from cranking out sappy
love letters to writing sex-death stories for the *National Star Chronicle*
in college.) In any case, I realized I could get rich by writing poems,
quarter by quarter. And while I was disabused of my foolish get-rich-
quick scheme pretty quickly, I did gain the admiration of boys, the interest of teachers, even the wonder of parents.

Night after night I sat up in bed tossing out poems about anything I
could think of—baseball, sunset, dreams, trees in the storm—a kind of
release from my hours of pounding the piano; it didn't feel too hard at
all. I didn't especially want to be a poet, but I did want to become an
artist, any kind of artist—painting, music, theater—it hardly mattered,
just so long as I could be some kind of Jean-Christophe creator. I
dreamed often of my heroic death conducting Beethoven in front of
the philharmonic. I would clutch my heart but wave off all help until
the end of the movement, and then fall to the podium, expired. Franny
Foxe would be in the audience, and she would burst into tears of love
and writhe in agonies of guilt.

Ronnie's real death intruded instead. I had gone on with my hard-
on fantasies while the hideous cancer took its course through my
brother's lymph nodes, and when he died the week after I stuttered out
my Chopin waltz for Abram Chasins, I was stunned. Ronnie's wide-

open, blank eyes drilled into the hospital ceiling and bored into my soul.

Right after the funeral, perhaps to ease my grief, my mother suggested that I try writing the epitaph for the tombstone. I grabbed at it as a sacred task, laboring hard, tears filling my eyes, agonizing over creating the smallest possible but most appropriate and unique tribute to fit on the face of a stone. I came up with a small poem that ended in yet an even smaller couplet:

Time will walk, and only snatches will be kept,
But we loved, and we will not forget.

This the funeral home took, although by the time the poem reached the artisan who carved the stone, the lines had become the standard "We Shall Never Forget." I didn't feel slighted, though. My words had been tossed back to the familiar cliché, where they belonged, but each of those words was now filled with real meaning, which I knew existed only because I had cried as I jabbed at the typewriter.

After Ronnie's death, writing poems became a darker, more sorrowful pursuit. But it also became fun. In high school I discovered the thrill of what we called "obscurity," the knack of hiding our meanings or ignoring them altogether, a case of bad T. S. Eliot. I wrote a story about a conversation with a strange woman I had met on the Q-5 bus on Merrick Road, a Miss Gimbel (a distant relative of the founder of Gimbels department store). I played out the reality into fantasy, turning the encounter into her bizarre seduction of the narrator, then his grisly murder. It was a laugh, in a tortured, horny sort of way, but even more amusing was the response of my enthusiastic teacher, who winked knowingly at me and seemed to find all kinds of deep symbolic meanings in the story. I had no idea what he was talking about, not a clue, but I was pleased that I had done something so well that even I didn't understand what it meant.

Then one Saturday, while riding the E train to the Donnell Library, I read *Howl* in that tiny black-and-white City Lights edition. The wheels clattering and the tunnel booming, I sat on the edge of the wicker seat, swallowing Ginsberg's mania, roaring through Molochs, skipping the Fifth Avenue stop and not getting off until I was finished rolling off "Holy! Holy! Holy!" somewhere in Brooklyn, dazed, all of life instantly transformed.

I had discovered something—the blast of words, the slangy newness, my own queer shoulder to the wheel. I no longer wanted simply to write poems, I wanted to *be* poems: I wanted to live the beat bardic spasm, be a Dada poet of action on a mystic quest, a lunatic holyman seer, a combination Whitman, Nietzsche, and Groucho Marx. I began hanging out in the Village, grabbing every odd, new book I could get—Ferlinghetti, Corso, Kerouac—especially the small mimeographed experimental magazines and chapbooks. I went to café forums, listening to Paul Krassner, Seymour Krim, LeRoi Jones all rant and laugh and tear at each other's brains. And in school I became, as they called it then, "a nonconformist," a beatnik.

One late afternoon after school, as I sat by the dining room table, my pants open as I ate cookies and milk, my mother walked in through the back door. "I have someone for you to meet!" Behind her came Lana Koenig, long dark hair, black beret, with one of those over-large black leather artist portfolios under her arm. I stood up from my milk and cookies to say hello, and my pants fell to my knees—which caused her to laugh as I quickly bunched them up again.

My mother, returning from the Brooklyn Museum on the Long Island Railroad, had met Lana—who went to the High School of Music and Art but lived only a few blocks away—on the train. She mouthed off about her son, as Jewish mothers do, and hauled Lana off to meet me right then and there. I should have realized that my pants dropping down to my knees did not bode well, but I almost immediately fell terribly, hideously, impossibly in love with her.

Lana was an artist who put "Eine Kleine Nachtmusik" and the "Trout Quintet" on the record player as she painted huge abstract canvases. She read Herman Hesse and *Summerhill*, and she would go with me to see *The Premise* or *Second City* or *Mother Courage* and laugh in the middle of Sheridan Square and talk about Van Gogh and "problems." Lana was everything about the High School of Music and Art that my stuttering Chopin waltz in yet another miserable, failed performance at the entrance audition had kept me away from ever knowing. Plus I thought she was beautiful.

This time I wrote—even built—a whole book. I typed out all the poems and slipped them into those plastic three-ring see-through page holders; then I cut two plywood slabs, sanded them down, carved the title of a J. Alfred Prufrock imitation love poem, "Just By Me Be By My Side," on the cover, shellacked both boards, and hooked it all together with silver rings.

Lana was delighted, truly entranced, and visibly moved. No derision, no teasing, she expressed only deep admiration for the art and the painstaking work that had gone into that wooden tome. But admiration was all that I would get, for my Pinocchio would never come to life. Lana enjoyed being "friends" with me, while she persisted in dating schmucks on motorcycles, and I dutifully kept on playing at being "friends," whimpering after her like some chubby pup until I couldn't take it anymore.

At least I had a way to focus my poetry, to sandpaper sexual fixation flat and smooth, so to speak, and thereby keep myself out of the mental hospital.

Dream the Night Before Starting
Graduate School Late in Life
1991/1964

I could smell it as I walked down the steps to the classroom in the basement of Lewisohn Hall, that familiar stench of plastic chairs and air
conditioning and antiseptic, that ineffably sweet, half-sickening perfume. I pushed open the door. Leonie Adams sat at the head, and all
the other students from the poetry workshop that I had taken the summer of my junior year in high school ranged around the seminar table
listening to her talk. In the dream, they all looked up at me, surprised,
as I stood in the doorway.

There was Margaret. Originally from Georgia, for twenty years she
had lived in New York City with her reporter husband. In her forties
and white, she was finishing her graduate degree in order to teach literature at a Negro college in Atlanta. She was going back to her South
in that summer of Chaney, Goodman, and Schwerner to save what she
loved. Once she had brought me to an elegant restaurant to teach man-
ners to the young Jewish smartass: "You must know etiquette for when
you dine with diplomats and royalty," she drawled, showing me how to
arrange my fork and knife, and then discoursed on William Carlos
Williams and Martin Luther King.

Norris also sat at that seminar table, a tremulous homosexual from
Greenwich Village before the days of Stonewall, and everyone kept his
ill-hidden secret to themselves. He would smile darkly; we smiled back.

Sister Mary would crack a toothy grin when I read my turgid, mas-
turbatory poems about throbbing tree trunks. As a nun, she seemed to
have studied mercy very closely, for the prohibitions and uptightness I
expected of a woman wearing an ugly black habit were simply not

there. She could talk directly about everything, even sex, accepting and forgiving all of life. In her thirties, she seemed too experienced, too worldly wise, to be a celibate, splicing Freud and Marx and Teilhard de Chardin to Jesus in thick, symbolic Gerard Manley Hopkins verse.

Others sat around that table, too, yet the faggot, the Southern lady, the worldly nun, and the high school kid clung to each other, forming our own little Canterbury tale. After class we would all stroll over to the Graduate Students Lounge in the Philosophy Building. Passing the statue of Rodin's "Thinker" hunched in front, we would sit and drink iced tea in the cool precincts inside and talk. Acutely—sometimes awkwardly—aware of how odd each of us felt, so different from each other, we nonetheless craved each other's company, each of us driven to nibble Oreos and sip tea by the same, irrational passion to write poems.

And then there was Leonie Adams. As I stood in the doorway, she sat as she always did, at the head of the table, a cigarette dangling from her fingertips, the attenuated ash continually building up, teetering precariously, growing longer and longer—our eyes ever fixed on its impossible length—until it dropped onto her blouse, unnoticed by the poet. She listened to our execrable poems, talked only about what she liked in them, and, instead of cruel critiques, offered choice words by Yeats and Eliot and everyone else on the art of writing verse: "Poetry should be at least as well written as prose," she quoted Ezra Pound with a smoker's thick phlegmatic laugh.

Ezra Pound made her sad. She would slump in her chair, the eternal ash dangling from her cigarette, and she would tell us anecdotes about the mad poet. Because Leonie Adams served as the Library of Congress Poet in 1948, she had the melancholy duty of paying visits to Pound at St. Elizabeth's mental hospital; and when he won the Bollingen Prize, she was the one to deliver the news. Her eyes drooped down with her ashes as she told the story in slow, drawn-out sentences; her face, framed by graying brunette bangs, looked like a child's. How sad she felt to have seen the genius—the crazy, fascist poet—to have seen him so, as he sat raving at her and everybody else, ignoring the honor. Then she looked up to recite by heart a poem by Elizabeth Bishop, a kind of "This Is the House That Jack Built" on how much Ezra Pound meant to the whole edifice of poetry. All of her students sat entranced, all silent, wrapped in her cigarette smoke, each dangling like the ash.

Sarah never came to the class, her health not allowing it, but in my dream she too sat around Leonie Adams's table. An elderly woman, she was too brittle to leave her cramped SRO hotel room on 113th Street, so Margaret and I would visit, bringing Chinese food or juice or some other treat. Sarah had begun writing ten years earlier, had had several stories published in little magazines, and was getting recognized as a "promising new writer." She was part of that class, even though she did not have the strength to sit at our table, and she would nod with a small smile, her hands in a little tepee under her chin, as we read our poems to her and told her every word that Leonie Adams had said that day.

One afternoon, Sarah looked up at me from her chair by her over-flowing desk and said, "You know, they call me a promising new writer. Imagine that!" She chuckled, and I smiled. "There is so much I would like to write about, so much really. Do you realize that I am eighty-two years old, *eighty-two*?" She took my hand, the young man's hand, and continued, "Do you know, I am eighty-two years old—and yet I am *still* afraid to die? Still afraid? *I am terrified!*" As she whispered these last words, a look of horror swept across her face, and she squeezed my fingers until they were numb.

"You will have to learn fear, Hilton," Margaret later confided in the same tone she used to impart tips on etiquette. "There are some lessons you cannot learn in school. Fear is surely one of them, especially fear of death." But as I turned to walk down Broadway to my grandmother's apartment, she held me by the arm and added, "However, I suggest that you become a promising new writer *before* you reach the age of eighty."

In my dream, all of them sat in the classroom, their heads bobbing up, all looking startled at the stranger who had walked in.

"Hey, it's me. Remember me? It's Hilton," I said. They still peered at me with perplexed expressions. "I was here many years ago. Have you forgotten already? Don't you remember me?"

Then a thick, phlegmatic cough erupted from Leonie Adams, and she smiled. And all their expressions around the table turned bright in recognition.

"Indeed, I do remember," Leonie Adams replied, and she gargled out a laugh that tossed her bangs while keeping her elongated ash intact. "Yes, I do remember you, Hilton"—the smoke curling from her blouse, her face lighting up—"Where have you been all these years? *We've been waiting for you for a long, long time.*"

College Poet
1965-1969

When I applied to Columbia, Leonie Adams wrote a letter of recommendation for me. I am positive that letter was the only thing that got me as far as the college's waiting list. Certainly my uneven grades, my unimpressive SATs—especially my math score—would not have gotten me in. Only Leonie Adams's praise of a young poet's promise would have made the admissions committee think I was at all worth noting. Getting taken from the waiting list was not impossible—it meant someone else had also been accepted to Harvard—even though I held out little hope. But when I finally did get chosen, I was more scared than surprised.

I had fully expected to go to Queens College or CCNY—Columbia was not in my league. I was no "Tweed," as the preppy students were called, but even more important, I did not feel smart enough. From the very first day of school, I felt out of place, as if I had sneaked in under the curtain, an uncouth guest from another planet called Queens. Then I met all the other writers, the long-haired freaks, the "pukes," many of them also Jews, and I thrived in a real scene. Columbia had only just done away with its policy to limit the number of Jews admitted to the college a couple of years before my freshman year, and that odd sense of being out of place was shared by many more than I first realized. We were walking in the precincts of the Episcopalian elite that had ruled New York City for more than a century. Most of us were not religious at all, but neither were we cleaned up and cultivated like Lionel Trilling. We were unruly, raucous, and radical.

Kenneth Koch now became my writing teacher, with his warmth, his giddy affability, his easy praise by way of jealousy—"I wish I had written that," he would respond to a student's poem—his way of making writing a pursuit of pleasure in which we were all equally horny. Language became fresh air and exciting, malleable, cut up and tossed randomly around until words formed new, surprising combinations; poems became wild blasting comic strips, able to be funny, manic, and silly; poems could be common delights like Frank O'Hara's lunch, could mug people on the subway and steal their secret thoughts, could laugh and be hard-boiled and pulpy; poems could be slobs, untidy and slangy; and words could be invented or reinvented, syntax garbled, grammar gutted, stories driven off the cliff. It was a new world.

I forgot all about Leonie Adams and her dark memories of Ezra Pound. I had written a thank-you note right after I was accepted, but other than that, she simply dropped from consciousness. In all the four years I spent at Columbia, I never went back to see her, not even once. I was more interested in laughing at Ron Padgett and Ted Berrigan's *Bean Spasms*, and watching them and the rest of the gang from Tulsa kibbitz during their weekly poker game at rotating Lower East Side apartments; more interested in chatting at St. Mark's Poetry Project parties with Anne Waldman, who always insisted on pressing herself emphatically too close to make each conversation a sexy put-on; more interested in sneaking Allen Ginsberg through the police lines during the strike; and definitely more interested in dropping much mescaline with Alan and Les to uncover great gobs of Oneness. Years later I felt overwhelming shame in never returning to the ash dangling from her cigarette, but by then it was too late: Leonie Adams had become feeble and was sent off to the old-age home.

"You can m-m-make love—or you can write a poem about m-making love," Kenneth Koch stuttered to our writing class one day. "They're really t-two different experiences—and m-m-most of the time, if given the choice, I'd prefer to make love." We all laughed, but his zany wit hit me like deep words of wisdom at the time—I would try for the sensation and leave art for other things. Then Koch gushed over someone's poem with the remark that it was so "terrific," he wanted to take the poem into a bathtub and rub the words all over his body.

"Terrific," Koch had said. The operative word at Columbia was *terrific*. If someone wrote something we liked, it was "terrific," and we'd pop the word out with that slightly clipped, hesitant Koch style or with Ted Berrigan's pills-and-Pepsi Tulsa twang. "Terrific" in the sense of being so good it was beyond belief, as good as sex or rock-and-roll; but embedded in the pleasure, bored into the word itself, was "terrific" in the sense of "terror": "terrific" the way a great acid trip could be shit-loads more "terrific" than anything you could ever dare to imagine (and you were relieved simply to come down in one piece).

Being a poet at Columbia was just such a mix of pleasure and terror, of giddy joy and utter fear. How otherwise with the likes of David Shapiro? David—his first book published in high school, already hailed as a new comet across the sky—could shoot off lines or recite whole po-ems by Apollinaire or Wallace Stevens or François Villon at the drop of a hat. David could toss off anecdotes and witticisms about Wittgenstein or Alban Berg or André Breton or Frank O'Hara the way some boys spewed out batting averages and RBIs. He knew everything—or at least he seemed to know everything—about poetry, art, music. And his wit—armed with such an arsenal—would just blast away, demolishing with ridicule every puny, average intellect in its path.

But David's poems really were terrific. It wasn't his fault that he ex-ploded with culture like pimples; he couldn't be blamed for emerging, fully formed, out of John Ashbery's head. Yet, even so, Shapiro was an itch impossible to scratch, a model of the writer I could never be.

There were other impossible models, of course. For example, for a time I dated Helen Wilson. She was delightful, chummy, alternately flighty and brooding, and only after a while did I learn she was the daughter of Edmund Wilson. This fact only made her more intriguing, more alluring, even though I could tell that being known as the off-spring of The Great Writer was something she could do without. In any case, I wasn't really interested in having sex, even vicarious sex, with her dad.

During the summer of my sophomore year, she invited me to visit her home in Cape Cod. I awoke in the morning before everyone else, and I tiptoed around the snug wood-frame house. I soon found myself peeking into a darkened room the dimensions of a good-sized living room, but this chamber was stuffed from floor to ceiling with library stacks separated by aisles, each stack bursting with all kinds of books, many specially bound, all arrayed according to some kind of personalized Dewey decimal system. It was hard to believe that one person could actually read all these books. I had never seen so many books in someone's home before, and as I squeezed through the dim, narrow aisles, I realized I was slipping through the secret loops and folds of Edmund Wilson's brain. Feelings of awe and panic came together in one thought: *So this is what a writer is like.*

I couldn't imagine possessing a room like that, much less reading all those books, and I was overwhelmed with the utter impossibility of becoming a writer. Suddenly, I heard a noise. I gagged with fear and guilt, and slid out of the library and into the kitchen.

There I spied the great librarian himself as he sat in his bathrobe, unshaven, newspaper open, hunched over a cup of coffee. Helen's mother introduced me; he tilted his head a fraction, glanced over his glasses at whatever specimen might be pawing his daughter this time, coughed out a garbled word, growled, and then abruptly resumed his morning ritual, utterly contemptuous of the trembling jerk-off who stood before him. *(So this is what a writer is like!)* Relieved to have survived the dark ogre, I went with Helen to the beach, where her kindly mother lent a sympathetic ear to the anxious dreams of a college poet.

I suppose all the writers at Columbia groped for a model, often searching for it by humiliating each other. We certainly all felt the insecurities and rivalries and jealousies of being shoved up against each other, and we were intoxicated with the idea that any of us could be a prodigy like Shapiro. Maybe it had to do with the fact that Columbia was an all-boys school—and it did feel weird, after going to a half-black co-ed high school, to be surrounded only by boys, almost all white boys at that—so the competitive jockeying in such a scene was probably no less intense than around the jocks. Yet each of us found ways to survive: One would retreat into quiet, wry humor to write surrealistic detective stories; or there was David Shapiro's roommate, Mitch Sisskind, football player as well as poet, who developed elaborate practical jokes—such as when he hung a large butcher knife from a string over his pillow so that he would sleep each night beneath a real sword of Damocles, all designed to drive David up the wall with the thought that he might awaken the next morning to find a bloody blade sticking out of his roommate's forehead, and then Mitch would write tales of eerie, gothic wonder through a child's eyes. Alan Senauke brooded over his mandolin as he played along with Bill Monroe records, repeating riffs over and over until he got them right or drove everyone out of his room in exasperation. Paul Auster drifted across the campus in his long, threadbare overcoat clutching volumes of Tristan Tzara, burrowing darkly into his translations, keeping his nightmares to himself.

But I found my home, most of all, by teaming up with Alan and Les. I had other good friends, of course, but I felt bound to them like brothers, the three of us like Mark and Ronnie and me before Ronnie died, the threesome we could no longer be.

Alan—short, with wiry black hair, dense eyebrows, and a round nose that made him look a little like a mole—would often seem to have dark storm clouds over his head as he brooded over words or music or, more likely, fucked-up relationships with girls. But when his face lit up with a joke, or, better yet, when he offered a "That's terrific!" after I would read him a poem, bright rays of dawn broke. His own poems had a flat quality to them, a prosy oddness, not the breathy, overexcited rant-ing I would automatically fall into, and no matter how I tried, I couldn't imitate his wry, offhand, talky tone.

Alan was demanding, of himself and of everyone else, and even on acid trips he would rarely slip into a purely aimless silliness. He was looking, searching, always seeking for the mystical core that would open up like a lotus into a new riff of his soul—and when he would find it, he would laugh with acute wonder, his face brilliant and open and filled with light, and I loved it.

I also loved to watch him practice his mandolin and guitar, playing his licks over and over. All of his walls were covered with records from floor to ceiling—treasures I never had known: Bill Monroe, Jimmie Rodgers, B. B. King—and walking into his room was like entering a chamber of secret delights. He never learned to read music, but he would listen to his records and copy guitar riffs. I envied the seemingly effortless way his ears made his fingers imitate whole phrases, harmonies, everything I could do only by laboriously decoding black dots on lines. Also, what was oddest of all was that his fingers seemed too stubby—no, they *were* too stubby—they were too short for a musician's, and at first I couldn't imagine how he could even try to pick the strings. But maybe just because of his apparent impediment he worked even harder, making music into some kind of metaphysical pursuit. It was an amazing sight to see him reach and grab impossible notes, kind of like watching a circus high-wire act and always feeling anxious that this time the trapeze artist would surely miss the bar, although he rarely did.

Les had crazy long brown hair, a wild beard, a large nose, and great protruding, bulbous eyes that, magnified by his round John Lennon glasses, looked like they were just about to pop right out of his head: He looked like a jock's worst nightmare of a freak. He had taken a leave for a year, finished up, and was now done with his master's degree, so he was the older brother, more worldly wise, cynical, had met Ginsberg (who had tried to seduce him) and everyone else years before, and he loved early Elvis, Screamin' Jay Hawkins, and the Rolling Stones.

Les was very thin. When he was a boy, he'd had intestinal surgery, so that he needed some special plumbing I'd never quite figured out. This seemed to make him even thinner, no matter how much food he ate. Periodically, his stomach would growl or make squeaking noises, and he'd touch it and laugh. It was as if another person always came along with him—his awkward stomach—and this double, with a mind of its own, would recite its own poetry whenever and wherever it wished. This didn't prevent Les—the Les of bulging eyes and exploding hair—from producing his own squeaks and rumbles, wild crazy poems that jumped all logic, pushed all boundaries, freaked out all decorum with total daring.

Les found poems everywhere—in trashy tabloids, overheard conversations, mad rants from street-corner preachers, bathroom walls, from any far-out recess of insanity or imagination.

Only Les, after a John Ashbery reading at St. Mark's, would lean over to me and whisper, "Look at Ashbery."

"Why, what do you mean?"

"He's been dead for forty-five minutes."

I peered at the poet, trying to figure out his wisecrack. At the party afterward, we studied Ashbery's pallid, vacant face, that placid, enigmatic half-smile as he gossiped. I realized Les was right, as we rolled down Second Avenue, laughing after we left the party. Of course, that explained all of his art: Ashbery is dead for forty-five minutes—always!

That brilliant, silly insight opened up Ashbery's poems to me, totally illuminating their eerie quality in ways I had never perceived before. Ashbery is a zombie controlled not by a single evil genius but by the whole world: Words flow into him from every tributary—all kinds of words, phrases, sentences: from movies, telephones, paintings, traffic —and then they pour right out. Only a dead man can write like that— an empty vessel of the world—and only Les could make such a discovery.

One time Les found stacked on top of a garbage can a pile of letters by a crazy woman to her doctor: "JOE TIME has taught me through the thought waves that there are two Moons, both egg-shaped, that is as if a giant egg had been cut in half. The parts facing us are Gold concave Mirrors, made Gold by HIM." On and on the letters went about JOE TIME and how the Germans had taken over the Left Moon to broadcast evil thought waves—utterly driven tales of paranoid logic all signed by Hope Gordon.

We studied the Hope Gordon letters and the adventures of JOE TIME in His fight against the Germans. We laughed at their nuttiness, but we were also awed at how one fantastic story jumped to another, how the language effortlessly, unselfconsciously zinged with excitement. We cherished the Hope Gordon letters as great works of art and wondered how they had ended up being tossed on top of some garbage cans on 107th Street. Only Les would have thought of fishing out the scraps of paper, only he would have shown me how madness snaps words in new ways, and only he would have made me look and listen to everything, especially things not supposed to be poetry or art, for psychic word blasts.

My friendship with Alan and Les was a kind of nostalgia, an attempt to re-create the bond I'd had with my brothers. I always felt like the youngest of the three, just like with my brothers, and I craved to be in their presence. I felt special and whole and needed. But this bond was more than a yearning for what was gone forever—for not only death but age and temperament had kept me from getting any closer to my real brothers than I did with Alan and Les. Poems wove us together; cops at Low Library pounded us into one, pulpy flesh; and *The Tibetan Book of the Dead* (chemically assisted) zipped us into the infinite.

■   ■   ■

Alan's band had rented a place in Shady, just outside of Woodstock, not far from Bob Dylan's place, where they practiced to make a record. Van Morrison lived down the road, and he had promised to listen to them play, at least according to a friend who knew him. I went to join Alan and Les (who was manager of the band) to write the introduction to *A Cinch*, the anthology we were editing, a month or so after I graduated. Now I was out of Columbia, and I was ready to escape New York, to split for the territories and blow up every conceivable bridge behind me.

We labored over that introduction for over a week. We wrote it — purposely, consciously — to produce as silly, as whacked-out, as inane a goof of hip sophomoric humor as we could concoct: a parody of a put-on of a hoax. It was *Janet Benderman* in an evening gown. The end result was a pyrotechnic display of idiocy akin to purposely shooting yourself in the foot. Yet we had so much fun writing it that we kept blasting away again and again, even after we had shot off all our toes and begun working up to our knees.

In the beginning you go to school, and we edit the *Columbia Review*. Did you know what these amazing works were going to do to you? You shall knuckle under. Almost unknown, almost unavailable, the *Columbia Review* is on the moon. For the last ten years it has been the only magazine to do this. It's the truth. Up your brains!

The "May-I-touch-your-pants,-Mr.-Pound?" editors of the 1950s got phased out by people like Ron Padgett and Jon Cott. R. P.'s poems were strange gash huckleberry. This was the start, the new language antagonizing the klunkhead academics . . .

Night after night we sat around the wooden kitchen table, after the band was done rehearsing. We'd smoke joints, sip tea, or drink beer, and howl again and again, coming up with ludicrous gems like "Up your brains!" and other slogans of the moment. We banged our fists on the table, Les popping each wisecrack into the Underwood. We said everything required of an introduction — the history of the magazine, sum-ups of the contents, descriptions of the authors, even grateful praise of Koch — only we gave it that extra twist of the inane.

Kenneth Koch was "the Charles Atlas of writing teachers . . . an in-describable white light"; kid wonder David Shapiro was "a new gunslinger in town" and "a vociferous esthete" who "hysterically ripped up staff meetings"; we described how, when the deans "flipped over all the references to shit" in one issue of the magazine, Phil Lopate bottled up censorship with freedom-of-the-press outrage ("The deans turned cheddar-orange, having violated their own kaka, you bet"); we characterized Tom Veitch's works as "His stories you are nobody home"; we mock-boasted how "the audience blemished" at Johnny Stanton's antics when our Poem Team gave wild-man "poem readings" at high-class girls' colleges like Vassar and Sarah Lawrence; and we noted how new "maestros" like David Lehman would now run the "magazoon." We howled, we gagged, we rolled with each idiotic remark or mala-propism, spewing out a complete Silly Symphony.

"Boogaloo Down Broadway" was the original title we had wanted for the anthology. And we boogalooed plenty, laughing and screaming—as we did whenever we wrote collaboration poems, each of us taking a line and riffing against the previous one in a quick, spontaneous madman's colloquy. We also knew we were taking extreme, probably stupid, risks. Even if the piece succeeded—and we thought only a few would get hip to the stoned-out play we were doing—we knew no one would allow this as legit poem lingo: We would be run out of town. Columbia University Press had given us an opportunity, put a book right in our hands—and we went and blew it up.

The academic klunkheads would never take me back. After *A Cinch* came *The Noose*.

Before launching into the customary acknowledgments, we concluded our introduction with a final Pound-esque Chinese poem of leave-taking:

> Who lives?
> Now Les Gottesman will not see you again.
> Editor Obenzinger is troubled and on the road. Alan Senauke is
>   working on his car.
> Wild birds on the roof call insistently. It's dawn, and we just want
>   to thank a few people . . .

Alan and Les would go off to the land of Van Morrison and Bob Dylan, and I would be "on the road" with a name even more unpronounceable than Kerouac's. We cracked up at our Li Po flatness, but we also knew it really was the end. Although we vowed to hook up to write again—maybe put out a small magazine even more terrific than *C* or *Evergreen Review*—we were scattering in all directions, the bonds broken, each to spin into new orbits—or burn up on reentry.

With the introduction to *A Cinch* done, I would go away the next day. Alan's band would keep on rehearsing, preparing for its big moment with Van Morrison. I would leave Alan and Les behind—I was "troubled," and I was hitting the road.

Amy and I agreed that we would both head out West. Amy needed to visit Madison, to connect up one last time with old friends, but after that we would hitch due north and cross the Canadian Rockies to Vancouver. The draft board made Canada a tourist attraction worth checking out, of course, but there was also a feeling of dread if we stayed in New York. The Revolution was beginning, it was time to pick up the gun, and the concrete pavements of New York were closing in. I felt that I had to flee, that my Revolution was out there, somewhere in the anonymous gut of the West.

For our final destination, we zoomed in on California—Berkeley or San Francisco, naturally, but we also thought maybe even Eureka. Paul Spike had some friends who lived there: He worked the stove and she waited the tables at the Denny's downtown. The previous summer, Amy and I had hitchhiked together up 101, got past Eureka to the rainforest and the elks, so we could picture ourselves living in that small logging town with its soupy fog and acrid pulp-mill smell. Eureka, Vancouver—it didn't matter where we ended up, really, only that we would get out of New York, as far from New York City as possible. Eureka was very far indeed, but just about anywhere else would do, just so long as we were close to the country, in a place with trees and greenery, and not a maze of concrete, and we would be gone from the wars erupting all around us.

Once we commenced moving, we would keep going until something made us want to stop—a mountain, a beach, whatever spirit would decide to grab us—and that would be the place we'd stay. Every two years or so we would move—just to experience different parts of the world—so it wouldn't matter too much where we first planted ourselves. Eureka seemed a good place to start. I could work the pumps at a gas station or maybe shovel wood chips into a tepee burner in a paper mill and write poems. Amy could get a job waiting tables at Denny's.

We would disappear.

It was a terrific plan.

BUSY DYING

JULY–AUGUST 1969

Yukon Thunderbird

Madison was too green. We went to some coffeehouses, drove around a lot, and joined Amy's friends for a party. In high school, Amy had once dated Dylan when he was still Bob Zimmerman, so her old friends didn't find me too much to speak of. I didn't mind. We would be hitting the road, once she took stock of her past, and that's what counted.

Finally on the road, we had no destination, just a direction, just possibilities, and everything was left to chance.

Once we got outside Madison, rides were not too far apart, although most were just short hitches. A smiling farm-machinery salesman pointed out the virtues of North Dakota with great pride as he dropped us off at the Fargo city park to sleep that night. We rode to the Canadian border inside a prefab shell of a house hauled by a Mack truck. We had started to climb up to the cab after the rig rolled to a stop, but the driver jumped down to open the door to the trailer home instead. When the truck started to roll, we had nothing to hold on to, and we began to bounce against the naked, unfinished walls of the empty living room. Letting out jittery laughs, we tried to hold tight to the bare frame with our fingernails, only to be hurled against the other wall at the next bend in the road, a couple of giggling loose cannons.

We crossed the border on foot. Miles trekking in searing hot sun, full backpacks, there was nothing but high-plains flatness with undulating heat waves wiggling up from the asphalt. I don't think I'll ever forget how hot it was, how the bottoms of my boots felt like lava. The Canadian border guards only smiled, passing the hitchhiking kids through, and we were unnerved at how easy it was, how anticlimactic to flee Nixon, even on foot: not quite *The Sound of Music*.

Then we took the bus to Winnipeg in time to catch the train to Vancouver. When we overheard two men speaking French over beers in the lounge car, we really knew we were in a foreign country, and we were relieved. Everything felt so easygoing on the train, the feel of a new place rolling under us, the drowsy flat miles crossing the plains, the panorama of the Rockies lunging up at us, plus we could perceive an unaccustomed calmness in the way people on the train behaved, and we liked the sweet civility.

Canada was truly a different place. No doubt with lots of problems, but still, it really was somewhere else. The vicious psychosis of WAR had not set in, as it had below the border.

By the time the train reached Jasper, the mountains were simply too beautiful, and we had to get off. Our instant scheme was to camp out in the Rockies, then to hitchhike the rest of the way to Vancouver and see the land. Canada felt like it could be the right place to end up, even before the Pentagon dug my lottery number out from under the ashes of my draft board, so we wanted to stay, to get a closer look.

Only when we went to hitch out from Jasper did it dawn on us just how great a mistake we had made.

Four roads met—North South East West. One headed back to Edmonton, one went down to Kamloops, another went on to Prince George, and the fourth went to Banff.

People stood with thumbs out in all directions at that junction—the place was jammed—as Winnebago after Winnebago, almost all with U.S. plates, lumbered by the clustered tufts of sad-sack hitchhikers. The traffic seemed to be almost nothing but faceless uptight straights spit out from American suburbs, one camper after another crawling up and down the pristine Canadian Rockies, each protecting its respective cocks, cunts, and kids from the strange, hairy creatures that populated the sides of the road.

Hours we stood, as camper after camper slowly wound its way through the crossroads, passing us by.

At night we ate some fruit and milk and cookies we had bought in town, and bedded down away from the other stranded freaks in a thin cluster of evergreens, a cushion of soft brown needles under our bags, just twenty feet or so from the road.

The next morning the miserable army rolled back out and took its positions once more. But hour after hour went by, and it soon became clear that the line of trenches in this war would never move.

Dull throbs of desperation pulsed through our brains as we thumbed on the road heading west, and we began to imagine spending night after night on our bed of needles, trapped. How hopeless everything seemed—we couldn't even get back on the train—and all we could do was hang there and watch the traffic pass.

"Whoever stops to pick us up has got to be a lunatic," Amy concluded as the parade of Winnebago straights went by. "He's got to be out of his mind to go against this flow."

Moments later, someone did stop. Why ours were chosen out of the thicket of thumbs, I'll never know, although the driver's pale blue Thunderbird marked him not so much a lunatic, but as someone who was, at the very least, not so straight; someone sporty, a free spirit of sorts. No matter—we had gotten a lifeboat out of this Sargasso Sea, and we swiftly squeezed ourselves into the backseat before our ride could change his mind.

Larry seemed about thirty or so, wore a tan turtleneck, and had the translucent, almost white, blond hair, slightly receding forehead, and youthful smooth yet ruddy face of a ski bum. At least that's what Amy, who knew of such things, labeled him. Next to Larry sat Doug, who appeared to be about fourteen years old, a blond kid himself, although not as albino-like as Larry. He wore a plain white T-shirt, and on his lap a small, pug-nosed bulldog pup squirmed and yipped.

The puppy soon calmed down, and Larry told us he was an accountant from Colorado, a financial consultant for major corporations with a little time to kill between contracts. Then he asked us the usual hitchhiking questions—a variation on journalism's classic who what where when whys—to which we responded with our typical *Reader's Digest* Condensed Book version of vague lies, skeletal half-truths, and fake Henry Fonda sincerity.

Larry had decided on a whim to see Mount Robson, the tallest mountain in the Canadian Rockies—the view from the highway was said to be stupendous, he informed us. It was a ride of only about eighty miles, but it didn't matter, just so long as we put some distance between us and Jasper's congested hub. We would have much better luck with rides if we were the only ones on the road.

After a while, Larry stopped asking us questions and left us to ourselves in the backseat. This was a big relief—being freed from the inevitable obligation to entertain our hitch—and we stared at the soaring, jagged peaks in happy silence. We were even able to take our scrambled eggs by ourselves when we stopped at a café.

That's where we ran out of cash. With Larry impatiently fingering his own check behind us at the cash register, I had to pull out a traveler's check from the orange backpack. It may have looked impressive —a little book of checks—but it wasn't, and a few checks, a couple of hundred dollars, amounted to all we had to set ourselves up at our unknown destination. It was embarrassing holding up the show to yank out a check just to pay a dollar or so.

Larry had made some vague remark about buying a hunting lodge, but when the road sign marked a viewpoint, he pulled over to take photos of the snowy peak of Mount Robson, and we parted company to scout out a spot in the shade to stick out our thumbs once more.

After a few minutes, Larry ambled over to us.

He told us that he'd been considering driving up to the Yukon, up to Whitehorse, to scout out opening a hunting lodge, some land he was thinking of buying, and he'd decided to go ahead and do it and go up north.

"The two of you could help me out a lot, help with the driving," he suggested. "It's a long trip, but there's no place like the Yukon for wildlife. I have to head first to Prince George to check out the land office, so you don't need to decide until we get there. Take some time to think about it. Anyway, if you're heading for Vancouver, Prince George is on your way, so you're welcome to come along at least that far, no matter what you end up deciding."

We were overjoyed to make the next hop so easily, not even needing to stick our thumbs out, since Prince George was a good two to three hundred miles away, so that alone was fantastic.

But going to the Yukon? All I could conjure up was starving Charlie Chaplin eating his boiled shoe in the Klondike gold rush. I saw the tramp daintily sucking up his laces like spaghetti, then transmogrifying into a plump chicken in the snow-blind eyes of his corpulent yet hunger-crazed partner. But we did know that the Yukon was far, very far away, and it was wilderness, another world. We figured we would check out Larry a little more over the next couple of hundred miles, and if he seemed cool—well, this could be just what we were looking for.

Doug didn't like the idea, though. He had a girlfriend back in Colorado, he complained, and he insisted that he wanted to go back home to see her. Larry told him to shut up. It would be just a few days' round trip, Larry reasoned, and they'd be back in Boulder in no time. Doug did shut up, finally, and was left to stroke the bulldog pup as his only consolation. I figured he'd rather pet his dick instead, and I felt sorry for him, but he seemed resigned to his fate, at least for now.

For the most part, Larry rambled on about life as a big-time financial wizard—how he lived in a condominium in Colorado; how he went skiing all he wanted, drove racing cars, traveled everywhere; how he enjoyed himself like he was some real-life Steve McQueen.

But after a while he quieted down again. This turned out to be his best argument for us making the trip with him. No talk was a big selling point, especially since, after his first interrogation, he didn't ask us anything more about ourselves—he never even asked us for our last names.

We began to imagine driving a couple of days and getting out at Whitehorse, just so long as we didn't have to play Miss Congeniality all the time or—worse yet—get into intimate, awkward conversations about Vietnam. Besides, when Larry did yak, it was generally about things like cars, which I knew I needed to learn something about, and he didn't seem to mind my ignorance.

But Prince George clinched it. The town is no Manhattan, of course, but it is in fact the largest city that far north, a regular little urban patch with stores and movies and restaurants and all the other fixings. We realized that Prince George was only a hint of things to come if we were to thumb ourselves back down south toward the clogged, congested, citified border.

Our only other choice was to just keep heading west to Prince Rupert on the coast, but when we spread the B.C. road map on the café table while Larry headed for the land office, and we saw the even wider, blanker spaces toward the very top with only a few, scattered names like Dawson Creek and Steamboat Summit, our minds were quickly made up. Larry and Doug didn't seem too bad—in fact, they were thoroughly tolerable—while the idea of roaring up to the Klondike in a sleek, baby-blue Thunderbird blew our minds.

Once we were out of Prince George, everything became an endless swirl of nonstop driving. Northern B.C. stuck up like a giant version of Abraham Lincoln's elongated stovetop hat on the map, which told us nothing of just how far away Dawson Creek and the start of the Alaska Highway really was. Stopping only at gas stations or to stoke up on berry and rhubarb pie and coffee, and to let the bulldog pup—Butch was his name—scamper and piss, we kept eating up miles, driving in shifts, always inching our way too slowly up the one road heading north to the very top of Honest Abe's hat.

All kinds of wild berries were ripe, and all the cafés—which were sometimes only little cabins, just about every one with a huge stuffed grizzly or brown bear tilting menacingly up on its hind legs by the front door—served the greatest pies we had ever tasted. We ate almost nothing but pie and coffee the whole trip. And with the absence of night —or at least the deep well of darkness that we used to know as night— meals, days, mile markers, everything ran together like all those juicy pie fillings oozing out between the crusts, as we drove nonstop, sleeping in the car in shifts.

At Dawson Creek, the Alaska Highway officially begins, the road running past the tall grain towers and on to the Yukon. The Alaska Highway we discovered was almost all gravel—which was smoothed and flattened and oiled down, but which nonetheless meant we were facing hundreds and hundreds of miles with no real pavement. The sleek Thunderbird was comfortable enough, although only a two-door, of course. The seats felt soft, the Naugahyde plump, and the two of us could nestle in the back. While the radio got almost nothing but static, the constant crunching of the gravel road masked our voices and turned the backseat into a private cabin, almost like a kangaroo's pouch.

We took turns driving. Amy would take over the wheel, and I would sit beside her; then the two of us would shift to the back again. I had told Larry that I only had a learner's permit—Alan had given me a few lessons on the back roads by Woodstock in his lumbering Chevrolet station wagon, which didn't keep me from flunking the driver's test in Kingston—so I was pleased that he would sit beside me to give me some tips, not at all perturbed because of my inexperience.

Larry told me how to place my hands on the steering wheel in pilot's lingo—right hand at two o'clock, left at about ten. That way I could swivel the wheel either way to make quick turns if need be. He showed me how to keep the pressure on the gas pedal even, judging the ups and downs of the road, when to apply my foot, when to drop it off. Not too many cars or trucks were on the highway, which wound its way in long easy curves and vast straightaways, mostly, and I got used to the gravel surface very soon. Just so long as I didn't have to navigate the Thruway or parallel-park in Manhattan, my lack of experience mattered little, and I felt at ease.

During my lesson, Larry talked about cars. We knew we would need to buy one wherever we ended up, so I kept the conversation alive by asking for his advice. He weighed Fords and Dodges in the balance, explained engine blocks and transmissions and other items I knew nothing about, and then went on about the advantages of a Camaro, a car clearly too sporty and too expensive for us.

I asked his opinion of a 1955 Buick. Of the Buicks my father had owned when I was growing up, I liked his '55 the best—especially its toothsome, boxy grill and its brake lights in a sidelong W with its big center nub. The following year, the big nub turned to a little button, an embarrassing nipple, the W transformed to a V, and I never liked Buicks again.

Old Buicks didn't impress Larry much, and he kept insisting on the virtues of a Camaro to the exclusion of all other options. Nothing else seemed to tell me more that I was far away from who I was in New York than when I let Larry ramble on about Camaros and, after this topic was exhausted, Harley-Davidsons.

Amy could match Larry when it came to car talk, but I could only ask questions, act interested, and nod, which meant that, after a while, we simply drifted into great calms of silence. After my stint, I switched with Larry, riding shotgun, while Amy, Doug, and Butch kept on snoozing in the back, and I occupied myself by looking at the vistas of forests and isolated ranches along the Peace River.

After so many hours of sitting, I began to feel numb, so I reached to the roof and then bent down to grab the front underside of the seat to un-kink myself. After stretching a few times, my hand brushed something under the seat. Reaching further underneath, I pulled out an old book. Actually, it was more a book cover and spine only, since most of its pages had been torn out.

"What's this?"

Larry glanced over, brushing back his alabaster hair with one hand. "Oh, that. What do you think?"

"Looks like it used to be a book." The title page was still intact, and I read it out loud: "*The Spiritual Diary of Emanuel Swedenborg, Being the Record During Twenty Years of His Supernatural Experience.* Translated by Rev. James F. Buss, 1902. A pretty old book, too."

I was startled to find, of all things, a book by Swedenborg. He was the mystic that Emerson and Blake had found so remarkable, which was almost all I knew about him. But little as I did know, I couldn't imagine Larry knowing anything more. It was hard picturing him reading Swedenborg rather than *Popular Mechanics*, unless he was secretly one more Jimmy hunting for God's fingers or other holy body parts.

"Yeah, I picked it up in a used-book store in Denver. Just a kick. Trying to figure out what made my great-great-great-grandfather tick. A hobby, I figure."

"Great-great . . . that's pretty far back." I didn't know if I was prying or not, so I just fingered the book, asking distractedly, "Swedenborg, huh? You're related to Swedenborg?"

"No, of course not," he grinned hugely. He seemed to get a kick out of my confusion. "I'm not related to *that* guy—I'm related to Johnny Appleseed."

I thought of the gangly character with a giant Adam's apple in the

Walt Disney cartoon, and then realized I was mixing him up with Ichabod Crane. "Johnny Appleseed? Naw—he's a tall tale, isn't he?"

"Sure, he's a legend, but he was real, too—and he was my great-great-great-grandfather." Each "great" clopped out slowly one after the other in a distinct, clipped caravan. "His real name was John Chapman. Look." He squirmed and pulled out his wallet, flipping it open to his laminated Colorado driver's license. "Lawrence John Chapman," it said, with a Boulder address underneath.

"See? Chapman. My family knows all about it, and I heard the stories ever since I was a kid. There wasn't much to it other than that—it's not like we go around trying to pick all the apples he left behind," he chuckled.

"But what does Swedenborg have to do with apples?"

In the course of the next thirty miles or so he told me.

John Chapman, although born a typical Protestant, had become a follower of the Swedish mystic. After his bride-to-be fell ill and died, he grew sick at heart, and he wandered into the wilderness of the Ohio Valley at the beginning of the previous century so that his grief would be stilled. There he began to meander with his famous bag of seeds far ahead of the frontier, so that when the settlers finally did arrive, they would already see God's fruit blossoming, and that would help them to understand the correspondence between the visible and invisible realms.

But John Chapman not only planted trees. He would sit in the woods and talk with angels, who paid him regular visits, conversing about all the secrets of heaven and hell. The Indians, regarding him as some kind of holy man, left him alone, and they became his friends, his protectors.

Only rarely did he leave his bower, but one day he came out with a child in his arms, and he brought the boy to one of the isolated settlements along the river. His mother was no angel but an Indian squaw. She too had died, and Chapman's family took his son—Larry's great-great-grandfather—back to New England to raise him as a proper Presbyterian, while Johnny Appleseed went back into the forest to commune with angels and drop more of his seeds.

Although his trees made him into a legend, he scattered more than apple seeds and semen. He also carried bags filled with tracts by Swedenborg to give to the settlers as they crossed into the wilds, his personal evangelical mission. This was so that, as the pioneers entered the mysteries of the forest, they should understand the links between the divine and worldly realms. But he felt the demand to be far greater than the supply, and it was no small matter obtaining books so far from Boston or New York.

As he sat beneath a tree, he conversed with an angel, who gave him the solution to his distribution problem. The angel told him to tear off a single page of the book and nail it to that very tree. Some distance away, the angel told him to tear off the next page and affix that to yet another trunk. In this way, page by page, trunk by trunk, he worked through Swedenborg's books, nailing leaf after leaf—a whole new foliage—to the trees.

There was no guarantee that any settler would come across the posted pages in the order they were written, but he calculated that any small flicker of Swedenborg's light, no matter how fragmentary or how out of sequence, could illuminate an entire soul. These were the spiritual seeds—these torn sheets of Swedenborg's vision—that he was truly intent on planting, while the apples were merely a demonstration, a pedagogical device.

The legend stuck to the apples, though. Perhaps such crazy missionary work—the wanderings of a man who spoke with angels and who tacked up sheets by yet another man who also spoke with same—perhaps this was just too much for the settlers to bear. In any case, only a few professors knew of Johnny Appleseed's Swedenborgian mission besides Larry's family, although the Chapmans made very sure that all the descendants of the mystic and the squaw kept squarely within the four walls of Presbyterian orthodoxy and away from the visionary Swede.

"So I wanted to see what this Swedenborg guy had to say," Larry went on, "and I couldn't figure heads or tails. It seems in this book I got —and he wrote dozens—Swedenborg takes a trip to heaven and talks with all sorts of dead people. It's like some kind of travel book."

I leafed through the remaining pages. Swedenborg met Moses on December 3, 1764: "He was at that time in his own place, below, where the ancients are in a tranquil state. He also came to me, and I spoke with him. He was a grave man."

"This is far-out stuff," I declared solemnly.

"No, it's just crazy bullshit. Great dreams, but it's still bullshit. Even so, I decided to try out Old Grandpa Johnny's trick. Driving up from Colorado I tore out one page after another and Scotch-taped them up in men's rooms. Sometimes I left them under coffee cups at the truck stops, a couple of times on telephone poles."

"Did you drop pot seeds along the way, too?"

"No, just tore up a book," he went on, ignoring my joke. "For a while it was a gas. But then I got bored—I figure you really got to believe— so I shoved it under the seat."

"Amazing."

"Well, I don't tell people that story too often. Most people don't believe it—they don't even believe Johnny Appleseed was a real person—so I just let it go."

He took the book from my hand and tore out a few sheets without looking. "Here, take this," he said, shoving a crumpled page into my hand. Then, with his left hand on the wheel, he hefted the rest of the dilapidated book with his right and in a seamless arc flung Swedenborg's spiritual diary out of his half-opened window.

"Wha—!" I exclaimed.

His grin filled the windshield. "You think I'm a litterbug?"

"No, just that—"

"Now the bears can read it. By winter it'll be mulch."

I liked him. Whether he was bullshitting me or not, his story spoke of mysteries that I never would have thought tumbled around in his head with Camaros and Harley-Davidsons. The impulsive way he tossed the wrecked book out the window made me think he really could be heir to the same looniness that made Johnny Appleseed invent the ultimate cut-up poem long before William Burroughs got his first fix.

He didn't say anything more about it, though. The story was done, the book gone, except for a few pages he stuffed into the glove compartment, and the page he had shoved into my hand, which I slowly un-crumpled.

"What does it say?" Larry asked.

"Nothing. It's blank. It's an endpaper or something."

"Bingo! Well, you probably got the best page in the book. You can go and talk to an angel, then write it up yourself."

I folded it neatly and stuck it in my pocket.

Blank Page

Amy was very political, but in her own way—and that usually came out in terms of sex.

She was Linda LeClair's friend, and when Barnard busted Linda for living with Peter Behr after they were anonymously interviewed in that stupid *New York Times* article about "The Arrangement," Amy flipped out. She got as maniacal about Linda's case as JJ or some other SDS crazy got freaked out about the war.

Linda had gotten permission to live off-campus by making up a story that she worked as a live-in maid; then she quietly shacked up with her boyfriend. They had a relationship, a serious trip. Linda didn't go around fucking every hippie on the street. She wasn't "a glutton for sex" the way William F. Buckley sneered about her on his TV show. She didn't "flaunt" anything—yet how could a "good" girl live with a guy and not be a WHORE?

Linda and Peter owned a mimeo machine, and Amy helped them crank out leaflet after leaflet lambasting such idiocy. They organized meetings. Sixty Barnard girls signed a confession that they too violated housing rules. Hundreds of girls jammed Linda's disciplinary hearing: Barnard had no right to meddle in their personal lives—they could take responsibility for their own sexual conduct—sex and love were good, not evil, and they could do whatever they pleased so long as they didn't harm anyone else. Besides, Columbia boys didn't have the same housing rules, so why should they?

The disciplinary committee sweated and squirmed, clearly ill at ease at being dubbed Puritans. The committee ended up merely slapping Linda's wrist for fibbing to the administration about the live-in job. As punishment, if you want to call it that, she was banned from eating in the school cafeteria—which, considering how horrible the food was, everyone regarded as a blessing.

Victory was sweet. But all of this had boiled up just before the strike, and when the buildings were occupied in April, the whole fracas was simply swept away in a flood of red flags and billy clubs. How could Linda's living with her boyfriend compare to Columbia lording over Harlem with its imbecilic Jim Crow let-the-niggers-in-through-the-back-door gymnasium that the university wanted to build in Morningside Park, a public park at that? How could it match Alma Mater pumping up the War Machine with Secret Death Research Institute for Defense Analysis crackpots? Yet, like I said, Amy thought it did.

"When girls can do as they see fit," she argued, "then the fucked-up gym would collapse, the war would crash to a halt, and skin color would be just the color of skin."

When she and Kate and other Barnard girls took a photo of themselves sitting on a couch in miniskirts sporting matter-of-fact, seductive looks above the bold caption, "GIRLS SAY YES TO BOYS WHO SAY NO," I got the point—or at least part of it. The poster was terrific, and playing up the eternal horniness of boys to fight the draft made the right connection, just the right Madison Avenue ploy to drive General Hershey Bar nuts.

To Amy, expanding sex consciousness—blowing minds—was key, the real Revolution, and the ideas of the women's movement were just beginning to percolate. I agreed with her, except that I thought we would have to break up the government no matter what, and we batted around the which-comes-first, the-chicken-of-change or the-egg-of-consciousness, for miles. Amy knew some people who had come to the defense of Valerie Solanas, the brilliant maniac who had tried to assassinate Andy Warhol. Les Gottesman had bought a copy of her *S.C.U.M*

(*Society for Cutting Up Men*) *Manifesto*, and we would read it out loud, a rant so crazy, so extreme, it was sweet Dada derangement. We loved it—"The male has a negative Midas touch—everything he touches turns to shit"—and the fact that Solanas had actually gotten to the point of shooting the Brillo box man himself was so crazy it was art. But Amy took her far more seriously than we did, getting to know the women in her defense committee. They argued that Warhol had dangled false promises of recognition, and that Solanas had been driven insane because of his manipulative male-chauvinist mind games.

I had met Amy Freeman on the charter flight to Paris two summers before, and we kissed a few nights later as we strolled along the *quai* while admiring Notre Dame bathed in floodlights. "*Vos papiers!*" the gendarme brusquely demanded with his coy Tommy gun, and we showed our passports; and the interrogation, with its tingle of danger, only added to our desire: You couldn't get more romantic. Amy was staying at her older sister's Left Bank apartment—she was a top gymnast who had dropped out of college in order to become a circus trapeze artist, and she had gone to Paris to learn her chosen craft. No matter, we went there to make out, the tiny room at the top of the stairs bright with moonlight splashed across Paris rooftops.

Finally, I had met a girl who liked poems and art and revolution and, unlike Lana and the other girls I had fawned over in high school, she actually wanted a relationship—I mean a real relationship with feelings *and* fucking, none of this artsy Platonic stuff. This wasn't the first time I had had sex, of course. I had gotten over that hump, so to speak, in my dorm room during my freshman year, despite the humiliation of my father walking in. Nor was this the first time I had ever had a relationship—there was Kate, who was now going with Les, but she was too sultry and stormy for me.

Amy, with her dark brown hair, her intense brown eyes, and her incisor brain, was exotic. She wasn't, of course, as exotic as Kate, whose father was a CIA agent conducting Operation Phoenix assassination plots in Vietnam and whose mother came from an aristocratic family of anti-Franco Spanish colonials from Spain and Cuba and the Philippines. Honey-haired and fair-skinned as they come, she liked to hang out with photojournalists from Puerto Rican newspapers. But Amy held her own: She was a Jewish girl from Wisconsin. Other than Les, who was from Oregon, I don't think I had ever met any Jews from farther west than New Jersey—except for Howie, who was from L.A., but he had to transfer back home to UCLA after his freshman year because, amazingly, his doctor diagnosed that he was actually allergic to New York City air. Amy seemed so much more American than anyone else I had ever known. She even knew how to ski.

Ed Freeman, originally from Pittsburg, Pennsylvania, where his father was a supervisor in the steel mills, had eloped in the thirties with Amy's mom because her parents disapproved of his impractical dream of becoming a Broadway actor. Their predictions bore out—he did fail on the Great White Way—but then he ended up in Madison to become a successful and very rich investment banker. Now he was taking an early retirement in order to return to his first love, acting. He had rented a comfortable apartment on East 63rd Street from which he trooped every day to auditions, rehearsals, modeling gigs.

Toward the end of my senior year, I had flipped to the back page of the *Times* to see a photo of him in a full-page ad for the *Wall Street Journal*. The paper was tucked under his arm as he strode by a lamp on a mahogany desk in a gentleman's club, his gray mustache giving him the look of Adolphe Menjou. He was much in demand, typecast as the elegant and courtly gentleman, although he was not the dapper bourgeois prick that the ad made him out to be. In fact, he played in an off-Broadway production of *The Bald Soprano* that spring, vomiting out Ionesco's wild verbal avalanche with gusto. Mr. Freeman was free-spirited, hip, a mensch who wore his wealth lightly.

The family's troubles had begun in the winter of my senior year. Robert, Amy's younger brother, had just started NYU, and he had some kind of nervous breakdown after an acid trip. After much distress, the family checked him into a hospital, but by April he was doing well enough to come home. He had joined the many others who left their minds, aided with a little LSD, to discover their inner world. He had gone through the inevitable freshman freakout—that first-year-of-college scary mix of enlightenment and horror that I had come to know only too well—but it seemed he would heal. Little by little he began to piece together a personality for himself while staying at the home of a friend of the family in Madison for the summer.

Preoccupation with Robert's recovery was soon overtaken by shock at Rebecca's sudden strange behavior. Literally overnight, Amy's younger sister had turned from a nervous and shy sixteen-year-old into a bona fide flower child. Amy didn't think she had ever dropped acid, so when she began walking with a dreamy look and syrupy smile while clutching a single white lily or red rose in hand and pontificating only in parables about OnePeaceLove, it took everyone by surprise. At first we thought it was an act, even a joke, but all our attempts to shock or tease the girl guru out of her trance only ended with her casting an even more beatific smile on all of us who were deluded by materiality.

As disconcerting as this may have been, the kid's family eventually learned to live with a saint. They would be brushing their teeth or fixing lunch or chatting in the living room when Rebecca would suddenly and silently float into the room in her flowing white gown with her white lily and idiotic grin, and they would just go on brushing or chewing or chewing or gabbing, mildly bemused but no longer alarmed at the apparition.

But one day she found that she could not stand up without getting dizzy and fainting, so she began to spend days in her bed or on the couch. This was no act, and her parents grew deeply worried. They sent her to doctors who ran dozens of tests. Nothing could be determined, and her condition remained a mystery. Finally, one neurologist diagnosed that she had a rare nervous disorder with a strange name I could never remember. The symptoms I could always remember: Whenever she was vertical, she would lose her sense of balance, the blood would rush from her head, and she would black out. Those were the symptoms, clearly, but the cause and cure remained mysteries. Little was known about the disorder, except that she was not expected to die as a direct result of it. She would have to live flat on her back until they could discover a cure.

Rebecca learned to live with her condition. She could tilt herself up slightly on pillows, but most of the time she had to lie flat, staring at the ceiling. I think I would have gone nuts in such confinement, but instead the girl guru became truly spiritual. Her parents contorted in grief and worry, as the doctors experimented with one failed treatment after another. But the thin wraith in the white dress on the couch remained calm, and she became more and more beatific.

The young girl studied the cracks in the white ceiling, and she found them beautiful. She tilted her head to see the clouds scudding across the little patch of sky outside the window, and she found those almost too beautiful to bear. Eventually, her parents rigged up a hospital gurney so that she could lie flat on her back as they rolled her to Central Park. The birds and trees were almost too much delight for her.

The beauty of the world brought tears to her eyes, and she became a source of consolation to everyone around her. When she was rolled into the hospital for yet another treatment, she would beam at all the other patients and share how splendid were the visible and invisible worlds. Robert, untangling himself from his acid demons, came to see her before he went off to Madison. She held his hand and smiled, and he felt bright beams of clarity and peace stream through him, and he knew he would be well.

Now it seemed that Ed and Miriam Freeman really did live with a saint. Wherever Rebecca was wheeled—to the park or the hospital—people would be drawn to her, and she would heal their souls. Any awkward sympathies or condescension on their part would be short-lived, and ordinary people would begin to see the dazzling universe that the girl flat on her back would share with them, and they would be brought a little bit closer to something they thought they would never know.

If her parents had been religious, maybe they would have thought of her saintliness as a blessing, but they did not. All they saw was a young girl who would be robbed of the joys of marriage and children and all else good in life. They wanted a daughter, not a visionary, and they came apart at the seams. They desperately needed help, and with their oldest daughter, the trapeze artist, gone to Brazil to join a circus, it was left to Amy to rescue her parents.

Amy stayed with her bewildered parents for days on end to calm them, and they clung to her desperately. Out of the blue, two daughters and a son had suddenly gone off to other worlds, and they had no idea why they had been sucked down this maelstrom. The fact that the son had seemed to recover, that the oldest daughter decided to defy gravity and swing from the rafters, and that their youngest child had achieved a very special state of grace did not relieve their anxieties.

They needed consoling, and Amy provided hours of heart-to-heart talks. She was their hope, their anchor. She wasn't recovering from mental agony or flying through the air or lying flat on her back—she was just deeply, comfortingly solid in a world of phantoms.

In the past I had observed the Freemans and their fortunes from a safe distance. Naturally, I would come over to have dinner with Amy's parents, I would go with her to visit Rebecca in the hospital when she went in for treatments, and I would go backstage after *The Bald Soprano* to congratulate her dad. I would drop by to say hello to Amy's mom in the Madison Avenue boutique where she worked. But the Freemans generally enjoyed their privacy and, happily, never sought to entangle Amy's boyfriend in their eccentricities or problems.

Amy would cry, and I would hug her. She wept often enough during those days, but when Amy got overwhelmed by events, she had the protective habit of plugging herself into an obsession. In this case, Apollo was halfway to the moon, and she glued herself to the TV, eating up every moment of lunar theater. At the job she had taken right after graduation—at a scientific publishing house, after all—the TV was kept on all the time to follow the moon landing, and she allowed herself to be entirely folded into the arms of the cosmic event.

As I said, Amy always found comfort in private mania. During the student revolt, for example, she had kept herself buried in writing a massive research paper on John Donne and other metaphysical poets, a seemingly irrelevant, quixotic preoccupation when everybody else at the university was consumed by flames. It wasn't that she was opposed to the demands of the rebellion, but she thought the tactics would end only in useless violence. She would go to demonstrations and yell at Grayson Kirk, but she didn't barricade in with us at Low or even hang out at Fayerweather. Instead, she spent each evening in her room uncoiling Elizabethan conceits, although she kept the radio tuned to the Columbia student station at all times. In this way, she found peace in a sea of troubles. With her family on an extended acid trip of sorts, the moon would serve as her Thorazine: Apollo became her salvation, and her eyes filled with outer space instead of tears.

Rebecca's condition was chronic, maybe even incurable, and Amy felt smothered by the need to bolster her parents. She had to find her own life—her own world—and she was taking off with me, fleeing New York, both of us seeking something, anything, just so long as it was far away.

And so we were chewing up the Alaska Highway, Larry doing maybe sixty, even seventy, with such skill and grace that we felt safe enough to blab or argue with ease behind our noise curtain of crunching gravel. We were even private and cozy enough to hatch Third World Revolution or Sex Freedom in our snug compartment. We had broken free of Nixon's America, and we felt free in the vistas of Canada.

I didn't think we would ever get tired of talk, but the miles were greater than even our mouths. Eventually, Amy started staring blankly out the rolled-up window and we fell silent. Only the whoosh of tires eating up gravel could be heard.

"One thing for sure," she sighed, finally. "The last time there were so many kids in this country was 1776—it's a demographic fact—and look what happened then."

With that irrefutable truth, Amy buried herself in an Eric Ambler novel, gone.

I can't read in cars without puking, so I kept looking out at the huge sky filled with its crisp, thin, azure light, staring at the endless miles of woodsy carpets and rolling hills punctuated by grassy meadows and glens and lakes and rivers. I had never seen so much country, so much wide-open, unpopulated, dense wilderness sprawling right before my eyes.

I looked and looked. I pressed my forehead against the window and looked. I twisted into contortions and looked. I slumped down and looked. I tilted my head, folded my legs, picked my nose and looked. Boundless swatches of splendor swept beside us, and I kept staring at it all, the vast distances and immensities becoming common, ordinary sights as the car knifed its way up the lone road.

I had no idea what I was looking at. I didn't know anything about the lives of bears or wolves, of course, but I didn't even know the names of any trees or flowers. All I knew were the flattest, stupidest tags for things. This was "tree." That was "mountain." I dumbly gawked at all the wilderness, unable to pin a word on any of it.

Amy hardly knew any more than I did, despite her green Midwest background. Maybe Larry could have told us what kind of forest we were passing through. He never did, and I didn't want to ask. Larry kept quiet, except every hundred miles or so, Doug would start pestering him that he wanted to get back to Colorado to see his girlfriend, Laurie, and they would yammer at each other for a while, their strained voices tearing through the envelope of road noise, until Doug would simmer down and miles of silence would resume.

I found myself staring yet not seeing. In the foreground, everything blurred as the car swept past, but the grand panorama beyond the road's shoulders slid slowly across the window, huge, teeming, wordless, empty, and I simply "took it all in," like they say.

Of course, I had been taken in myself, a captive of sorts. I felt no danger, and I had willingly cooped myself up in the baby-blue Thunderbird, but I knew I was hurtling through this void sealed off from its unknowable blankness. No suffocating panic overcame me, but the more I sensed the enormity of the wilderness on all sides, the more the smallness of our Thunderbird space capsule pressed in.

For some reason, the blank vista brought the page from the Swedenborg book to mind, and I pulled it out of my pocket. The sheet had a nice grain to it, that kind of careful weave old books have, and when I ran my thumb over its surface, I could feel all sorts of satisfying bumps and ridges.

"What's that?" Amy peered over Eric Ambler.

"Nothing. Just a piece of paper."

I hadn't told Amy anything about Larry's Johnny Appleseed tale. At first I had just wanted to keep the story to myself, my own private property separate from the other cluttered memories we were forced to share on the road, but I really don't know why I still kept it secret. Whatever cloudy reason I had initially, I still didn't feel like telling her.

"Maybe I'll write a poem," I joked. She knew I couldn't write in a car, either.

"Just make sure you don't barf all over me," she advised, turning back to her mystery.

The last time I had been a captive was in the Tombs. Even before that, I had been a willing one for days on end in the Low Library Commune. I realized that the blank page in my fist and the tumbles of undifferentiated chlorophyll spinning by the window were equivalents of sorts.

Both waited for invisible words.

I folded up the paper, put it back in my pocket, and peered out the window again. As I looked, the vast, naked page of wilderness flashed with scenes, smells, faces, memories expanding like the darkness of my dreams.

Once again, I felt myself waiting for the bust in Low Library. Again

I dangled in that long, endless moment when everything, the whole world, changed right before our eyes.

Then I remembered Ronnie.

. . .

I am consumed by the piano contest at Carnegie Hall and Abram Chasins's cruel rebuff, my humiliation. "Just try again," Ronnie says, and I see the plastic bracelet, his hair curling around his jaundiced wrist. "In case I die, they know I'm not Catholic so they won't need a priest to say last rites." "Oh, someone else might need last rites, but not you," I think, the notion of his dying as remote as his conversion to Rome, and I withdraw into the ruins of my musical ambition.

That week my parents are hardly home as I trek to JHS 59 and return to lonely egg rolls at the Chinese restaurant on the corner of 225th Street and Merrick Road. Still, everything is normal, although it is St. Patrick's Day, which means little to Jewish kids except an excuse for yet another party. Annie Moskowitz's padded bra crackles as we slow-dance, her hair, teased and sprayed, plastered to my cheek, her thick perfume lacing my nostrils. But I feel no joy, no wistful hard-ons, and I sense that somehow something is wrong. I sit through "At the Hop." Finally, I call home — I don't know why — and Mom tells me to come back. "We have to go to the hospital," she says. "This is it. I'm afraid we'll be too late."

The familiar smell of stale urine wafts through the empty Long Island Railroad waiting room as I pace, waiting for the late-night train to Penn Station. How could I have wasted time at a party? I wring my hands, walk from one end of the dim, narrow room to the other, chattering.

"Does he have the *will*?" I ask her.

"A will?" she answers, distractedly. "No, he doesn't have a will. He didn't write one — what does he have to give away?"

No, no, she misunderstands me, not a last will and testament, but the will to live. I want to know he will fight until I come to help him. Does she think I want his varsity jacket, his track shoes? Does she think I am so selfish at a time like this, that I want to split the pitiful loot even before he dies? I flush with shame, but before I can answer, the train roars in, and I stare out its window at the darkness, anxiety pulsing with the clatter of tracks.

We race through Penn Station to the cab stand, eyes forward, silent, dogged. Green trash of St. Patrick's Day. No moment to spare; our arrival can forestall doom. Was he all this time so sick, *that* sick, sick enough to die?

Why didn't I know?

People stare at us. The graveyard shift, the debris of all-night New York scattered in the station, subway creatures, the scattered weirdoes up at all hours, they all can see the mother and her son driving forward, heads down, grim. We have crisis stamped all over us, disaster weighing down our shoulders, and those few people in Penn Station peer after us, wondering at the mystery printed on our faces. The cabbie notes the destination, Sloan-Kettering, and our impatient silence, and he too eyes us knowingly, not saying a word.

Running up the steps. Hushed hospital darkness, only dim nightlights on. One intern on duty in the lobby expecting us. Nods, points. Elevator rises, lights climbing up numbers. A gulping, a breath, doors sliding open. Putrid green hospital hall, excessively quiet, still. Footfalls to his room.

Dad stands by the head of the bed, Grandma and Aunt Zosia toward the rear of the room.

"Too late," Dad chokes out, hugs me, sobbing.

Over his shoulder I see Ronnie is on his back, his lips slightly parted, breathless, not moving, his face neatly shaved, though the dark stubble breaks through as always. His eyes are open, wide open, bluish as ever, staring up at the ceiling. I gape. I look up at the spot on the ceiling overhead. What does he see? His open eyes grow larger and larger, fill the room, great empty orbs.

I had not arrived in time. All along he was dying, and I should have known. Suddenly I realize the subterfuge of my parents, the incessant Polish, the small lies I had told myself. My teenage self-absorption. The sad irony of "In case I die . . ." All of it makes sense—and now I am too late. I look at his blank eyes as he gazes up at the institutional green paint of the ceiling.

Dad throws himself on his chest, wailing, while Mom holds his hand in silent grief.

I stare at his eyes. Can I look in if he can't look out? Can I touch him? I don't. An intern cracks open the door and softly asks us to quiet down. We are disturbing the other cancer patients, our cries frightening them with thoughts of their own demise.

Dad tells the story of his final moments. Before Ronnie lapses into a coma, Dad holds his hand.

"*Daddy, I'm afraid. I'm afraid, Daddy,*" he reports Ronnie's last words.

Daddy clutches his hand tightly, even as the doctors pound his chest trying to beat his heart back from cancer. We wail again. I feel strange, as if we are all violating some rule. How can they let us all crowd into his room like this? *Aren't we forbidden to see death?*

I stare at his lips, which seem almost to smile.

Grandma strangely cuts an apple with a little knife, her hand steady. Between her tears, she quarters the fruit and offers me a piece. I don't want an apple. How could I be hungry at a time like this? Why are you feeding me now? But she nudges me again to eat. She's a survivor of the Nazis, and even when she fled with her daughter Zosia through the streets of the Warsaw Ghetto and into the sewers, she clutched her pot of *krupnik*, her barley soup. She knows death only too well. I take the slice of apple and hold it.

I stare at his face. It does not rot, does not dissolve, it's still his, it's still Ronnie. His face, his open eyes burn into me.

"*Eat*," Grandma says, "you're upset," and she holds up another wedge of apple already slightly brown.

Why doesn't somebody close his eyes?

■　■　■

The rest of the world may have been hung up with men on the moon or with troops in the Mekong, but up in the Yukon all the news was about the *Manhattan*. Not the concrete island that Amy and I had just fled from, this Manhattan was a huge oil tanker outfitted as an ice-breaker that was just now navigating the Northwest Passage. While submarines had cruised beneath the Arctic icecap before, the *Manhattan* was fast becoming the first surface vessel to bridge the gap between Atlantic and Pacific that had eluded explorers for centuries. We hadn't even known of the escapade while living in the other Manhattan, but the *Whitehorse Star* we picked up in the café touted the *Manhattan's* progress not only as big news, but also as something of a disaster, which was a little surprising.

"That *Manhattan* gives Ottawa a mighty fright," the old-timer explained to us over coffee. "Outsiders—I mean Canadian outsiders— only get worked up about the North when the Americans do something to scare 'em. First it was Klondike gold, then buildin' the Alaska Highway during the war and gettin' plenty nervous what the Americans were going to do with all those soldiers after the road was built. Now they're all agitated about the Northwest Passage."

In fact, Ottawa got so agitated that they loaded up a plane with politicians from Parliament to fly over the *Manhattan* as a reminder that Canada does in fact hold sovereignty over the barren landscape, just in case the Americans should happen to forget. While the tanker worried "outsiders" because of the perennial suspicion that, once again, the giant of the South harbored ambitions to steal the North, the great feat also irked "insiders," everyone who lived "north of sixty," since now it was possible for the oil discoveries of the Arctic to be shipped out in huge tankers (the newspaper even entertained speculations about jumbo submarines) instead of the crude getting pumped out through pipes across the muskeg and tundra.

"We can watch the tankers wreck and spill their guts out all over MacKenzie Bay," the grizzled cat operator complained. "At the same time we can kiss good-bye all those jobs layin' pipe we thought we had comin' to us."

He had done his own wrecking, having gotten drunk and demolished some heavy equipment, which accounted for why he was no longer working for the Imperial Copper Mine outside Whitehorse. But laying pipe or not, there seemed to be plenty of jobs around, if he could just stay sober long enough, and he presented all his gripes with a friendly wink.

Larry Chapman had struck up a conversation with the drifter moments after we had taken our seats at the lunch counter. Larry had some kind of magnetic power—maybe it was that Johnny Appleseed aura of affability—and he had a knack for striking up a conversation with just about anyone. Wherever we stopped, Canadians were drawn to Larry's blond radiance like moths to a flame, and they would quickly open up and give us news or tell us their hard-luck stories in response to his ready grin.

We had time to talk because we needed a new tire. The blowout had occurred during my stint driving, and even though I pulled the Thunderbird over, decelerating very slowly, my arms taut, until we rolled to a stop, the tire was in shreds. Given my inexperience as a driver, I was shaking like a leaf once I got out. Maybe if I had jammed on the brakes I could have stopped sooner and saved the tire, but Amy told me we could have spun out of control if I did something as foolish as that. There was no other choice on a gravel road but to ease off and inspect the chewed-up remains. Fortunately, the rim seemed undamaged.

Still, I felt responsible and offered to pay for the tire. Once again, Larry said the trip was on him, but this time he confessed that he was running a little low on cash and no one would accept an American check. If we could lend him the money until we reached Whitehorse, where he expected to find a pile of dough waiting for him at the Western Union, that would help out. Of course, we were always free to bail out and hitch another ride any time we wanted—and he nodded toward the road. He would just wait a couple of days at the next pie-and-coffee until a cashier's check got to him by mail.

We figured we would be chipping in, no matter what. We did go with him into the Western Union office back at Prince George to wire his secretary, and if he was half the successful wizard consultant he said he was, we wouldn't bother ourselves too much over his overwhelming need to be generous. Besides, taking off on our own in the Yukon was no easy prospect, and we didn't want to get stuck at night with bears on the prowl if we couldn't hitch another ride.

We peeled off a few traveler's checks and cashed them at the counter, while Larry excused himself to tend to business at the adjacent garage. Now we were alone in the coffee shop with Johnson, the still-sober old-timer, and we asked him about the kinds of jobs a couple of outsiders like us could land.

"*You?*" He squinted at us through an invisible microscope. "A bunch of college-kid cheechakos like you?" He shook his head in disbelief. "Have you ever stayed shut in for seven or eight months until the ice breaks up on the Yukon River? Do you know what *real* cold is like? Can't tell now with all the sun, but do you know how stir-crazy and even bloody-minded men can get when they're locked up for months at a time inside a dark icebox? No, no, my friends; go back to the temperate zone. Where you from? Wisconsin?" he nodded at Amy. "They got cold enough winters there. Even so, you don't know cold and dark and cabin fever till you get stuck inside for a winter here."

"Wisconsin is not exactly the tropics," Amy retorted.

"I'm afraid it is," he chuckled back. "Winter in Wisconsin compared to the Yukon is time for a swim and a suntan."

We kept insisting until Johnson reluctantly offered his opinion.

For college kids like us, most likely a job in Whitehorse with the government being bureaucrats was a good bet. "A sure bet, though, is schoolteachers—they always need teachers for the Indians out in the bush. But I'm warning you: The cold and the dark have been known to drive many a cheechako insane. You know, when they built the highway and all, they figured on people pouring in for development. A lot came, but the road also turned out to be a good way to get out—and you can bet a lot of people can't wait."

A cheechako, we learned, was a tenderfoot, and the only way to outgrow that status was to hold out through one winter until the ice broke on the river the following spring. There was something so God-awful about the pains of surviving months of frigid nighttime that we found ourselves oddly attracted to the prospect, and we figured we would check out the government offices when we reached Whitehorse.

Once we hit the road again, things went on in their usual way, except that Larry had to keep asking for cash to cover gas. Amy recorded all the money we put out, even noting the cost for pie and coffee at each stop in her notebook. Rocks smashed the headlights one after the other—and we helped out again by paying for the replacements. Considering how rough the road was, we were lucky the muffler wasn't punctured or the windshield wasn't shattered from a chunk flung back by a passing truck. Blowouts and busted headlights were to be expected, we soon learned, and travelers often carried more than one spare, along with extra headlights and big cans of extra gas.

Amy snoozed in the backseat with Butch, the little bulldog pup, curled up on her lap, and I gazed at the rounded-off hills and the endless immensity of wilderness, so benign in the warm sun it was impossible to imagine the harsh blinding whiteness of winter.

Soon we would be in Whitehorse with the prospects of a new life before us.

Nothing to do now, nothing but sit and think and dream of Whitehorse or invent names for trees or return to the past, and after a while I remembered Ronnie's eyes.

Then I remembered Miguel's smile.

■　■　■

That night we were sitting around the kitchen table in the ninth-floor apartment that my friend Benjamin shared with Bob, Steve, and

Miguel. They had all been tripping on mescaline, and I had too, although not with them. A day or two later we were still coming down, smoking grass to ease re-entry. We sat around the table, stupefied, drifting with the remembrance of the visions. Miguel slipped into the kitchen quietly, hardly making his presence felt. A Jewish boy from Bogotá, he was not wearing his wrinkled blue pinstriped double-breasted blazer lightly dusted with dandruff, the too-formal jacket that had become his trademark. I also noticed he didn't have any socks on either, while his shoes were only very loosely tied, which seemed a little odd. He smiled absently, and everyone nodded and went on bullshitting as before. After a while, Miguel got up, offering one last faint smile, and then he backed out of the room without having said a word.

Soon after, a profound thud, a concussion, shuddered through the building. What the fuck? We all looked up, startled, but, after a moment speculating on the mysteries of the city night, there was little else to do than return to bullshitting. A half-hour later the doorbell rang. Bob got up to answer, and he stepped out the door. When he didn't return, Steve looked out the peephole and saw cops in the hallway. A bust! Quickly Steve flushed the grass down the toilet.

Soon Bob returned with some cops. It turned out that Miguel had jumped out his bedroom window while we had sat in the kitchen vacantly bullshitting. The thud that had shuddered through us had announced the deed. Down the airshaft on the concrete covered with cat shit, Miguel was spread-eagled on his side. Bob had gone down to identify him. Half his face wasn't there. Only blood and brains and one eye left wide open. He had left his shoes neatly placed side by side beneath the open window, then dove out.

The university called Miguel's parents long distance in Bogotá.

Then we waited. Now we realized that he had come to the kitchen to say good-bye with his faint smile.

Why? Why did Miguel do it? What was wrong? No, it wasn't the mescaline, we reasoned. (We comforted ourselves from guilt by saying that, if anything, the hallucinogen was just a catalyst.) But what had driven him to dive out the window? We all described the last days we had seen him. A week before, we had sat together in Ferris Booth lounge—John Berryman was going to give a poetry reading—and Miguel asked, "Do you know Nietzsche?" We were reading some of his books in Humanities, but Miguel, as was his style, was reading all of them. "Nietzsche says that there are those who deserve to live," he went on, "and there are those who deserve to die."

"Well," I teased him, "I always heard that Nietzsche was a Nazi."

Miguel lifted his eyebrows and smiled.

We began poring through his notebooks, looking for clues, as if discovering why this brilliant boy from Bogotá went flying out the ninth-floor window would somehow change the fact of it. His notebooks were filled with scribbles and doodles, with phrases in English and Spanish. Drawings of spirals, circle upon circle. *Platero Y Yo.* "El Puzo, the Well." Steve remembered that Miguel was always carrying around *Platero and I,* by Juan Ramón Jiménez. Sketches of donkeys. Simple addition. A drawing of a rustic well, very nicely done, in the margin of his physics notebook. The same sketch over and over, losing its definition, becoming circle upon circle until the paper was torn. We went to look for *Platero and I,* digging through his clothes, opening his private things.

Bob grabbed the book from under Miguel's blue jacket. Page by page we looked. Then Bob turned to the chapter called "The Well."

There was the illustration, the rustic well of Miguel's sketch. Bob read it out loud; it was only a page. The narrator addresses his donkey, Platero. Describes the well.

> Night comes and the moon shines down there in the bottom decked with fickle stars. Silence! Along the paths life has gone far away. Down the well the soul flees to the depths. One can see through it to the other side of the twilight. And it looks as if from its mouth the giant of the night, master of all the world's secrets, were about to come out . . .

Bob could no longer read. He faltered, overcome, and Benjamin took the book to continue.

> Platero, if one day I throw myself into this well, it will not be, believe me, to kill myself, but to catch the stars more quickly . . .

We gasped, astonished. Could Miguel have been killed by a poem? It seemed too strange, and suddenly we insisted that we had to go to the morgue so that each of us could see Miguel's smashed face. Bob alone had had the shock of that hideous sight, and at the weird words about the well we all suddenly felt as if we had to see Miguel one last time. We wanted to grasp the horror as more than some dream from a book. We had to make Miguel's death real inside of us, we wanted the evidence of gore, we wanted to become, like Bob, true witnesses to the results of his farewell plunge.

Just as we had gathered ourselves to take the subway downtown, the doorbell rang. Miguel's parents arrived, and we stayed to mourn with them instead, our gruesome pilgrimage to the morgue abandoned. His father was a surgeon, and he listened to our stories of Miguel as he unconsciously peeled an apple with a pocketknife in a single perfect curl of skin. I remembered my grandmother quartering apples in Ronnie's death room, that same distracted, automatic slicing. I sat in awe of the surgeon's steady hand, of the couple who, eyes red and downcast, did not cry before their son's friends, who kept precise habits of care and sustenance instead.

When I phoned my parents about Miguel, they wanted me to come home to Laurelton right away. They were frightened, even angry, that something as bizarre as a suicide plunge could occur at such a place as Columbia. I told them the story—minus the mescaline—and when I came to the point of Miguel's father expertly peeling the apple's skin, I broke down. "When I saw his parents, I thought of Ronnie," I began to cry, "I thought of you, of how you must have felt when Ronnie died." When my mother hugged me, I sobbed in her arms with an abandon I had never felt before, as if I had finally plumbed the depths of grief, all my grief, and pulled out some strange prehistoric fish. And I would never get the chance to cling to my mother like that again.

That was when the wound of Ronnie's death finally began to change, if not heal. I never did see Miguel's one open eye, yet so much of the shock, so much of the horror had been the same, even to the point of Miguel's swirling, incessant doodles of wells so insistently tearing notebook pages so much like my own obsessive drawings of eyes.

"To catch the stars more quickly . . ."

I had imagined my parents' sense of loss before, but now I felt their grief, how much their lives had changed, too. Soon after Ronnie's death began my father's endless, inconsolable mutterings to himself as he pounded the steering wheel while cruising down the Belt Parkway, as did the sudden whitening of his hair and the onset of diabetes. My father wailed at his funeral, sitting shiva on the step leading up to the bedrooms, crying out that Ronnie was a prince. But my mother became catatonic, silently cooking meals and dusting, until my Aunt Zosia took her to the Art Students League, told one of the teachers what had happened, and insisted that she paint her grief. Soon she turned from the conventional still lifes and nudes of a suburban housewife artist to violent abstractions torn with garish, clashing colors, expressionist nightmares, and grotesque, unquiet pietàs and crazy figures of the dying Prince. Her wails stood out on canvas.

Their lives had changed, and there was nothing I could do, nothing at all; and in that moment, in my mother's arms, I had wept for them. Watching the Yukon roll before me, I realized that those sobs amounted to a kind of confession, an acknowledgment of further guilt, a realization that my selfishness had even extended to the claims of pain.

But confined to the Thunderbird, I could not avoid more thoughts, and I peeled back other realizations about the suicide, considered consequences that I usually kept hidden from my waking life.

With Miguel the trauma of Ronnie's loss had been repeated, not in fantasy but in reality. This time I was not simply *feeling* guilty for having been oblivious, for repressing the knowledge, tormenting myself for having hidden the enormity of Ronnie's disease from myself. Even if I had known, I could not have stopped the course of my brother's decline. No matter how much I felt I could have intervened, the will to live would never have been enough. But Miguel's case was different. Here I really was responsible for his death, for if I had not kept myself from knowing the truth, if I had not willfully cast blind eyes on obvious signs —the feet without socks, the Nietzsche, the expression on his face—I could have halted his suicide plot. The thought had nudged me before, but I had managed to nudge it right back into its dark recess. Yet now, tucked into my two square feet of Thunderbird backseat, I could no longer hide from the realization.

Miguel had actually stepped into the kitchen to say good-bye. Why hadn't I comprehended his awful state of mind? Why hadn't I reached out to him, grabbed him, pulled him by my side, kept him from the window ledge? Why did we allow him to trip out on mescaline if he was freaking out? Why didn't we know?

The fact of the matter was that his friends could have saved him, and we didn't. I could have—and I didn't. Sure, his roommates were closer to him than I was, and they should have read all the signs more clearly, and maybe they tried, but I was there in that kitchen, I was there when he passed before us, and I should have known.

Miguel's life had been within my grasp, and I failed—again.

■ ■ ■

"Look!" I pointed out across the windshield.

A deer—no, it was too big, its antlers too wide, too thick to be a deer—an elk—no, a moose stood in a meadow of tall grass.

It was a little after midnight, but in the couple of hours of twilight that passed for night this far north, it wasn't too hard to make out the darker presence of the beast. As Amy kept the car crunching over the lone white band of endless gravel, the hulking moose lifted its head with casual ease, no alarm, its antlers tottering like a too-big crown.

"Wow!" she gasped in a whisper, keeping her voice down. With Larry and Doug asleep in the backseat of the Thunderbird, we spoke in a private hush, even though the constant growling of the gravel beneath the tires provided its protective wall of sound.

I swiveled to watch the moose as long as I could, and I tried to burn its image into my brain. But by the time we curved up an embankment to catch a long ribbon of river glittering by mountains under the half-light, the gray, grassy meadow and its dark beast were gone.

"That must still be the same river we saw back at Muncho," I said. Amy didn't answer, and we fell into a long silence.

A hundred miles back I had gone to pee when we stopped for gas, and propped up behind the slimy faucet of the sink was another crumpled page of Swedenborg's diary. Larry had gone in before me, and it looked as if he was keeping Johnny Appleseed's odd mission alive with the few pages he had stuffed into the glove compartment before he flung the remains of the book out the window.

I had taken the sheet, and after the moose went by, I uncrumpled it from my pocket to read in the dim in-between light.

When Amy asked, I told her that I had found it under the seat, from an old torn book Larry had found, Emanuel Swedenborg's *Spiritual Diary*, and she knew as much about the mystic as I did.

"How weird to find something like that in the Yukon," she marveled. "And from Larry, of all people."

It was just an old book he had picked up somewhere, I explained, so it wasn't as much of a marvel as it seemed. It was junk to Larry, though it might be portentous junk. The book's connection to Johnny Appleseed I still kept to myself.

"Read it out loud," Amy insisted.

"'I conversed with angels respecting the fact that it is believed that it is difficult to tread the way to heaven, because so many things must be done and all lusts forsaken, besides many things more," I recited. "Wherefore, as occurs in the spiritual world, the matter was shown by means of a road, which signifies truth which leads.'"

We both looked up at the gray ribbon of gravel ahead of us before I continued.

"A road? How freaky," she observed.

I continued: "'A road appeared at the right, where both the good and the evil trod. It was the same road; but, when they reached to a certain distance, there was a great stone, in shadow, which the good saw but not the evil. From that stone, which is called the cornerstone, a road led to one side and another to the opposite. The evil went on the opposite side, which was behind and sloped downwards; but the good went the other way, which inclined upwards. The latter led to heaven, the former to hell. That stone signified the Lord and His Divine Human. Hence was shown that the . . .' "—and the text on the page jumped to the next, missing page.

"What's on the other side?" Amy asked.

"It's the page before—nothing about any roads. It's about magic."

"Well, read that too."

" 'Others practice magic by means of written characters, by which they know how to direct themselves to their hells. There is magic with those who are roundabout; magic with those who are below; magic by means of words, and, the worst kinds, from the Word; fantasies by means of thoughts; fantasies by means of various affections: in a word, there are innumerable kinds.' "

"Sounds like Andy Warhol." Her tone was subdued, not sarcastic. "Directing himself to hell."

"Swedenborg says that these magicians glow, they shine in the forehead. Maybe it's like a glowing third eye."

"No, I don't think these magicians are the good kind—but what do you make of the road?"

"Bullshit," I replied, "but it's funny that the one mystical thing we find is kind of a road map."

"The Alaska Highway goes up and down through the shadows," she added. "And these mountains, maybe they're the cornerstones."

"So, are we going to hell?"

"By the way the road slopes up and then curves down, I'd say we're going to heaven *and* we're going to hell—both."

"You can't go to both," I corrected her.

"Why not?"

"Either you're good or you're evil. You turn right or you turn left—you have to choose. That's the way they make the road maps."

"Maybe there's another way. The fork-in-the-road business is old hat, it's Robert Frost, and it's trite."

"The guy is having visions—give him a break."

"Things are even more complicated than Swedenborg thinks," she continued. "If the sun can shine at night, if *Manhattan* can float over the Arctic, then heaven and hell can be in the same place at the same time."

Just then, our headlights turned on a pack of wolves slinking along the edge of the road. About five or six of them in the hush of the bright Yukon twilight trotted by in a line, the lead wolf glancing up in the instant our headlights beamed on the pack. The blinding dazzle of light gleamed momentarily in the predator's eyes, and then he pushed his head down low to lope along as before.

We rolled by without a word, more surprised than the pack, which just went on with their business, trotting along the shoulder in the disappearing red glare of the Thunderbird's brake lights.

"*Wolves!*" Amy finally hissed as the pack whisked off the rearview mirror.

"Are there wolves in heaven?"

"Wow."

"Amy, just think. Here we are, with giant rivers and moose and wolves and endless wildernesses, barreling up and down the road."

"Yeah, it's far out," she whispered.

"And we're zooming right past it. Soon this ride will be over, just like every other ride, and it'll be gone. Now we're in New York—now we're hitching—now we're seeing a moose—now we're fucking—now we're in heaven, now we're in hell—now—"

"Stop!" Amy snapped.

We could feel the gravel chewing up mile after mile, and I saw Miguel drifting away from the kitchen table with his wispy ironic grin, and I could see him slip out of my grasp, and I let him die. He had come to his own fork in the road, and I hadn't even known it was there, so who was I to know where we were speeding to? Heaven might as well be hell, so I didn't need to needle Amy with the news.

We kept silent for a few miles. The sun, which had barely dipped down to the horizon, began to climb, and I fell into a drowsy meditation of roads.

"Just before we left New York, a strange thing happened," she broke the silence at last. "My dad—a strange thing with my dad."

She hesitated, as if she wasn't sure what to say or was afraid to confide.

"I came to the apartment to visit, and when my mother opened the door, I saw my father sitting on the couch. He looked so very old and tired."

She stared ahead at the road, her hands absently coaxing the steering wheel.

"Is that it?" I prodded.

"He didn't know who I was," she said, simply.

"What do you mean?"

"He didn't recognize me. He looked up with a blank look on his face. He didn't know who this person was who had just walked through the front door. It lasted about a moment, this strange look—a long time, really. For that whole time I was a complete stranger to him. I just stood there staring back at him, and I could see it all in his eyes—how baffled he was, the panic and the fear, the confusion—and it was like—well, I don't know what it was like."

"I don't get it."

"My mother came up to him and took his arm, and it was as if her touch brought him back from the dead. His confusion lifted away, he returned, and he knew who I was again. But I was shaken to the core." She hesitated, keeping her eyes on the road. "I wasn't sure who *he* was anymore."

Her mother recalled other incidents when he had seemed to check out from the world, brief moments but increasing in frequency, and they became alarmed. Wife and daughter took him to doctors, who said that he was probably on the verge of a nervous breakdown. He was too young to be senile; he was simply disoriented from being exhausted, emotionally fried, and he just had to rest, catch up on sleep, eat well, and they gave him some tranquilizers.

"I want to believe them," she said.

"Why not? What else could it be?"

"I'm not sure, but when I saw that look in his eyes, how completely empty, scared, and confused he was . . . " she drifted off. "My own father didn't recognize me."

We sat in silence again, and I realized I had been so embroiled in my own sorrows that I had no idea what kinds of sorrows and anxious worries bubbled up inside of her. I still didn't know Amy, and as absorbed in my own grief as I was, I would never know her. Girls were always a mystery to me, and I realized I would never penetrate to their depths, which I accepted as a part of what made up the two sexes, though Amy's brain was especially difficult if not impossible to fathom. But here was another fork in the road, a hole in Amy's heart, a great soul-pain, and all the other clichés, and I was still ignorant, as blind as ever.

It was my fate to be always the last to know.

"Amy," I put my hand on her shoulder, "you can't—"

"YES, SIR!" Larry whooped from the backseat, just waking up. "We got some prime hunting country here. *Great God Almighty! What we need is to get us some rifles, go out for a hunt, and bag us a moose!*"

Whitehorse Monday

"The real thrill of hunting is the pursuit," expounded Larry. "You don't even need to bag something. But you do need to smell the dirt, get real close to the ground, spot little flutters in the brush. All your senses are keener than they've ever been before. You can't smoke, can't drink, otherwise your prey can sniff you out and you can't smell worth a damn yourself. Time gets real slow—and with all this daylight up here I guess time would just about seem to stop, and we'd have no fear of darkness, no dangers of the night here, either. You get small, invisible, blend in, and you learn the real meaning of patience. You follow signs when you hunt. That's the real fun, not just blowing the brains out of some deer, but tracking them down, reading the signs, getting close . . ." His voice trailed off, his eyes radiating.

"Don't get me wrong," he resumed in a more normal voice, "when you finally do get some moose or, better yet, some huge brown bear in your sights, that's a feeling that can't be put into words. You pursue and you corner the critter, his life is in your hands, he's square in your crosshairs, and all you need to do is squeeze the trigger." He squinted through imaginary sights. "*Bam!*"

Ever since the tire blew out, Larry had begun to crow more and more about the joys of the hunt, and every half-hour or so he would put in a plug on how great it would be to go tracking a bear or a moose in the wild. We had never seen him so passionate—even when he spoke of Camaros, he had kept a certain professional coolness—and that passion was, naturally, infectious.

We thought it would be a terrific thing to do, at least to go out in the countryside, but you couldn't just get out of your car and go take a stroll or a hike, because so many wild animals lurked in the bush. Everybody carried a gun. We'd see people coming out of their houses with a rifle dangling from one hand just to walk to the highway to empty their mailboxes. Brown bears and grizzlies abounded—those huge stuffed beasts stretching on their hind legs in front of the coffee shops testified to their menacing presence—so people always had to be on the lookout. We started to anticipate Larry's frequent rhapsodies on hunting, and I thought I could even detect a little of Johnny Appleseed's fervor to nail up Swedenborg's revelations every time Larry gushed on about the thrill of the pursuit or the virtues of different-caliber rifles or how to read bear shit for signs.

Of course, we never imagined ourselves trying to bag a bear, but we did enjoy the notion of being able to see the wilderness up close while Larry did his thing and protected us at the same time. So as we neared Whitehorse, we figured we would check out how much it would cost to rent some guns.

We knew we were approaching Whitehorse when the road got smoother, small stretches were even paved, and heaps of dirt like small hills from road construction started to pile up on all sides. There were just sixteen thousand people in all the vastness of the Yukon, and most of them seemed to be clustered in Whitehorse, with the town appearing to be in the midst of a building boom. The place was impressive, considering the fact that every other name on the map amounted to nothing, either a bunch of trailer camps for crews working on the highway or in the mines, or one of those ramshackle gas stations attached to a general store and a café parked along the mile markers.

But Whitehorse was a regular town. There were plenty of trailers, of course, yet there were houses too, and it had Indians who lived on one end of town and the thick Yukon River nosing along one side. Most of all, it had everything that went into making a town, at least one of each. One hospital and one library, two movie houses, one bookstore with English editions of paperbacks, and a single post office with a picture of Queen Elizabeth. Quite a few people spoke with English accents, and they were so friendly and the town seemed so snug that we immediately started figuring Whitehorse to be the place for us. Odd, though, were the little boxes on the street that looked a little like parking meters but were actually heaters that people used during the winter to plug in their cars when they parked. Otherwise, they'd come out of one of the movie houses and find that their engine block had frozen solid in the middle of the film.

Larry and Doug went off to hunt up the telegraph office, while we wandered around, sent postcards to friends, and eventually made our way to the government office, a modern aluminum and glass box a few stories high, to see if we could apply for jobs as teachers. But it was Friday and everything was closing up—we had lost all notions of which day of the week it was, much less what hour of the Arctic day—so we had to come back on Monday. As we walked out, we saw Larry and Doug chatting with a short, husky gentleman—he was one of the few people around town who wore a jacket and tie—and when Larry spotted us, he waved us over to join them.

"Come here and meet the commissioner," he called out, and introduced us by our first names to what looked like a nondescript, minor clerk in a Wall Street office. The clerk smiled broadly, greeting us with an English accent, and handed us a business card that identified him as James Smith, the Commissioner of the Yukon, which was the equivalent of territorial governor, Larry informed us. The ability of Larry's gregarious magnetism to attract people blew our minds as never before. He had somehow struck up an instant rapport with Commissioner Smith, who said he had been serving as the Yukon's appointed executive (it wasn't an elected position) for several years. Before that, he ran a tour-guide business and tourist shop in Whitehorse, but now he wanted to go back home to England.

"I consented to the appointment only with the promise that I would have a direct line to Ottawa and they had to consult with me on everything. Naturally, they go ahead and make deals without my knowledge, despite their promise. For instance, they just agreed to build a company town for a new asbestos mine—building the town was just to add a little sweetener to the deal—but the territorial government is supposed to pay for the schools out of our own budget, so of course they only inform us of our new expense after the fact. A bloody headache," he confided to Larry.

"But I can't complain, really. I've made my fortune. There are no conflict-of-interest laws here, you know, so I've been able to invest freely with the wisdom supplied to me by the mining concerns—and now I'm ready to go home."

He spoke of what sounded like big-time corruption with such openness and ease—all while Larry offered friendly, knowing nods—that it seemed quite natural to equate "development" with lining your own pockets. I was amazed—all the crap of America didn't stop at the border—but the commissioner smiled so broadly, seemed so congenial, and I suppose it all was, as he said, strictly legal to use inside information for investments. More important, he became curious as to the kind of work Larry did, and after discovering that the American was some kind of corporate accountant, Smith asked him if he needed a job. We were just standing there, listening in on their chat, but now the two of them went off to Smith's office, and we were left with Doug to gape in our considerable astonishment, and we occupied ourselves by watching Butch begin his dog job of sniffing along the little strip of pavement in front of the government building to find a spot to pee.

Twenty minutes later, Larry came out of the glass building, a toothy grin adorning his white crew cut and albino-like face. Monday he would meet again with Jimmy Smith and talk over prospects for doing some work for the territorial administration. We were dumbfounded. What an unbelievable stroke of luck, it seemed, although we had a hard time comprehending that the crumpled, chunky clerk actually ran the whole shebang, a happy little crook. At first, Amy and I thought the guy must have been a phony, the whole act a put-on, so as a test we asked the lady behind the counter at the restaurant where we gobbled some eggs for dinner to name the commissioner of the Yukon. "Jimmy Smith," she announced with no hesitation, and that seemed to clinch the case.

Now everything pointed to Monday. We needed to check back to find out about teaching on Monday, Larry needed to check back about his job offer on Monday, and, after learning that he had gone to the Western Union office and found it had closed and wouldn't be open until after the weekend, we also had to return on Monday just to get some cash. When we suggested that we could visit the hunting lodge that Larry had intended to go scout out, he just waved the idea off, saying he had already called them up and the place had been sold in the meantime.

"Why don't we rent some rifles and head for the hills?" he joshed instead.

So we went to see about renting a camper—and there were plenty of Winnebagos and the like all decked out with equipment at a lot— but they cost way more than we could possibly afford. We just wanted to tag along for the hunt, expecting that we would put up the dough in the meantime but that Larry would pay us back come Monday; and when we went to check out guides and guided tours and gun laws, we found out that you could easily rent a gun and get ammunition without a license. But there was a hitch. They also had a law that you had to have a guide for $70 a day, and he would supply food and everything for another $140 a day. I suppose Jimmy Smith and the territorial government had kind thoughts in mind of protecting city-slicker tourists, although the idea of drumming up some trade for his tourist business and tax revenue for his government no doubt added some relish to the regulation.

Larry looked at us expectantly like a dog tugging his leash for a run through Riverside Park, and we all agreed that the rule that you had to have a guide was a shuck. No matter what, we didn't have anything close to the amount of cash needed to outfit even one of us, so the adventure was totally out of the question, simply impossible. Maybe it was that puppylike look on his face, but it suddenly dawned on us when we ditched the idea that Larry may have really expected us to shell out all the green for the entire escapade, our treat. The notion was ridiculous, but that made us ponder the situation. Though we felt comfortable chipping in a little, the amount had begun to add up. We had loaned out quite a lot of our limited dough to Larry, and we really did want to get at least some of it back.

Monday and its visit to Western Union loomed even larger than before. But what could we do to kill time until then?

Doug piped up about Colorado and his girlfriend again, but the three of us just ignored him. Too much hinged on Monday to turn back now—but we knew we had to keep on moving. After so many miles in the Thunderbird, the thought of camping out in downtown Whitehorse for two entire days was as unthinkable as Doug's homesick wet dreams to turn back. Fairbanks was too far down the Alaska Highway, but why not come back on Monday morning to find out the answers to all our questions after a short jaunt to Alaska anyway? We could get to at least a sliver of Alaska if we kept heading west until we reached Haines Junction and then took another road south, which cut through a little nub of B.C. before crossing the border to end up in Haines, a small town tucked on the Pacific in the northeastern armpit of the Alaska panhandle. After stocking up on soda and chips, we jumped back into the Thunderbird, and in short order we left the town's pavement behind to feel the gravel's familiar growl under our tires once more.

Haines was just a few hundred miles away, so the trip was nothing, ten hours or so. We kidded Larry about his new job prospect, and he went on about how we would be his assistants flying out into the bush in a little Piper Cub to check out good hunting spots. Doug didn't relish any of it, smoldering with his puppy on his lap, but we got high on the idea of becoming factotums for Larry the big honcho of the Yukon. What a trip, we marveled, and as we took the turn to Haines and the road climbed up alongside what seemed to be huge chunks of glacier ice tucked in rocky crevices while great snowcapped mountains soared along the border, the idea of our new careers in the territorial government seemed more and more plausible. Why not? Who could have imagined running into Jimmy Smith in the first place? It didn't take too much effort for us to shrug off qualms that the commissioner was a two-bit crook, and Larry would be, too. Everything was possible, and a Yukon of adventure stretched before us.

Larry pulled over to pick up a hitchhiker, the first one we had seen along the entire Alaska Highway. Hitchers usually made their bids for rides at the gas stations and didn't spot themselves along the roadside, since the blast of gravel of a truck barreling by could hit you like shrapnel, and why would you stand in the middle of nowhere, anyway? So this wiry guy a little older than us in a blue T-shirt with a backpack and bedroll by his feet was an unusual sight. He was from Alaska, not the panhandle but the main body of it past Fairbanks, a forest-fire fighter on a break. He was a man of few words, as country people often are, but after the usual pleasantries we asked him what he was doing in the middle of nowhere, and he told us he had had "a little run-in with a bear" just a few hours before.

He had left his last ride with the intention of camping out by the glaciers, but when he walked around a bend in the path not too far from the road, he stumbled upon a mother grizzly with her two cubs. Startled, he backed up very slowly around the curve he had come from, got down, and played dead. Nothing could be worse than getting on the wrong side of a grizzly protecting her cubs, and he had no gun, just a Bowie knife, and he would have been mauled badly before the enraged, protective mama would even notice the pricks of his blade. But the ruse worked, and after a few snorts and sniffs she was satisfied that the firefighter was no threat, not even worth a nibble, and she moseyed off with her cubs.

Amy and I were wide-eyed, and our giddy dreams of hopping planes through the bush were brought swiftly down to earth. He had recounted his brush with death with such calm matter-of-factness, the same steady manner of relating incredible events as had Jimmy, that mystic handyman of the summer stock theater, when he related his vision of the finger of God. The firefighter told the story, and then he didn't say much after that, getting out soon after we crossed the border, once again to vanish down a side road. He was simply the bearer of a commonplace tale, stolid and taciturn, and he was just as suddenly gone, swallowed up by the wilderness, as if he had never even existed outside of our consciousness. The story was so vivid yet so transient, like the hitchhiker himself. Amy hastily wrote it down in her notebook alongside her daily tally of money for coffee and gas, just so that the sudden encounter with the bear wouldn't end up a figment of our imagination.

The border itself was unremarkable — the guard spotted the Colorado plates, checked Larry's license, opened the trunk, peeked into our backpacks, then waved us through — but what was truly remarkable was the way, immediately upon crossing into Alaska, the road switched to a fine, smooth asphalt blacktop that made the tires hum, as if loudly announcing that we were now in a country that had enough dough to pave over everything in its path.

Haines turned out to be a fishing port pushed up against steep hills along a little bay with snowcapped mountains behind it. Amy and I went off on our own to look at the boats and talk to the fishermen, who seemed excited about the salmon coming in; then we headed for a small café for burgers, although when we found out how much a single burger cost, we just about freaked out and settled down to bowls of chili instead. Everything was too expensive in Alaska, but the lady behind the counter told us we could pick up some smoked salmon real cheap, and she directed us to a certain house a few blocks away, where the folks shipped it down to the Lower 48.

When we told Larry, his face lit up, and we all piled back into the car and drove up and down hilly streets looking for the place. We finally spotted a hand-scrawled sign that simply said "Smoked Salmon," but when we knocked on the door, two goofy black Labradors came galumphing out and slobbered all over us while Butch cowered under Doug's legs, and a woman in her forties next door told us that it was the neighbors who sold salmon but they weren't home, and after a little chat she invited us inside to wait.

The house was cozy, a real home with a couch and a dining-room table with four brown colonial chairs, even a TV, and one of those reclining leather easy chairs with her husband, a little paunchy, lying back in it. Larry's charm kicked in, and pretty soon they were showering us with hospitality. In fact, after they heard how long we'd been on the road, they began to shower us with actual showers, her husband ordering Doug to get into the shower while she scooped up all our clothes and tossed them into their washing machine. It was a whirlwind of hominess, and while we waited for Doug and Larry to finish up, we sat on the couch and listened to their stories. It was as if they were spiders who had waited patiently for someone to get tangled in their web, and now that we were there, they were not going to eat us, just smother us with their unrelieved loneliness.

She was forty years old, and he was in his fifties, and they had gotten married not long before. She had only recently come to Alaska from New York, where she had worked at *Time* magazine—something about checking out facts. "I hated the job and I hated New York, but I had to stay to take care of my mother, who was terribly ill," she explained in a soft voice as it slowly rolled up and down without pause like a road winding through gentle hills. Her mother had been on the verge of dying, but never did, and the daughter stayed to nurse her while her married sisters took care of their own families in Virginia and California. She didn't want her mother to die, of course, but she hated New York, though she never let on to her mother, who managed to linger on year after year.

"She lasted a little more than six years, and so many nights of those six years I cried my eyes out, until one night she finally did pass away. I wept that night too, but this time also with joy that I was free, and after the funeral I decided to get up and leave, to get as far from New York as I could, which is Alaska, of course, and I never ever want to read *Time* magazine again," she explained, her singsong ending with a tiny laugh.

"People come to Alaska because they're running away from something," her husband added with gruff sagacity from his reclining throne. "You just ask anyone, and you'll find out they're here because they had to get away from their folks or some big mess they're ashamed of, or they got broke and bankrupt, or they have some other dark secret. Alaska's the place to go, the last place to hide out."

We explained that we were sort of running away from New York ourselves, trying to get away from all the concrete and congestion and craziness (we didn't specify the war or the FBI or anything), so we could truly appreciate Alaska's attraction. The king of the reclining chair offered to square me up with a job right then and there. He worked at a logging mill, and despite all protestations, he tilted forward to pick up the phone and called a friend—the foreman, I guess. When he hung up, he said I could begin Monday at $4 an hour, which sounded like a lot, but with the prices in Alaska so high, it really wasn't that much. Still, I could hardly believe that yet another turn of fate had even landed me a job. I thanked him with some warmth, although I wasn't sure I wanted to stay in Alaska, which was, after all, still the United States, and I still held to the idea of tucking myself safely away in Canada. Now we would have to decide which Monday we would take —Monday in Haines or Monday in Whitehorse.

"What ended up bringing *you* to Alaska?" I asked my new benefactor, just to make some conversation while contemplating our choice of Mondays.

This turned out to be a mistake. It quickly wiped out our dilemma over which Monday to choose, for the offhand question triggered a rambling, fitful monologue, only vaguely comprehensible. It was as if he had told himself the story so many times without explaining who was who or any of the whys or wherefores that all connective tissue had been dissolved from the bones of the narrative.

He had joined the 59ers, that group of midwesterners who had trekked up the Alaska Highway in a long caravan in 1959 to settle in the new state. They were hailed as new pioneers in all the newspapers, and like the old pioneers, the 59ers were itchy for elbow room, and they were sick of the ills of urban life, which I suspected really was code for the fact that they didn't like black people. After a big spread in *Life*, they were soon forgotten by the rest of America as they staked out claims to their homesteads. Most of the 59ers made the trek as families, but he went alone, driving an old Hudson because "I told her I wasn't coming back for ten years, and here it's been ten years, and I still won't go back. Besides, they said it was murder, but it was self-defense. *It was self-defense, plain as day.*"

His eyes did not glaze over; the pupils instead screwed up into little sharp moons, as he squeezed the armrest of the reclining chair tightly with one hand while crunching his beer can with the other. His face, already deeply lined, began to crisscross with furrows like the canals of Mars, while his forehead, exposed by a receding hairline, throbbed with pounding intensity. He went on about the barroom brawl that apparently caused him to kill a man, landed him in the stockade, and booted him out of the army with what sounded like a dishonorable discharge. His voice rose, sputtered, and though we couldn't make out exactly who the "she" was that he wouldn't come back to, it was "she" who the deadly fight was about. We just sat, not saying a word, waiting for the rage to spew out of him, trying not to move and have him flip out into a bad-trip flashback and lunge after us, while his wife simply wrung her hands, quietly praying that the explosion would be averted. Finally, he pulled the beer can he clutched to his lips, which seemed to signal his return to 1969, his eyes resumed their typical dullness, he looked up at us, and he asked us in a pleasant voice if we would stay for dinner.

The change back to what seemed his normal, hospitable self was so abrupt that it struck me as almost comical. His balding pate seemed to deflate, and the deep canals across his face became mere lines once more. I didn't laugh, of course, and Larry, who had returned to the living room fresh-scrubbed from his shower with his clean laundry in his hands just as our host began his tale, beamed one of his ebullient, empty smiles and responded in John Wayne plain-talk, "Why, that's mighty friendly of you," as if the balding man in the easy chair had not just confessed to killing a man.

"Do you folks have a place to sleep?" our host continued.

His wife, who appeared more and more anxious, started to squirm. "Well, I'm not sure we have ..." she began to interject.

"Sure we're sure," he exploded, and in an instant the recently married couple began arguing loudly, and we found ourselves witnesses to a furious domestic spat. She didn't want us there for dinner or to sleep over, it was a terrific burden putting up four people out of the blue, and he had extended invitations without even consulting her, and what right did he have to ...

We just sat, horrified, fearing to move, not wanting to set off the murderer on another rampage. Then Amy whispered to me, "Let's get out of here." I was about to get up and unobtrusively slip out the door when I noticed Larry tipping backward on one of the colonial chairs, that vacant smile still attached to his face as if nothing were amiss, while the raging couple continued to lash out at each other. Larry did not find the murderer's tale at all disconcerting, so why should a little tussle over inappropriate offers of hospitality deter him from accepting a meal and a bed? Doug just stroked Butch, bored and inattentive, his head down, and I felt as if I no longer knew which way was up. Witnessing the ugly domestic squabble was disorienting enough, the two fugitives from the Lower 48 yelling at each other as if no one else were around, but the fact that Larry didn't seem to notice any sort of problem, that he was impervious to the heightening threat of violence and just sat, slightly bemused, made me dizzy. Was he making believe nothing was happening, exercising a kind of slick tact, or was he simply incapable of reading the obvious signs of danger and distress? Bear shit in the hills he could decode, but did the human voice convey nothing at all, did the contorted face send no message, did the angry word mean zilch?

Amy caught Larry's eye and jerked her head to signal we should leave, but Larry just stared back vacantly. In a few minutes the newlyweds had exhausted themselves and fell silent. Still panting from their rage, they turned to Larry expectantly, as if the blond ski bum could fix everything, and he did beam back at them, although his bemused smile was turning ever so slightly to a smirk.

"Well, it looks like the laundry's done, so we'll be getting on now," he said, as if the fight had not occurred. "Much obliged for the hospitality."

Everyone shook hands, Amy and I offered our thanks, we grabbed our clean clothes, exchanged a few pleasantries, and took our leave, the whole episode quickly and quietly closing up behind us as we stepped down from the porch.

"Weird," Amy and I sighed to each other, but Larry didn't say a word about the couple. Again, it was hard to fathom exactly what was going on in his head, and we didn't pursue it. Maybe he knew that we had to let the storm pass before making any safe move to depart. Whatever his thoughts, he didn't share them, and we just had this deepening, eerie sense that Larry did not look upon the universe the same way we did, not in the least. Besides, it was getting late, the twilight that passed for night was getting darker in the nook of the little town, and we had to find a place to sleep. We drove around until we found a gas station that had closed up for the day, and we bedded down, safely scrunched up in our seats next to one of its pumps.

When we awoke, the gas station was open, and the attendant let us use their restrooms to wash up. Coming back from the john, we were startled to discover that one of the tires had gone flat overnight, right there in the gas station parking lot, which pissed us off, although we were happy that Goodyear had decided to crap out in such a convenient location. The Thunderbird had a mind of its own, we figured, and it was going to argue in its own way. Luckily the tire was not ruined, and we were able to hit the road pretty early in the morning after the attendant slapped on a patch.

"A good goat year," the mechanic told us as we cashed yet one more traveler's check. Some state officials, trying to assess what the limit was going to be for hunters, spotted eight hundred head of mountain goats from a helicopter. He also told us that the salmon were at the peak of spawning. "It's something to write home about, if you've never seen it before."

The mention of salmon reminded us of our mission from the day before, and we drove back to the "Smoked Salmon" house. The slobbering Labradors came out to greet us once more, but this time their masters were home. Thankfully, the house of the previous day's encounter stayed still and quiet next door. We bought a package to eat right then and there, while Amy sent some back to her folks in New York. It was amazingly cheap for salmon, just a few dollars, and it seemed like a good sign. No more insane refugees, no more strange encounters, no more flat tires, just sweet smoked salmon.

It was Sunday, it was time to head back to our rendezvous in Whitehorse, and Larry took the wheel. He kept a lazy pace, especially considering the eighty miles an hour he would clock on the gravel, but we had plenty of time, and with the blacktop so smooth, so silent, it felt dreamy whirring gently along the road. We were jerked out of our reverie, however, when, not too far from the border, Larry suddenly swerved off to the shoulder after crossing a little bridge over a stream that a sign announced was King Salmon Creek.

We got out and looked over the railing. The creek, only about twenty-five feet wide, was packed shoulder to shoulder with huge swarming salmon squirming and wiggling and jumping upstream, the quivering mass single-mindedly going through its spawning ordeal. They were beautiful, huge fish, three or four feet long, and to see so many jamming together was an incredible sight to behold. They must have been the king salmon of the creek's name, and we could clearly understand why they had received their royal appellation, for what huge, lordly fish they were, their incandescent scales glittering in the sunlight as they broke the surface of the water. It looked like a stream of diamonds in foam.

"Far out!" escaped my lips, and Amy responded likewise with her own gasp of amazement, but Larry simply stood, zonked out of his mind, his eyes giving off those same throbs they did when he tripped out about the virtues of the hunt. He positively glowed, and in no time he scampered down the embankment to the shore and stuck his hand in the water. The fish were so thick he could easily grab one, and he tried wrestling it to the shore in his arms, but its four-foot torso flailed and slithered out to continue the salmon's frenzied upstream course.

Pretty soon he climbed back up to the bridge, gathered a few huge rocks, and, lifting them high above his head, began hurling them down on the boiling mass below. It was almost impossible not to hit one, and as soon as a fish was clobbered, it would flip and flop into the air and drop back in and start floating back downstream, unconscious. Larry stationed Doug along the shore below the bridge, and as the knocked-out salmon would flop by, he would scream at Doug to grab it and haul it in. A sign on the bridge read "No Fishing When Salmon Are Spawning," but such a technicality hardly stood in his way. Larry seemed half-titan, half cartoon character, lifting small boulders high above his head and then hurling them down at the rush-hour crush below. This, we supposed, was the thrill of the hunt he had spoken of, but our increasing disgust, which we did little to hide, did not even register. He had been transported to another world, a planet of blood lust, and nothing inhibited him, nothing pulled him back, and his frenzy to kill matched, even surpassed, the salmons' own frenzy to climb up the creek to drop their eggs.

Each salmon was heavy, maybe thirty or forty pounds, and while Larry could easily knock one out, Doug could hardly hold on as the stunned fish flopped and slithered out of his arms.

"Go down and help out Doug," Larry ordered me.

I glanced at Amy, and silently we agreed I had little choice. With me at his side, Doug was able to grab a huge one, and I wrapped my arms around its tail while he yanked its nose to the shore. Larry ran down the embankment in triumph, and he grabbed its body to check if it had eggs, and a huge quantity began to gush out. He squeezed the fish until all its pinkish, creamy caviar had spewed on the shore, a sight both dazzling and nauseating. I could see no reason for doing this other than the sheer delight a little kid has in setting ants on fire, and Larry chattered and grinned with what seemed a similar joy. Killing the fish, stealing it away from its destiny was one thing, but watching its load of life-giving force spurt into the soil was yet another sort of perverted pleasure, an orgasm of exquisite waste.

We had all but disappeared in Larry's eyes, so we figured we might as well split from the grotesque scene. We decided to make our way into the fields to find a secluded spot.

We wanted to fuck. It had been nearly two weeks since the last time we had sex in Madison, we hardly had a moment to ourselves, and we were increasingly bemoaning our horniness. With Larry and Doug now lost to their lunatic hunt, we figured this was our best and probably only opportunity. The frenzy along the creek—whether the spawning or the spoiling—could not keep us from our own biological urges.

We walked through the high grass until we passed a clump of trees, far enough away so that Larry's shrieks would not be heard, but not too far to risk getting lost, and at a level spot in the clearing we spread our jackets on the ground. Under the circumstances, this was the best we could do, while flies and other insects buzzed around our heads. As awkward as it felt, we kissed and squirmed with great determination, Amy nervous that someone could still see us, while I brushed away flies.

Suddenly Amy froze. "What was that?" she whispered.

"What was what?" and I listened, hushed. "It's nothing," and I resumed my fumbling effort to kiss her.

"No," she leaned up on her elbows. "Listen."

I rolled onto my back and listened. Nothing. I was about to try again when I did hear a sound, a slight snap of a branch, followed by a crackling of dry grass.

"Just the wind in the—" My reassuring denial was interrupted by a soft yet deep, guttural grunt, a growl pitched so low that it seemed almost beyond the range of human ears.

In a flash we both jumped up and started hopping and stumbling back along the trail even before we could button our clothes back up. Adrenaline pumped through our groins instead of sex as we dashed through the field ahead of whatever monster lurked behind those trees. Breathless, we bumbled back to the road and could see the now-reassuring sight of Larry's back as he lofted yet another boulder over his head to kill more fish.

We caught our breath, laughing nervously, and stood alongside the car to watch Larry carry out his slaughter, unaware that we had been gone. By now, three salmon, including the huge one whose eggs I had watched him squish out, were stretched by the side of the creek, but for every one they caught, nine or so were knocked out, hurling back downstream. Given how much competition there was, and how tiring the climb upriver, it was easy to assume that those KO-ed fish would never make it to their spawning grounds, so the havoc Larry caused was multiplied many-fold. Yet he was our only means of escape from the bear, and we kept a wary eye on the field and clump of trees from which we had just fled, just in case the grizzly decided to squeeze the eggs and sperm out of us. Even as Larry pummeled the fish, another creature was getting ready to prey upon us. We had no choice but to put up with Larry's blood lust until it was exhausted, and we just leaned against the hood as Butch, locked inside, whimpered and howled, clearly in need of a walk.

"Say, Larry, what about letting Butch out? He needs to take a walk," Amy called to him.

He just waved his hand, not to be disturbed with such trivialities. As much as Doug petted and loved Butch, the two of them did little to take care of the puppy that was still not yet completely housetrained. This had greatly irritated us; especially when, sleeping on our laps, Butch would pee and even once had taken a shit on the floor by our feet. With the windows rolled up most of the time because of the gravel and choking dust flinging off the tires, the car had become a smelly dump. Larry didn't seem to mind, as if he would simply toss the car away and get another one once the Thunderbird was thoroughly spoiled. But as Larry took charge of driving more and more, sometimes sharing the wheel with Doug, the backseat had become home to us, and we did not appreciate the stinky shit-hole it was fast becoming.

Amy just opened the door and let the dog out. He relieved himself immediately, and then began to sniff up and down the bridge, soon wandering off into the field we had just fled from, despite Amy's calls after him. "No, Butch! Come back, Butch!" The puppy ignored her, sniffing his way until he disappeared into the brush.

Amy gave me a pleading look.

"No way I'm going to chase after him," I answered her eyes.

Larry had decided that three was his limit, and to my relief he hollered for me to help him haul the salmon up the embankment to the car. Taking some oily blankets he had in the trunk, he soaked them by the side of the creek and wrapped them around the fish to keep his catch moist and fresh; then we hoisted them up and stuffed their carcasses into the trunk against our backpacks. He announced that we would eat the two smaller ones, while the large one, whose eggs I had watched him squeeze out, he would stuff as a trophy. I had no idea how he planned to accomplish any of this, but all that mattered was that we were finally leaving King Salmon Creek and we would get back to Whitehorse by Monday.

With the stuffed trunk slammed shut, only the missing Butch kept us from hitting the road. Doug joined Amy in calling after the dog, and after a few eerie moments of silence the puppy shot out of the woods, squealing and yipping in fear, then bounded into the boy's arms. We reckoned Butch had met up with the deep-throated beast himself, although instinctively we chose not to tell our car mates of what lurked in the woods. Doug just thought the bulldog was excited to see him.

Soon we were at the border, and we were worried that the Canadian border guard would turn us over as poachers to the Alaskan Fish and Game, particularly since the fish smell from the trunk began to pervade the entire car. But he just glanced at Larry's license, not even bothering to look at our IDs, as he waved us through. Now that we were back on the Yukon's endless gravel road and we had to roll up our windows, the stench from the salmon broiling under the hot sun grew more and more pungent.

That's when we decided to get married.

I didn't ask Amy, and she didn't ask me. We were just clutching each other in the back seat, horny and happy to have escaped the monster. Enveloped in the aroma of very ripe fish and puppy pee, we turned to each other, the idea dawning in both of our heads at exactly the same moment.

"Let's get married!" we both whispered, laughing at our mental telepathy.

The logic of it was basic, overpowering in its obviousness. We had talked on and off during the long ride through B.C. and the Yukon about the notion, so it wasn't as if the idea came as a total bolt from the blue. But for some reason, the massacre of the salmon, our disaster at sex, our terror of the beast, all the disjointed, bizarre events since we hit Whitehorse seemed to point in that one direction with inexorable logic.

We were getting scared, I guess.

Commissioner Smith, the hitchhiker, the murderer and his lonely wife, Larry's blood lust, the bear—all of these encounters came and went like discrete particles, and only the road, only the forward motion of blacktop and now the crunching of gravel provided the string to hold them all together. We needed more than the road, though. We were together, we would stay together, we would be stories twirling around each other, and that flow, that fuzzy yet real vibration would group every incident and every encounter together as nothing else would. The increasingly putrid Thunderbird could not hold the universe, but we could.

Getting married was the instrument that would allow us to link one thing to the next.

We were ready for Whitehorse Monday.

Heaven and Hell

Monday was a total bust. Disappointments and disasters tumbled in an avalanche, and by the end of the day we found ourselves speeding back down the Alaska Highway toward Dawson Creek and on to Prince George trying to stay just ahead of the crashing debris.

Getting a teaching job was no problem, we learned, but our joy at the discovery soon faded when we were told that we needed to bring our own trailer: Housing was so scarce that nothing else was available. Besides, the supply of teachers was no longer so tight, which meant the Canadians were hiring far fewer Americans than they had the previous year, and because we were not citizens or even new "landed immigrants," the paperwork was especially complicated. The best advice the woman behind the desk could give us was to head back down to Vancouver and get things worked out there. No trailer, no papers, no dice.

Meanwhile, Doug was getting more and more anxious that Larry would accept Jimmy Smith's job offer. "You can't take this job," he would plead over and over, "I don't want to move up here." So when Larry came back from his meeting with the commissioner saying only that he was going to think it over, while directing a wink at us, we thought at first that he had given in to Doug's reluctance, but only temporarily. We calculated that he had really agreed to take the job but held back from telling Doug in order to allow the boy more time to get used to the bizarre reality of moving to the Yukon — or maybe he was going to first haul the kid back to Colorado before he flew back to Whitehorse by himself.

But, really, we had no idea what had transpired between the commissioner and the accountant. We thought about it so long, mulling over the way Larry dismissed any more talk about his job prospect in so much the same manner as he had brushed off his interest in buying a hunting lodge, until uncertainty was the only thing we could be sure of, and we grew more and more to suspect that Jimmy Smith may have even rejected Larry. In fact, the more we meditated on all the events of our journey together, the less we believed that Larry had even been offered a job in the first place. We only had his word for what had passed between the two men, and the whole thing could very well have been a fantasy, a trick, a game, a big fat nothing.

Worst of all, the Western Union office didn't even cough up a dime. Larry's face flushed at the news that nothing was awaiting him, he stammered, he asked for the clerk to check again. None of this produced any money, of course. But after his first flash of irritation and embarrassment, he recovered his cool and wired instructions that the money should be sent to Prince George and kept there until his arrival. He apologized to us and offered to write us a check so that we could stay and go ahead with our business in Whitehorse. If we wanted reassurance, or if there were any problems with cashing the check, he reached into the glove compartment and pulled out another end page from the Swedenborg book to write out the address and phone number of his parents in Ohio, and they would straighten anything out. Otherwise, we could go back down to Prince George with him and pick up the money there.

Once again we could opt to split. This was a critical moment for us, another fork in the road. We wanted to stay in Whitehorse, but with only a few weeks before the autumn chill would plunge temperatures below freezing, we had no trailer and no way to survive. Besides, we needed the dough, and who would cash an American check in Whitehorse? Larry had tried to write a check at one of the cafés, and the answer was clearly no-can-do, although he assured us we would have no problem if we sent it to the Bank of America in Vancouver. But that ruled out getting the cash in our hands anytime soon—and we wanted the do-re-mi, our only money, in our palms. Now everything pointed south—first to Prince George and then to Vancouver—so keeping to our little selves in the cramped backseat compartment of the Thunderbird seemed the only reasonable alternative.

Our tale of three clobbered fish turned out to be the only thing that reached some kind of satisfying conclusion in Whitehorse. In a display of questionable generosity, Larry gave away the two smaller, rapidly decomposing salmon to the people who ran a café on our way back to Whitehorse—and the four of us were served up free pie and coffee in exchange. But the big one was Larry's prize, and we helped carry the behemoth to a taxidermist in a warehouse shed along the Yukon River in Whitehorse, and as he detailed arrangements to have it stuffed, mounted, and shipped back home, we could see the taxidermist eyeing him suspiciously. He asked Larry where he had caught the fish, and since we had no desire to listen to Larry's fabrications, we hastened back to the car, relieved at least to have all the pungent fish disposed of. After what seemed an endless half-hour, he returned, tossing his checkbook into the glove compartment and beaming his sunshine smile at us once more. "It's all taken care of," he announced. "Let's go!" For all we knew, they didn't take his check and he had just donated the carcass to the taxidermist with one of his affable devil-may-care shrugs. It was the same as his interview with Jimmy Smith: We could no longer assume that the story ended the way he happened to tell it.

The Thunderbird began eating up the gravel. Larry kept on yakking for a while, mostly about guns. Double aught this, caliber that, bore, sight, semiautomatic, on and on. We paid little attention, while Doug lapped it all up. Guns to the man and the boy were objects to be admired, revered more than cars even, and Doug shot back arcane questions that Larry answered with the wisdom of a Torah sage. We were relieved that we never did go hunting with him, seeing what kind of sporting job he did pounding in the heads of the spawning salmon, and after a while even the two gun lovers grew silent.

Larry did almost all of the driving now, although he let Doug take the wheel two times, despite the fact that the kid was surely too young even to have a learner's permit. It was Larry's chance to teach the boy how to drive, and he would scream at him again and again to keep his foot steady on the gas pedal. Naturally, Doug's foot bobbed up and down like a rubber duckie in a bathtub, and Larry would, as if on cue, bellow at him with every bob. The tension was unbearable, almost as agonizing as sitting through the domestic terror between the murderer and his wife back in Haines. But eventually Larry grew tired of "Driver's Ed," the master took permanent command of the wheel, and we barreled down the gravel road at racetrack speeds.

Occasionally, Butch would whimper and we'd badger Larry until he'd pull over to let the dog relieve himself, but for the most part we careened through the Yukon and B.C., only snatches of conversation drifting back from the pair in the front seat. The windows were rolled up, and with the vacant view whizzing past, nothing, no memories of Columbia or Ronnie or sex fantasies or old movies or Frank O'Hara poems, nothing rolled through my skull. I was rendered a blank, the walls of the Thunderbird pressing against my head, the front bucket seats pushing into my knees, and the window screwing itself inexorably into my scalp. I began to smother within the padded coffin of the Thunderbird; I was trapped, incapable of budging, buried alive at full speed; and the sensation of being bound, of compression and suffocation, tightened my chest, my abdomen, my whole being with the absence of possibilities. I could not move, and there was no place to move to if I could. I was able only to shift from side to side in slight gradations, to lean against wife-to-be, to push my bulk against the door, half-hoping it would fly open, to throw my head back and stare at the baby-blue Naugahyde on the ceiling just inches from my nose.

For two or three hundred miles, a captive in this horrible, speeding dungeon, I felt great bubbles of panic roil through my guts. This time there was no escape, no Ronnie to save me. I began to worry that I would flip out, flail wildly, and Amy would squeeze my hand until the freakout ran its course, the constrictions, the palpitations, all the fear and panic escaping through my asshole in soft, quiet farts. At least something could escape, and the freedom my rectum briefly enjoyed allowed the claustrophobic terror to relax its grip, if only for a moment, until the flatulent buildup of fear would travel through my gut once more. It would have been funny, if I could have allowed myself the perspective to enjoy my own torment, but I had no ability to gain any distance, strapped as I was in the torture victim's chair.

It wasn't that I was afraid of Larry. Clearly, he was a jerk, but I did-n't feel he was any sort of menace. All that the modern-day Johnny Ap-pleseed meant to me now was the means to recover our money and our hitching spot on the highway out of Prince George. But the long hours of constraining ourselves, of trying to remain polite while wishing with all our might to turn invisible, naturally took their toll. I felt like a baby being asked to sit still for a portrait in a photographer's studio, squirm-ing as if the ordeal took forever, only the shooting session really did last forever. What could I do? Nothing except press against the two square feet allotted to me and bottle up the mounting hysteria.

Just when I thought my fear-induced flatulence would explode in a mushroom cloud through the top of my head, the panic of captivity suddenly evaporated. I didn't feel high or liberated. I simply stared at the open, metallic sky of the North, my mind gone, the brain shifting to neutral, its load dumped, and I was relieved to have been emptied, utterly vacant. I had finally succumbed to the waves of panic, the body and soul no longer responding to the impulses of life. I wasn't confused or lost, like Amy's dad in that moment when he hadn't recognized her; instead, the tremendous vacuum of feeling tricked me into thinking I was free when in reality I had simply become resigned to my fate.

I watched in this daze as we rolled past the lush prairie farmlands of the Peace River, and when we finally reached Fort Nelson, the town's grain elevators towering over the prairie, I barely twitched as Larry parked in front of the municipal swimming pool. We would all go and take a dip, he advised. After my confinement, hardly anything more ab-surd could have been suggested. But we did — I unfolded myself from the seat and revived somewhat, enough at least to realize how odd it was to go swimming at this juncture, all of Fort Nelson's kids splashing and screaming around the strung-out travelers. Yet, after we were brought back to the ordinary itchiness of life, the rest of the trip to Prince

George went by swiftly. With money in our pockets, we would soon be back on the road, and the road would mean freedom once more.

But first we needed to make our way to the Western Union office, which we did as soon as we arrived at Prince George. Wherever Larry went after Prince George, for sure it was not going to be in our direction—we figured we would head down to Vancouver and he would go back to where he came from with Doug. The two of them started to fight about it, since Larry wanted to stick around Prince George, but we couldn't care less. Anxious to go our separate ways, we waited in the car with Doug, who slumped over in a bummed-out pout, while Larry went in to the office. But he returned with more bad news: The signals had gotten crossed again, and the money was now up in Whitehorse. Tomorrow morning they would straighten everything out, and he acted pissed off, really sorry, it wasn't his fault, etc., etc.

The thought of one more night with the two of them was almost unbearable. We were exasperated, at our wits' end, but there was nothing we could do but try to find a place to sleep. We were far enough from the Arctic for the late hours to resemble the nighttime we were accustomed to below the border, and true darkness began to blanket Prince George sometime after 11 p.m. Larry drove to the outskirts of town, turning left, then right, then left, until the pavement ended and the road became nothing but wagon ruts, and we began driving through darkening woods.

It was strange, almost as if he had been there before, as if he knew where he was driving. We just wanted to find a clearing where we could get out of the car and pitch our tent, but he kept on taking one side road after another, winding through incredible curves, the Thunderbird heaving, lurching from side to side, as if the car would never come to a halt, no matter how rough or clogged the road. The ruts seemed to get narrower and narrower, dense bushes pushing against all sides, and it appeared as if we were squeezing through knots of leafy nets, the branches and brambles scratching the windshield, the light from the headlights splintering against the twisted, black brush as the deepening blackness of night and brambles engulfed the car. We were entering some Bermuda Triangle, and soon we would be totally ensnared, sucked down into the depths, swallowed up in the dark gorge of prickly, scratchy brush. Yet Larry kept dragging forward, plowing through twigs and thorns, as if he were driving down a road he was inventing as he went along.

No one said a word. We just stared at the weird jungle about us, our nerves jumbling and crackling with tension. Where was he going? Why? Just when the scene was reaching what seemed an almost unbearable height of spookiness, Larry brought us back from the precipice. Suddenly, the Thunderbird burst through the dense vegetation, and we came upon a genuine road, still a country road, but one considerably more than an overgrown path — a paved road filled with life, a small thoroughfare with speeding cars passing in both directions. Perhaps he had known where he was going, after all — at least we were no longer lost in scary Hansel-and-Gretel woods — and we spent the night once again stuffed into our tiny backseat coffin pulled over in a turnout on the side of that road, the blinding lights of the passing cars comforting us with their presence.

The next morning we parked by the railroad yards, and while Larry went with Doug back to the telegraph office, we bought some fruit from a grocery and climbed up on an unused platform by the tracks to eat. We talked things over, speculating if Larry would really get the money this time, and we wondered if we would have to hop freights because we were growing so short of cash. They had left Butch with us, and he busily scampered up and down the old wooden platform, so we didn't think they would simply split and leave us in the lurch with the boy's bulldog.

After a couple of hours Larry showed up, a curious expression on his face. Some of the money had arrived—not all of it, but at least a little—and snapping a crisp, new $20 bill, he said he would split it with us until the rest arrived the next day.

We hadn't speculated on this development. We figured he would have the money or not, but this was an in-between thing, another song-and-dance act, yet one that showed at least a little return and the possibility of more.

We were relieved, disappointed, encouraged, confused. By this time there was nothing to talk about, only bad vibes between us, but there seemed to be no other choice than to spend yet one more night with the jerk from Colorado, and he decided to spend it in a motel.

He would, but not us. After renting the room, he unlocked the door, and we walked in with the two of them to survey the clean sheets and inhale the antiseptic smell of the bathroom. But the creep didn't say a word. He didn't offer to let us camp out on the floor, didn't even invite us to take a piss, much less a shower, and we turned around after sniffing the Mr. Clean and headed back out without saying a word. At least we would be alone. We did our laundry in the motel's coin machines and then curled up in the back of the car for one more night, pissed off.

The next morning Larry came out with a fresh Pepsodent smile, but no apology, no acknowledgment of anything strange. Doug stalled, locked in the toilet, until finally Larry hollered at him to haul ass, and he came out, his unkempt head down, a somber cloud of shame hovering over him. At first we were glad that at least the boy felt a little guilty for how his dad had given us the cold shoulder, but after a while we realized that Doug's dejected, hurt manner may have had nothing to do with us. Things had not gone well between father and son, we figured. Perhaps Larry had finally spilled the beans, laid it out, insisted that he was heading back to Whitehorse, no matter what Doug thought; and in the privacy of the motel room the argument had been settled with vehemence, maybe even with a smack to the head.

"I want to go home," Doug muttered through his phlegm, his head down, stroking his pup, and once again Larry told him to shut up. But Doug wouldn't stop—he went on about the guns, what about the guns they left back home, who would get the guns, he wanted his guns, the guns would be seized, confiscated, his anger seething. Larry became unusually alarmed, clenched his teeth, snapped at the boy to hush up, as if he had blabbed some secret, had opened a chink in a real criminal plot. We stared out the window, trying to look casual, like we hadn't heard anything, but I could sense Amy tense up alongside me. Something was wrong, something terribly fucked up, although we still couldn't tell what it was. Owning guns, even a lot of guns, wasn't illegal, but all this talk about firearms was too bizarre, too sinister. Either they had the arsenal of an entire army secretly tucked away—maybe the Viet Cong would level Denver during the next Tet Offensive—or the whole talk was a code for something else, something even stranger than a rifle-barrel fetish. Who could tell?

No more money had arrived at the Western Union office as of early that morning. Our frustration, our overextended patience, our suspicions all had started to gnaw into us, but we had no choice but to walk a couple of blocks to get some breakfast. We had coffee and English muffins, while Larry ordered for himself and his sullen offspring massive quantities of eggs and bacon and pancakes, all the fixings. Such a feast plus a cushy motel room seemed to add up to more than twenty bucks, and such extravagance aroused our suspicions even more. As they shoveled the mess into their guts, we told them we were taking a walk and we would meet them back at the car. We hustled to the Western Union office to check with the clerk, who told us that some money had indeed arrived the day before, but that none was expected that day. She didn't know if he had wired for more, and company rules did not allow her to reveal the amount of money he had received the previous day.

We waited in the car, more perplexed than ever. Was it simply that he had gotten all the money and didn't want to cough up what he owed us? Had he wired again? Soon Larry and Doug arrived at the car, toothpicks dangling languidly, and he offered to write us a check one more time. We had him this time, since there was a bank just two doors down from where the car was parked, so we suggested that he go in and cash his own check.

"Good idea," he responded without missing a beat, and he fished out his checkbook and disappeared into the bank. Yet when he returned a half-hour later he only shrugged, informing us that the bank refused to cash it because it was an American check. "But I'm sure you could cash it at the Bank of America in Vancouver," he repeated his offer, then tossed his checkbook back into the glove compartment with a lackadaisical flip, and off he went with Doug to reconnoiter the streets.

What to do? Leaving the car was out of the question. He might double back and, discovering we were gone, hit the road with all our money and our gear to boot. No, at least one of us had to guard the Thunderbird at all times. I stayed put while Amy headed for the bank, and when she came back she had the scoop. Larry could cash his check: He just had to pay the $2.50 for the call to his bank in Colorado to check out his account. No problem, we figured he had forgotten to ask, and now everything would be settled once and for all. But Larry was nowhere in sight, and we waited hours until we spotted him and Doug heading back into the coffee shop for lunch.

We dashed over, really excited, jabbering to him that we found a way to get the check cashed, and we would even pay for the call. He acted delighted, a real nice guy ready to help out any way he could, but it was Friday, around 2:30, and we had to make it back to the bank quick before it closed. First he had to finish his coffee, then his refill, then he had some pie, and slowly, too slowly, he inched his way over to the cash register to pay his check. We were nervous, anxious to meet the deadline, and to our utter relief Larry finally did mosey into the bank within minutes of closing. We had managed to beat the clock, despite his stalling tactics, and we stood there, anxiously awaiting the results of the long-distance call.

The time difference! We hadn't factored in the time difference! His bank in Colorado was already closed. Larry must have known, and now we would have to wait until Monday, languishing one more weekend in our baby-blue tomb. Larry shrugged, folding the blank check into his wallet. He tossed the checkbook through the Thunderbird's open window onto the dashboard before going off with Doug and the bulldog to take a little walking tour of the town.

Another weekend? How could we possibly live through another weekend with the two of them? We sat in the car as the hours ticked by, trying to figure out what was what. What would Mickey Spillane do? We easily slipped into the tough-guy detective mode, figuring it was the best way to scope out the scene, since we were dealing with some kind of sordid character here, although exactly what kind eluded us. Clearly, we were playing a waiting game, and we were so pissed off, so hungry for our dough, we swore that, no matter what he did, we would outwait the bastard.

We rolled that over in our minds for a while, weighing all the angles.

Then it dawned on us that maybe Larry had all the time in the world. Maybe he had nowhere to go, maybe he didn't need to be in Colorado, maybe nothing waited for him in Whitehorse, maybe Prince George was as good as any place to while away a weekend or a week or a winter. Larry was taking his good sweet time returning to the Thunderbird, letting us stew in our own juices, hoping we would get so fed up we would run out of time and simply cut out without our cash. Something would have to give, for sure—but we had to have our money.

Was Larry simply a con man, a crook out to soak us? If he was, why did he give us his parents' address and phone number? It could have been fake, of course, but the small town, the numbers, all of it looked too real. Then we thought of the checkbook. Grabbing it off the dashboard, we opened it to the record book.

ACCOUNT CLOSED.

No doubt about it, there it was in the bold capital letters of Larry's handwriting. Well, taking his check was impossible. Doubtless, he was willing to pass off a bad check on us—but why did he leave his checkbook out in plain sight? In order for us to read it and know he was conning us? What kind of con was that? He had seemed so respectable at first, and even when his tales unraveled, he wasn't much worse than any other creep. Was he really an accountant?

Then it struck us that we weren't even sure that Doug was his son. We tried to calculate ages, and it seemed that Larry would have to have been fifteen when Doug was born. OK, maybe seventeen or eighteen. It was possible, but he looked too young. And if he wasn't his father, who was he? And that night in the motel, Doug's shamefaced demeanor the next morning, his odd rage about guns—what did it all signify? It dawned on us that something might be going on, something too sickening, too twisted even for Mike Hammer to comprehend. What kind of unspeakable things was Larry doing to the boy? Was he a captive, too? What were they running from? Running to?

After all these fearful speculations, I finally spilled the beans on Johnny Appleseed. Amy listened, eyebrows arched, thoughtful, not saying anything for a long while.

"Larry is a new kind of legend," she responded at last. "He doesn't need the past to make him any creepier, but if he's really related to the original Johnny Appleseed—well, it figures he'd be the bad seed. I think I'd be even more surprised if he wasn't related, since all the other myths of America have turned to crap, anyway."

She paused for a moment, and then asked, "Why didn't you tell me this story before?"

"I don't know. I wanted to keep it for myself," I offered by way of explanation. I hesitated, and then continued guiltily, "He didn't ask me to keep it a secret."

"Do you have any other secrets you haven't told me?" And before I could even recollect anything, she hastily added, "Don't tell me if you do. I don't want to know."

It was getting late, although the sun still slanted at a sharp angle, casting deep shadows along with glints and eerie, luminous blazes on the sides of buildings as in an Edward Hopper painting. The downtown streets were empty, deserted, except for the Thunderbird, and we felt more and more alone, frightened, unable to decide what to do.

We needed help. When we saw Mounties cruise by slowly in a police car, casting suspicious eyes at the lone car with Colorado plates, we frantically waved them down to blurt out our story—we had lent this guy a lot of money, he owed us, no proof, closed account, bad check, what could we do? The Mounties listened a little too casually, we thought, and they offered that they couldn't do much of anything about personal loans—that was between the parties concerned—but they could check the plates to see if Larry was some kind of escaped convict or if the Thunderbird was a stolen vehicle. We should just sit tight for half an hour until they returned.

When they drove off down the street, we felt lonelier, more anxious than ever before.

We heard their footsteps echoing down the hollow, empty street even before we saw them in the glare of the slowly setting sun. Larry and Doug turned the corner barely a minute or two after the cops had taken off, and the duo came walking down the block toward the car. Had they been watching us all along? Did our calling over the Mounties trigger a countermove on their part? What would we do? My head swirled, panic crawling up my throat; the moment had come, and we still had no strategy.

In desperation I looked to Amy, the Amy of thoroughgoing logic, the Amy of cool determination.

"You decide," Amy hastily whispered to me when the duo was still half a block away. "I can wait it out or I can leave. It all depends on the vibes. You decide, decide on the spot. You're the man, they'll expect you to make the move, and I'll follow."

There would be no time for a conference, and all the cards would be in my hands.

Larry leaned through the open window, his big grin adorning his face, which looked even whiter in the strange incandescent glow of the northern light. "How you guys doing?" he inquired in an easygoing tone of voice that betrayed nothing; then he slid into the driver's seat, Doug quietly taking his position on the passenger side.

"Fine," Amy smiled back, "we've just been sitting around reading. What about you?"

"You'll never believe it," Larry went on, launching into the story of his day's adventures as he twisted toward the backseat. "We walked all over town, and then we found a place, a sporting goods store, where I could get a check cashed."

We perked up. We were unexpectedly drawn to what we thought could be the news that would signal our easy salvation, the quick end to our ordeal.

"Is that so?" Amy cued his next line.

"Yeah—but they would take a check for merchandise only." Our faces fell, but he maintained his grin, unperturbed. "I tried," he added apologetically. "But at least they would take a check if I bought something," he resumed his bright tone. "And look at what I got."

Larry drew out of the paper bag an enormous hunting knife, maybe a Bowie knife, a foot long and two inches wide. He held the thick, flat blade upright in front of my face, its point right between my eyes, like Jimmy's finger of God. The slanting sunlight glinted against it, the hard, smooth metal blazing and shooting out fiery light with the intensity of a nuclear blast, the vertical blade radiating across the broad, horizontal dullness of my face, bright, hard, sharp.

I opened my eyes wide. I opened them so wide that the brilliant flash of the knife's sharpened edge allowed nothing but pure white flames to pierce my retina. The glaring, reflected sunlight burned into my skull. For a moment I could see nothing, nothing at all, only the blinding light filling up the Thunderbird, Prince George, the sky.

Nothing else but light.

Then the gleam flickered as the knife sank down, and I stared helplessly while Larry plunged the blade's sharpened tip into my abdomen, driving it in again and again, blood and bowels spurting, my guts splattering against the baby-blue Naugahyde of the Thunderbird.

. . .

Perhaps my own murder should really have come next. And I almost feel that it did, at least in another dimension, that realm of choices not made, whole solar systems that we always leave behind except maybe for tiny sidereal splinters that get stuck in our butts to remind us of what could have been.

But that is not what happened.

Amy quickly grabbed Larry's wrist, the blade tilted toward my face. For a brief moment they stared into each other's eyes, the grin frozen on his lips, her knuckles tight, bone-white, squeezed around his wrist, and her face set, rigid. It was an eternity, and Amy held both of our lives in her hands.

"We'll take the bus," she said between clenched teeth. She pronounced each word slowly, tensely, her voice suddenly metallic, the words filling the void, while her eyes never moved from his, drilling into Larry's brain. "We talked it over," she continued, "and we figured we could cash the check in Vancouver like you said."

Larry kept grinning, his eyes never moving from hers, as he had throughout the whole confrontation, but he dropped his arm, and he slid the knife back into its sheath and into the paper bag. He grabbed the checkbook on the dashboard, and Amy, her voice suddenly reverting to a chatty, girlish lilt, argued with him about the correct amount he owed us, knowing full well we would never see a dime. She said later that she haggled over the amount to act like we weren't running away, just so that Larry wouldn't get any last-minute ideas about using the knife instead of his pen. Squabbling over how much he owed us seemed normal, and normal was what Amy wanted to be in Larry's eyes, just in case he suspected otherwise.

Larry took on his old affable self, chatting and smiling, as he drove us to the bus station, and by chance we arrived just two minutes before the bus for Vancouver departed.

I never said a word through any of this.

In no time we were sitting in our seats on the bus, speeding away from Prince George and Larry and the boy, with hardly a second to collect our thoughts.

In a flash, we were free. And the fact that our thick roll of traveler's checks had become pitifully slim hardly mattered at all.

"You saved my life, both of our lives," I told Amy as the bus curved along the Frazier River gorge. "I guess I owe you, not just love you."

"That's what I'm here for," she said, staring out the window. "I'm here to save you, my sister, my father, everyone—even when I don't want to."

In Vancouver we rented a room in a flophouse frequented by hookers. A very overweight older woman insisted on walking through the halls in her bra and panties and nylons, although we were not too sure her parade did much to attract business.

No Bank of America in Vancouver, which came as no surprise. But we were astonished when we dialed the number Larry had given us to have our collect call accepted by his parents.

"Where is our boy?" Mrs. Chapman asked in a creaky voice, and we related our escapade with her son to the Yukon. She was growing old and hard of hearing, so we had to yell into the pay phone in the hotel hallway. We described our money problems, and how Larry told us that his parents would make his check good, but they could not or would not hear a thing.

"My boy, my boy," his mother lamented. "He should be in the hospital. He is *supposed* to be in the mental hospital."

When we called a second time, she accepted our call again, but then she berated us for getting her son in trouble. Apparently, Larry had called her after getting picked up in Prince George for writing bad checks, among other more serious charges that she would not disclose, and he was being arraigned in court that very day. "My boy—now he is in such trouble, and he was not supposed to leave the hospital," she replied to our request for money. "He is a *very* sick boy," she said, then hung up.

The third time we tried, his mother wouldn't even accept our call. We didn't want to get in touch with the Mounties again, reasoning that we had more to lose than gain by getting involved with the cops, so our fate seemed clear: We were alive, but our money was gone forever.

In the end, all we learned was that Larry had escaped from a mental hospital. We had just spent days traveling to the Yukon and back in the company of a mental patient on the loose, perhaps an affable homicidal maniac. The fact that he was a madman explained some of his inconsistencies—why, for example, he did not seem to act enough like a real con artist. But who Doug was or exactly what the boy's relationship was with the older man remained as mysterious, as disturbing as ever, and the thought of our blindness and naiveté made us sick.

We took the Greyhound from Vancouver all the way to Eureka, and we crashed with those friends Spike had told us to check out. We got as far away as we could from Larry and Doug.

Dan was a fry cook at Denny's, while his girlfriend, Faith, was a waitress there. They rented a house on F Street, an old Victorian coming apart at the seams, and they opened their door with kind hospitality as soon as we arrived. Not too many freaks in Eureka, after all, so we were a welcome sight. The air was chilly, the fog constant, filled with that acrid sweet stink billowing out of the pulp mills from the towns of

Samoa and Manila on the spit of land across Humboldt Bay. Dan and Faith had almost no furniture and no heat except for a fireplace, which they stoked with wood from old crates and busted wooden chairs and slats from the walls. We would sit on the floor on our sleeping bags as Dan methodically yanked apart the few pieces of furniture left in the place in order to cook thick steaks and potatoes they regularly filched from the restaurant.

Dan, easygoing and taciturn, was an artist who told us he hoped his lottery number wouldn't come up in the draft, as he tossed a chair leg into the fireplace. The walls were decorated with his sketches and paintings, and among the cartoons of winos and hoboes in old-town Eureka and drawings of peeling eucalyptus trees that lined the road to Arcata were sketches and paintings of genitalia. I'd never realized how many angles, how many close-ups you could find in the folds of a vagina or the cauliflower of a scrotum. Was that painting of curling hair and flesh male or female? Was that round mass a breast or a penis or an elbow? In Dan's pictures, all sex disappeared as the organs became increasingly abstract and unrecognizable.

Faith was warm and voluptuous and smiled a lot with a sweet open mouth as she flipped huge slabs of meat over on the fireplace grill. She brimmed with robust milkmaid delight and chatted with sparkling chumminess, a fresh face among the abstracted sex organs tacked to the skeletal walls. I amused myself with imagining the intense artist of few words pushing too close between her legs, pencil in hand, eyes squinting at her pubic hairs, while his model chirped matter-of-factly about the fog or the odd tastes of customers at Denny's, like the one who ordered burgers with maple syrup.

We felt safe with Dan and Faith, and we were exhausted from our strange journey into Swedenborg's Heaven and Hell.

Dan told us they were looking for teachers on the Hoopa Indian Reservation, up on the Trinity and Klamath rivers. We contacted the school district, and we would be driving out to Hoopa for an interview in a day or so.

Meanwhile, I stared at the sizzling steaks in the fireplace, trying to make sense of all that had happened in the Yukon. It was as if we had passed through some ordeal, some test, though we were not completely certain what for or what it signified. Amy had seized the moment, had grabbed Larry's hand while I had sat frozen. I had been protected by another Ronnie, except she would be my wife.

Whatever would come to us next in Hoopa was probably just one more torn, out-of-order sheet from a crazy mystic book that we would find nailed to a tree, and I had to learn to accept whatever it would be.

I also had to accept that there would be things I could not know. Jimmy's fate with the finger of God would never be known to me. Had he been snatched by the Mafia or was he spending his summers fixing pinball machines in resorts in the Catskills? I wouldn't know the truth of Larry's strange doings either, I was sure of that. I would never know the real story, and even in the midst of it all we could never know, and maybe that was the real story, the lesson we were supposed to learn. Maybe there were just bits and pieces — endings with no beginnings or beginnings without endings — torn pages nailed to the trees.

I did have a dream soon after we arrived in Eureka. It marked, in a way, the transition, and I would come to have this dream repeatedly.

We were driving with Larry and Doug into those dark bushes outside Prince George once more. The undergrowth and tree branches got denser and denser. At first I felt afraid, panic jolting through me, as the darkness and the mystery and the terror closed in around us. But after a while Larry and Doug vanished, and even Amy disappeared, and the car seemed to melt away, and all that was left was the fact that I was traveling by myself, inexplicably moving through the thick growth, propelled by some magic momentum, while the branches and twigs kept twisting around me, slowing me down, fondling me, embracing me in their net. Amazingly, I felt no fear, just comfort and peace, calm and sweetness, entwined in all the branches. I kept moving, slower and slower, though still never quite coming to a halt—until I melted into the night, and I dissolved into the tangled arms of the dark forest.

At that point, lost in the embrace of bushes and branches, I woke up.

FINAL SUITE

MAKING THE PAST SAFE TO DIE

Making the Past Safe to Die
2005

The scholars received the request on their research email list. It was simple, and by the language and feel of the text, it seemed authentic. The little note at the top of the email said it came from a Native American in Alaska by way of a friend who was on the listserv:

> The army built a road in the Yukon during the war in the 1940s. They were afraid the Japanese would hop from the Aleutians over to Alaska and from there down to the States, so they wanted to build it in a hurry. With the road they would be able to send troops up quick, if they had to. An Elder of ours is over 100 today, and he was a guide for that road, at least on the Alaska side. It was the first time that he ever seen a black person. A lot of the workers were black, he says, and none of them were prepared for the cold. Because they were in a hurry, they worked no matter how cold it was, and it can get plenty cold and blow hard. Days

went by with it down to 40 below or colder, and once it even been 80 below. When they froze to death or died from injuries, they were just thrown by the roadside with no ceremony at all or buried. This upset our Elder a lot, and he never forgot it. Now he would like to have a ceremony for them so that he can rest in peace. Can you put me in touch with someone that might be able to talk to me about all of this so we can figure out how to do the ceremony? Has anyone even talked about the black people that came up here? Have they been honored for what they done for the USA?

I answered immediately, almost in tears. I told the history to the young Indian by way of the scholar who posted the request. Two crews from the Army Corps of Engineers worked to meet each other, one starting from British Columbia, the other from Alaska. About a third of them, the ones hacking their way through Alaska, were black, and it was a point of pride among them that they could do it. They had never been allowed to operate heavy machinery: The brass said Negroes didn't have brains enough to work a bulldozer, but the military was desperate for manpower, and they sent them north over the objections of General Buckner, son of a Confederate general. So you could imagine how adamant these men were to prove themselves. And they did, despite their losses. Their accomplishment was big news in the papers at the time, a morale boost, and the veterans still gather, although their numbers are dwindling. But I couldn't say if they were honored enough for their sacrifices, and I hadn't known about the dead left by the side of the road. That was a shock. I replied to the young Indian with some Web sites and email addresses so that he could find out more for himself.

I never got a reply. I didn't know if the scholar who had posted the note contacted the Indian from Alaska and if he in turn passed my message on to his elder. None of the other scholars replied. There was just silence. The discussion bounced on to other things, and nothing more came of it. I began to doubt if I had even seen the message, but I had saved it and I would call it up, and there it was as clear and sad as before. Was it only sent to me? Did the sender know that I had had my own small ordeal on the Alaska Highway? That I had spent time with Indians teaching on a reservation? Was it a cruel joke? Or had a spirit contacted me, sending a message from a different dimension?

I posted more queries to the list—to the list manager—but there was nothing, no answer, and every message seemed to vanish.

Forensic Life Histories
2003

Dear Hilton,

It was great seeing you at the big benefit for the Rosenberg Fund and learning about how you work with students doing research. I got a kick out of you describing it as leading a bunch of junior detectives— and how you're collecting stories of revelations or epiphanies. In any case, I figured I would send you a note, considering that once we were roommates—remember that place on Mission Street above the Zocalo Mexican restaurant?—and I am, as you know, a private investigator. You should get the real gumshoe perspective, although, as you no doubt know, being a private eye is hardly anything as exciting as they make it out to be in the movies. I'm now branching out, attending academic conferences on oral history and urban planning, sharing my experiences. I'm even writing an article for a journal.

Actually, I've coined the term "forensic life historian" to describe what I do, particularly since I work on a lot of death penalty cases for attorneys who represent indigent defendants. I spend hour after hour —hundreds of hours—delving into the lives of people, mostly men but some women too, who are facing trials or who are already condemned and are sitting on Death Row waiting to see if somehow they will be spared. I dig out how their private lives intersect with public records, and I try to find the storytellers who can explain all the factors, the pressures on a man's life that can lead him to explode in murderous violence. Jurors want to know the story, and if I can find and piece together the different stories by locating the key storytellers, then the jurors can begin to understand the defendant's life, and they can make a decision out of compassion and not just from fear and rage.

Well, I don't want to overstate it—but this may be very different from the kind of "detective" work your students are doing.

In any case, I want to add another story to your collection because it was a kind of revelation for me, and it happened when I was a college student at Columbia, so you may find it useful. It was before the strike. I was volunteering at a settlement house in East Harlem, tutoring students with schoolwork, trying to figure out what I could offer troubled teenagers just a little younger than myself, but also trying to share the political excitement of the time. One night I got carried away talking with one student, walking through Harlem for hours and not paying attention to the streets.

"Hey," I exclaimed when I realized I didn't know where I was. "I'm lost. How do I get back to Columbia?"

His reply was, "Look up."

At first I couldn't understand him. Look up at what?

"Just look up," he said again.

So I looked up. I was facing the West Side, and all I could see was the massive darkness of Morningside Heights Park, the sheer cliff that stood between me and the lights above. I had always looked down from Morningside Heights, and from there the park would stretch out beneath me and the streets below seemed to teem with life. I could look down from Columbia, from the heights down to Harlem and the East River—it was a great view, a lovely cityscape, and it was inspiring in its way. But I had never been in a position to look back from below, to look up, at least not at night. And now the park collapsed into an undifferentiated sheet of black wall, indistinct and impossible to scale, a huge dark monolith up above my head, so imposing, frightening even.

But that wasn't all of it. There above that dark wall I could see the very tops of the buildings of Columbia. And I could even make out the twinkling lights—they glittered like diamonds high above the dense black mound—of one of the buildings. After a moment I realized that I was looking at the chandeliers of the Columbia Faculty Club. Some professor was probably chatting over wine, his elbow patches grinding into a plush leather chair, and he did not even realize that I was there, far below, staring up at his ceiling, marveling at the dancing lights, with my friend.

This was one of my first experiences of what I came to call "the discipline of looking up." How you see a city—how you see a life—depends on your perspective. I had never before been in a position to look up. I had a new view, so distant and frightening, but so revealing.

This experience, this important discipline of looking up, had something to do with how I found my way to investigation and how I approach my job. Now, whenever I find myself with someone very different from me, whenever I try to delve into the stories behind some crime, whenever I go to a conference or to a courthouse or to a university, I say to myself, "Look up!"

I am always aware that there is another view. There's always one from the bottom, and you never really understand anything deeply unless you take that view. It became the motto for my life.

So, when are you going to invite me to lunch at the Stanford Faculty Club?

Looking up,
Joe Barthel

Fate
2005

The story was around for a few days—a brief mention on TV, a feature in the newspaper—and then it was gone.

The couple had gone to the same college, but they had never met there. He lived in San Francisco and she in Manhattan—he was a software engineer and she was a lawyer—but they met one summer at a party in San Francisco (friends of friends of each), and they spoke about traveling to Bhutan. He was amazed that she even knew of Bhutan, much less wanted to go there. He didn't take her phone number, and by the time he got in touch with her that fall, she had been diagnosed with cancer and had just begun treatments. He moved to Manhattan and began taking care of her, lifting her in and out of bed because she was so weak, and eventually the treatments did their work, she was free of the disease, and they had found love instead.

To celebrate her health and their love, they traveled all over the world. After the Himalayas and Patagonia and Nuka Hiva, they were walking down the Champs-Élysées when they passed an office of Iran Air. It was time to visit Persia—he had grown up in Saudi Arabia, his father working for an oil company, and he loved Middle Eastern culture—so they stepped in. When they got to Iran, they went to small villages and obscure towns, to historical sites far from Teheran. She was Jewish and afraid, but once she became used to the *hijab*, she felt comfortable.

When they visited the ancient mud city with the giant mud citadel, they stayed at a little guest house made of mud like all the other houses instead of the dull, modern hotel on the outskirts, where they had made their reservations. They were given a room with no window, but he did not feel safe there. What if there was a fire? How could they escape? Instead, they switched rooms and took the room with the window.

When the earthquake struck, the great heaving of the ground demolished the entire city of mud, burying tens of thousands, including the two of them. The ugly modern hotel did not collapse, and the room with no windows did not collapse, but the ceiling of the room with the window they had taken fell on their heads. They called out from under the rubble, and he made a joke about buying her an engagement ring. Rescuers pulled them both from the debris, but he was terribly injured, he was bleeding profusely, and he died in the ambulance from loss of blood.

Now she was alone. All of the ways that their stories had come together, all the decisions they had made—which party, which destination, which room—it all seemed to lead to this point, this juncture:

They should meet, he should bring her back to life, they should love, they should travel around the world, and they should come to the city of mud. And there he should die.

Discovery
1961

"What's that?" Mom cries out as Ronnie, bare-chested, holds his arms over his head to stretch against the walls of the arched alcove that divides living from dining rooms.

"The doctor at school said it was just a pulled muscle from throwing shot-put."

Ronnie smiles, winks at me sitting on the couch, as Mom becomes hysterical, typically overprotective—"Oh, such a Jewish mother," he nods knowingly at me.

But when I look up, I can see the lump as large as a small grapefruit in his armpit, along with his slight, bemused smile.

He quickly disappears into the operating room, and in the days that follow, my parents talk nonstop Polish, while I go about my business, not comprehending, not concerned. No assurance can be greater than Ronnie's smile.

He comes home after a while, seems to grow stronger. Mark too is home from college, and we're all at the house, even Aunt Zosia from Caracas, and Mark and I fight over what to watch on the big wooden TV. Zosia gets involved, wants to change the channel, and we gang up on her, kidding around, call her a "clodhopper," of all things.

"What is this 'clodhopper'?" she fumes, not understanding but aware that we're teasing her. She survived the Nazis because she was tough and feisty, so she is not going to accept being slighted or teased by a couple of kids. She shouts at us to explain, and we yell back, when Ronnie surprises us at the top of the stairs. He steps down the staircase from his bedroom to find out what all the fuss could be about.

He stands above us in chinos and a gray, threadbare Union College sweatshirt. Clutching the banister, he asks, "Why all the screaming?" Then he takes another step, pauses, weak-kneed, sways, and wobbles back and forth. So frail, he seems about to plunge headfirst down the stairs, but he just looks down at us in consternation, baffled at his body's sudden state of affairs. Silenced, our bickering is immediately forgotten, and all of us look up, all eyes fixed on him in his moment of frailty. He clutches the banister, quivers again, then regains his balance, his composure. He peers at us from his commanding height with a grin. Then he continues to make his way slowly down the rest of the staircase.

After a paralyzed moment of silence, each of us explodes into tears, our cries filling the house. Zosia runs over to Ronnie, grabs him, hugs him. Mom and Dad run from the kitchen into the living room, "What's going on?" No one can answer, wailing.

Dad also begins to weep, knowing that, whatever the cause, we are all now crying about the truth. Ronnie will die, and Dad clutches him, pounding his back with his hands, the inevitable course of the disease wordlessly known by Ronnie, that unspoken knowledge shared between father and son.

Counting Baghdads
2003

In 945 came the Buwayhids, and in 1055 the Seljuks. In 1258 the Mongols led by Hulagu invaded Baghdad, and in 1340 the Jalayrs; but then the Mongols returned, this time led by Tamerlane, in 1393 and 1401. Then, in 1411 Turkoman Black Sheep came, and in 1469 Turkoman White Sheep. In 1508 the Safavids, and in 1534 the Ottomans under Sultan Suleyman the Magnificent invaded. The Safavids returned in 1623, but so did the Ottomans, under Sultan Murad IV in 1638. The Ottomans stayed put quite a long time, until 1917, which was when the British arrived; in 1931 they installed King Feisal and left, but in 1941 the British returned to depose the pro-German government.

Finally, in 2003 came the Americans (along with the British, again), led by Bush, but this time they were going to do the job right.

The Rape of Nixon
1972

David Somerset was a quiet, wry guy who wrote labyrinthine detective stories in invented, screwball worlds. He was the student reading *The Big Sleep* as the police assault began in Low Library. He suffered greatly from his asthma, and his regular tugs on his inhaler were as much a part of him as the heavy acne that cobbled his face. "I'm a *lunger*," he once told me in classic detective lingo. The condition seemed to have driven him to a sensibility of laconic gothic excess and perverse wit.

In the early seventies David moved to San Francisco, where he worked at the docks in a lot that overhauled used industrial freezers. He did the bookkeeping while the crew of very large Samoans moved the freezers from one end of the lot to the other. He lived in the ramshackle abandoned office building in the lot, where he spent his extra time hammering away at his typewriter on his stories.

I had asked him to rent a post office box to use for receiving money, letters, fake ID, whatever was needed to help Mark Rudd and other antiwar fugitives and draft resisters survive in the underground. One day he came to see me, explaining that there was a problem with the mailbox.

David had written a letter to the Arlington National Cemetery inquiring if any babies were buried there.

"Babies? Why babies?"

He explained that he was writing a story based on a voodoo belief that the ghosts of those who die while still virgins cannot go to their rest in heaven without first having sex. These ghosts must fuck someone in order to find their peace. He told them that in the story he was writing, President Nixon walks through Arlington Cemetery and gets raped by a host of heavenly minded babies.

"I wanted to make sure that there were really babies buried there before I actually wrote it," he explained. "I told them I wanted it to be realistic when Nixon gets raped by the ghosts of babies."

My eyes widened as big as tombstones. What a crazy idea—and to send a letter of inquiry yet! I burst out laughing. David offered his wry grin and then took a quick blast from his inhaler.

"In any case," he continued, "I got a visit from the Secret Service yesterday. They had the letter and they just wanted to ask me a few questions. I think they thought I was threatening the president. I told them I was just writing a story, but I think the next time Nixon comes to San Francisco, they might pay me a visit again. I'm not sure if the mailbox is that safe anymore. Maybe they'll check my mail, you know."

He paused, and I just stared blankly at him.

"You know what else?" he added. "They wore dark suits, they didn't smile, but most of all they were actually wearing brown wingtip shoes."

You bet the mailbox was no good. Just wait till the *Brown Shoes*— that's what we called the FBI—checked out what came through that slot.

I told him we'd cancel the box right away. Then we stood around awkwardly, not saying anything.

"So, did they tell you if there were any babies buried there?"

"No, they wouldn't tell me," he replied matter-of-factly. "I suppose I was just asking for some top-secret information."

We kept standing around, staring at our feet, at a loss, digesting the idea that the number of babies buried in Arlington National Cemetery could be a government secret.

Suddenly we both burst out laughing.

On the Klamath
1969/1973

Soon after we arrived in Eureka, Dan and Faith told us about a job. Friends of theirs had been teachers up at the Hoopa Indian Reservation, and they knew that the school district was desperate for teachers, particularly for a married couple to teach at one isolated school far along the Klamath on the Yurok part of the reservation at a village called Pecwan or Johnson, the name of the former owner of an abandoned trading post.

I could get a deferral from the draft for teaching school, plus we needed jobs, and we had already entertained the idea of teaching in the bush when we were in the Yukon, so it seemed to make sense, and we went after it. The district superintendent drove us out to the end of the road along the Klamath to the school. Amy would teach kindergarten to third grade in one room, and I would teach fourth to eighth in the other, and as the husband of the couple, I would be the principal. There was a fairly new building, a generator for power, a radio phone, and even a teacherage, a small house with a plate glass window looking out at the school, which was surrounded by a cyclone fence and had a flagpole in front.

We were hired for the year on emergency credentials: We were white, we were Ivy League graduates, and all the district superintendent was interested in was for someone to take attendance so that they could collect federal money. We flew back to New York to get married in a hurry. We also studied up on Indians in the few weeks before school started, but we read about the wrong ones: Navajo students tended to be quiet and withdrawn in schools, while Yuroks were loud and rambunctious, a lot like New Yorkers. We were also surprised to discover that the two-teacher school was also the community center, with regular nights for volleyball and movies, and with the only radiophone connection to Eureka for emergencies, so we had to serve all kinds of needs, not just teach. We were soon in far over our heads, learning how to teach on the spot.

It remains the hardest job I've ever had.

Amy and I returned to visit a year or so after we left. We were coming down from Oregon, from a meeting of radicals, and we decided to drive up to the house of one of the families that had befriended us. When we arrived, we came upon an unexpected scene of sorrow and mourning. Not long after, I wrote a poem to mark the loss.

LAMENTATIONS AND DETERMINATIONS

Last time I went to Pecwan
more exactly, Klamath River Extension of the Hoopa Indian
    Reservation
(Yurok Tribe)
we drove along the river
The familiar cranky & crooked road
to see the Simpsons.
Night, finally, when we drove in
surprised to find maybe 25 cars parked
askew in the dirt ruts by the coop or down closer to the river:
Must be some party, we thought, sitting in our own dark vehicle.

Nervously we climbed the stairs to meet Hunsucker
who told us Cindy got drowned in the river
2 days before & they had all come to drag the river.

Still abundant Klamath of eel, trout, salmon,
even mammoth sturgeon lurking on bottoms
like succulent aquatic pork;
Klamath, still the old center of the universe, the juncture.
We turned to lean on the balcony of the A-frame

to look at it,
trying to see how far
we stood from it.

Barnfires kept watch on the bank all night.
She'd been swimming as she'd done 14 years
dove in, her skull cracked a rock
& Vicki couldn't hold on to her hair, then she was gone
into the current
after the first bob up.

My student, among other things.

I peeked at her 7th grade doodle in her desk
one day before school began
a nosey principal
"*Why must our people be in pain . . .*
INDIAN POWER . . . Love Peace Love . . .
Don't you think Tiger O'Rourke is *such* a bully?"

The river isn't as sentimental as I am, nor even so mean.
The river isn't a typically schizoid 7th grader either
tho now it seems she *is* the river,
a hitchhiker, enrolled in a new school, etc.,
yet the people won't leave the river alone with its catch.
This was no Ophelia or Mary Jo Kopechne, just a quick dunk,
as her life was in the first place, or yours,
suddenly deciphered like a secret telegram
in a shredding machine.
The men cruise, very quiet as a result of determination.
All the people bring food the women cook up,

endless batches, and discuss
equally endless exegesis of
what it was that made God angry at Cindy.

A year before, when the river came close
to a foot of the road
the rains abruptly ceased. We knew we'd be dry
that season.
No houses would float out
In the grayish-yellow, massive, uncanny river,
As in the great flood of 1964
past Requa by the sea
where Oregos, the old round rock outcrop at the mouth, looms out,
informing the salmon what the weather is
or if it's the right time to spawn.
People drove out to the bridge over Pecwan Creek to celebrate,
wine passed around. The white preacher & a visiting evangelist
were in a dingy navigating a giant eddy
away from the swifts, grappling huge logs
for the venerable full-blood who lived at the mouth of the swollen creek
to use as firewood.
Pistols out, we took pot-shots at the drift
Ever so often cutting close to Bjorke's dingy.
"Yahoo! Shoot the preacher!"
Tho nobody did. It was all laughs.
God isn't angry at Cindy.

Just before Thanksgiving vacation
we stood out front washing our car
getting set for the long weekend in SF

when a parent barreled up in his truck.
He reeled out drunk, demanded
that his 2nd grade daughter
get homework, lots of it
& that I get a haircut, despite the fact
that I cultivated short hair
"Git a haircut or I'll kill you!"
I talked circles, but he persisted, hinted at the gun
in his glove compartment, offered me wine:
"You fucking hippie!" then blubbered,
sobbing, **"I can't be no fucking hippie, I'm an Injun!
I'm a fucking Injun!"**

Lil had them in a washtub
a hundred or so—talking—all the while grabbing them,
slicing their lengths down the middle,
eel-blood sloshing up the galvanized sides, up her arms,
a broad grin as she gabbed.

Ollie's mom was very old, was reared by her grandmother
in the old way in the woods;
refugees from a massacre,
whenever they'd see *waugay* they'd flee.
Others, as children, could remember seeing the smoke of
the old ones across the river or beyond hills.
The story was passed on to Ollie's mom
of when the first whites came.
The Yuroks were aware the whites were down by the sea building
    houses.
As they were having a major dance at Pecwan Creek

word came from scouts the whites were sailing up river.
The festival broke up as they all
rushed to the banks—
it was pointed out to me at which bend—
to watch the boat sail by,
and as it did the wind came up,
capsizing the boat
& drowning those first premature invaders.
After Charles Manson inflamed the press,
Ollie's mom wouldn't talk to me anymore,
insisting that I was the devil, that I was a hippie
& all hippies kill.

Imperceptibly, word came up from the banks next morning
they got her.
Immediately, the teen-age boys heaved picks & shovels
in a pick-up & went to dig her grave;
her girlfriends in a hush went to prepare her room
for the mourning;
a truck came up, we knew she was inside,
& behind it, in single file, the men walked.

[AUGUST 1973]

Survivor's Guilt

1991

I started the doctoral program at Stanford in the nineties, the autodidact scholar returning late in life to the academy. It was strange being treated so deferentially, with professors and administrators doing everything they could to help me pursue my research. I was introduced as a "distinguished" writer. I came to regard "distinguished" as meaning someone who publishes books that hardly anyone reads — but that was fine. I figured that at least I wasn't "extinguished."

The campus was beautiful and spacious, a kind of Mission Romanesque dreamscape. It was so spacious that the Quad at the center of the campus never really filled up with people, and the people I did see were strangers who kept to themselves. Of course, I was lonesome, but the place always seemed empty, underpopulated, even when classes changed, and this was unnerving.

Soon, though, the empty place began to fill up with ghosts. I began to see the faces of dead friends and relatives float before me: Ronnie, Miguel, Cindy Simpson, who had drowned in the Klamath, Bill Wahpepah and the other AIM activists, the wedding guests I had met in the Sabra refugee camp in Beirut before they were all massacred, my relatives in Majdanek and Treblinka, even though they had been murdered before I was born, those hundreds of Iranian students I worked with who returned after the shah was overthrown, only to be executed by Khomeini because they were leftists, old friends who had fallen to cancer, Ted Berrigan and all the poets who had gone — their faces kept swirling around me, crowding in the too-big space of the beautiful campus. I wasn't lonesome anymore, but I became increasingly morose, walking around with tears constantly in my eyes, nodding to the faces of dead friends and relatives floating across the Quad.

I had previously studied at San Francisco State, so I went to visit Eric Solomon, my old professor friend at State, to get his advice. He chewed at his unlit cigar, mulling over my story of ghosts. At last he took out his cigar, leaned toward me, and squinted at me for a long moment. Then he spoke: "*Survivor's guilt*. You've got survivor's guilt. Nothing to it." He waved his cigar at me, and as soon as he did, I understood, and the ghosts flew away.

Hilton Obenzinger's *Retraction*
1983

In the last issue of *Hilton Obenzinger*, an item appeared that several readers found offensive. It was certainly not our intent to offend anyone, and we deeply regret having done so; we did not take into account how seriously some people might view our writings. We hope that all who were offended will accept our apology and rest assured that we will make every effort to be more sensitive in the future.

The Big Picture
1988

Helen Wilson came to San Francisco to exhibit her paintings at a downtown gallery. I had not seen her for two decades, since not too long after she took me to visit her home on Cape Cod and I had been growled at by her writer father, Edmund Wilson, and I was delighted that she had called me up to come to the opening. Still, it can be awkward meeting someone again after so many years, and it could be even more awkward trying to say something nice about their art, if it so happens that the work is banal or boring.

I walked into the gallery and I was stunned. Helen looked good—even more beautiful than I remembered—and I hardly recognized her. But her paintings were the astonishing thing.

They were done on small wooden boards, very small, placed against a large white wall. Yet each of them depicted in sharp-edged realism a huge vista—a seascape or a view of an industrial harbor skyline or a sky above a wide beach or an expanse of rooftops across a city—filled with some kind of dramatic light. They were immense, gigantic expanses, panoramas seen through tiny keyhole spaces, and the vastnesses expanded even more dynamically because they shot out from such very small spaces. These very small paintings of very big views were terrific, and I felt I had encountered an altogether different way of looking at the world, that I had been moved in some kind of wonderfully eerie way.

I laughed to myself at the thought that I was afraid her paintings would be banal. "This," I thought, "is what an artist is really like."

Some Final Thoughts from Hilton Obenzinger
1984

A porcupine drowns while trying to make love on a waterbed.

A black hole devours a Midwestern state and it isn't missed for a week.

Hilton Obenzinger prints an article mocking every major religion and no one gets offended.

A supermarket manager is arrested for making funny faces every time someone buys chicken breasts.

Hilton Obenzinger prints the word "breasts" without offending anyone.

An orangutan who can speak seven languages is arrested for illegal facial expressions.

Surrender
1977

Mark Rudd surrendered in September 1977, after years on the FBI's most-wanted list for conspiracy and bombings. Many of his charges had already been dropped, although he still had felony charges stemming from the 1969 Days of Rage riots in Chicago protesting the Chicago Seven trial. The swirl of events after 1968 — the splits in SDS and Weatherman's turn toward guerrilla warfare — had come to its end, and one by one most of the fugitives surfaced. There was a general feeling in the country for amnesty in the wake of the Vietnam War, but the fugitives were able to cut deals on even the most serious charges because the FBI had broken so many laws pursuing the Weather Underground that the government had deemed it wiser to keep its own misdeeds out of sworn testimony. That day in September, Rudd had to appear at Gerry Lefcourt's law office in Lower Manhattan at 8 a.m. He had taken the subway down from the Bronx much too early, and he had about an hour to kill.

Rudd walked up Broadway below Canal Street, slowly making his way as the neighborhood began to stir. At 396 Broadway, on the corner of Walker Street, he looked up and saw the sign on the storefront. "Hilton Textile Corporation," it said, and in smaller letters, off to one side, "Nat Obenzinger." What a surprise. He realized he had stumbled across my father's business, and he chuckled. It was so early in the morning that my father had not yet arrived, and he sat down on the small stoop at the front door to wait for his appointment to surrender. He felt comfortable sitting in front of the Hilton Textile Corporation, and he read the newspaper.

"I thought about you and me in Columbia, and during my time underground," he told me later. "And I thought about how you were faring in San Francisco. I hadn't seen you in a while, but I did know that you were still active in radical politics, running a printing press for the movement. I thought about our friendship and our political bonds, and how the two became intermixed, and how you helped me during those days underground. It felt great sitting there."

It was strange that he would suddenly come across the Hilton Textile Corporation. But there had been so many other crisscrossing occurrences, so many coincidences, that it didn't seem strange. It was logical, even inevitable that he would sit on that stoop.

After a while, Rudd got up, and he went off to turn himself in.

The Metal Box
2005

My father had a small metal box that he kept on a high shelf in my parents' bedroom closet. He would let me look at it from time to time when I was a boy. Inside were official papers — naturalization documents, diplomas, and the like — and a roll of crisp Polish zlotys from before the war.

He would keep silver dollars there, too. Each birthday he would bring his sons large silver dollars in quantities according to their age, plus one for good luck. I remember the delight of stacking the thick coins—seven plus one, eight plus one, and on. Eventually, the coins would disappear, gone back to the bank, but the pleasure of their weight, the rich substance of those dollars, remained. I suppose my father wanted to instill a sense of how important money was, and that we should love to possess such hefty coins.

There was also a little notebook bound in thin leather in that small strongbox. The writing in the notebook was in Yiddish, and by the way the words were arrayed line by line, it looked like a book of poems. This was the journal he kept when he left Lublin and came to New York, he explained, but he never translated the poems. He soon learned English, and he could speak it without a hint of his first language. Ironically, he had to learn Polish when he married my mother. As the daughter of a Polish nationalist—the highest Jewish official in the Polish government, and at the start of the war the *only* one—she knew only Polish, not Yiddish, so he had to smooth out his broken Polish to communicate with her at first. Eventually, her English became as American as my father's, and Polish became their private language.

Throughout my parents' journey through languages, my father's poems, written in neat Hebrew script, sat in that box, waiting to be read. As he grew into his nineties, I would find other evidences of his youth scattered among his photos. There was a whole envelope of negatives that, when developed, revealed him at the beach in a bathing suit and tank top posing with other fellows and girls in front of 1920s cars. It was the late twenties, he had been in America for just a few years, but he recognized no one in the photos, none of the girls who clung to his muscular arms; he couldn't remember that day at the beach nearly seventy years before. It was as if he were looking at someone else, except we could tell it was him, and he was robust and young and filled with joyous energy. This was your life, the photos were saying—whether you remember or not, here it is.

But what would the book say? His eyes were failing and he could no longer read his own writing, so I would have to find someone else to tell me. Yiddish is in no way a dead language, but it's also a little bit not alive, and it proved very difficult, even at a university, to find someone able to translate the verses, especially because they were handwritten in cursive Hebrew script. Eventually, a colleague led me to a young rabbinical student at the Jewish Theological Seminary, Ben Weiner. He worked at the book in between his studies, bit by bit making his way through the poems. He proved to be an able translator, and he even produced English transliterations of the Yiddish for a few of the poems. I was going to read them out loud to my father. But by the time Ben finished, my father was on his deathbed. I would not be able to recite to him in the voice of his youth.

The little book was titled *Beginnings*, and at the bottom of the first page was a note in Polish: "Immigrated to America 10/17/25." The author is inscribed, in transliterated Yiddish, as "Nachmen Obzinger." In the title poem, "Beginnings," which he wrote while still in Lublin, he considered his reader.

Naked, I take pen and paper
And sit at my table to sing.
This that you now hold in your hand,
This I have written for you.

Who was "you"? The first poem—"The Victim of Love," a story of rejected love and suicide—had the note at the top: "Lublin 5/3/25." The penultimate poem, called "Too Small"—"Too small and weak am I / To sing of you, dear mother"—was dated "New York May 11, 1926." The very last was simply noted "New York 1926" and titled "The Forgotten," a tiny story of shipwreck and of a forlorn young man, drowned and left on the beach. Sometimes the "you" was his mother, but were the poems also written for the love he left behind? Or was the young man addressing his older self decades later? Or speaking to his sons?

The book crossed an ocean, filled with poems of the unrequited love and morbid loneliness of a teenager, although the loneliness naturally grew deeper when he found himself alone in New York. He especially yearned for his mother, who had heroically kept her children together as refugees during the war. The book crossed over more than the Atlantic, as it documented that one year of change.

In *Beginnings* are comments on events, on the execution of the czar, and even satirical swipes. But he also writes, still in Poland, about a fire that burned a synagogue to the ground. It impressed him so much that he composed two versions. Did the fire actually occur? Or was it a symbolic story of the fragile existence of Jews? He made his warning much more explicit in another poem:

Look around, Jew.
As you can see,
You must not wait
Till they drive you out.

It took him many months of arguing for his father to allow the very young man to travel to the New World. Hiel Obcynger traveled back and forth between America and Poland for his shoe business, and he had been caught in New York for the duration of the war, leaving his wife and four children to survive on their own. That's when he had become a United States citizen, changing his name to Obenzinger, Germanicizing the name because he believed America would enter the war on the side of the kaiser. Despite his mistake, this gave his son the option of becoming a citizen, too. But Nachmen's rabbi father opposed his son leaving Poland, because a Jew could not be pious in America: The Gentiles forced you to work on the Sabbath. The rabbi finally did relent—an uncle testified that the boy was already a goy, since he would routinely go out to play soccer on Saturdays—and he allowed his son to travel to New York, where he waited for him while on yet another business trip. When Nachmen arrived, it happened to be Yom Kippur, so his father was in the synagogue and did not meet the ship. The young man, abandoned once again, wandered through the city until the end of the holy day before his father came to get him.

One poem addresses his father's absence during the war, when the rabbi was stranded in America and the boy had to fend for himself, scavenging for food. Upon his arrival in New York, his father soon returned to Poland. In the poem, he says farewell to his father, who, ironically, abandons his son once again, just as he had before the war:

NY 3/2/26

THE UNKNOWN FATHER

You leave again!
Like buzzing flies
Memories, dark and bright,
Flit before my eyes.

Mother,
With tear-stained face
Gestures towards the wall.
"This is your father,"
With closed eyes
And impoverished hands.
Feeling the warm kisses
Of my unknown father,
Hearing his quiet words.
"Do not cry, my dear son.
Before long
I will stay with you."
A life laid to waste,
Never still from youth,
My father came at last,
When I had been driven away.

"Driven away" because he followed his own admonition to the Jews. Nachmen does not wait in Poland for more pogroms. He makes his way to America, and he records the strangeness of what he comes upon, not much more than two weeks after he arrives and begins working in a factory firing watch cases:

I sit in the shop
Twisting, hunched over,
Remembering my mother
As tears flow from my eyes.

After nearly two months, he casts a picture of "the new land," its frenetic hubbub and its reach to all the peoples of the world; he also comes to know its driving force:

IN THE NEW LAND

Here
In the new land,
So far away.
The life
Is so strange,
And the thoughts,
And the laughter,
And the song.

Everyone runs
In a muddle:
White and black,
Arab and Chinese,
Like in a plague,
Like an animal
Through a hoop.

The great, omnipotent
Dollar,
Look at it,
See how it grows.

How he would have loved to sit around the Friday night table, no longer running through the hoops, to be in his mother's arms; and many of his poems are filled with such yearnings.

My father wrote his poems at about the same age that I went to college as an aspiring young poet. By that time, his watchwords were

"Everything is under control" and "Be practical." He had become a man who measured everything by practicality, by hard, cold reality. "Poems won't put food on your plate," he told me, and he had learned this cruel lesson himself. After six months in his new land, he ceased writing poems; he was engulfed by work, by going to school to learn English at night, by his dreams of success. He resolved that he would struggle to bring everything under control. He grew to love "making" money, the thrill of buying and selling, of watching his fortune grow, one hard-won dollar after another, clinking up like those piles of silver coins he gave me for my birthdays.

Even so, he kept his little book of poems, although he would eventually forget how to read them. "Nachmen" would become "Naum," then "Nathan," and finally "Nat," but he had not resented his youthful passions; he had not forgotten his soul's journey across worlds.

I saw something in the book I had not realized. He recognized himself in his son; and even though he believed I was foolish, he understood me.

NEW YORK 4/8/26

OLD THOUGHTS

You read these verses
From the poet,
And an image runs through
Your mind.

Ah! How he laughs
And mocks the world
That is so great and holy
And costs so much money.

Like a worn-out soldier
Whose sword has fallen from his hand,
Like one who has outlived and outlaughed himself,
He is ready to embrace the earth.

You, reader of these lines,
Have a good laugh.
The writer
Is not yet twenty years old.

ACKNOWLEDGMENTS

Grateful thanks to the following people who contributed to the research for this book: the parents, teachers, and students of Writer's Week at Los Altos High School, and the staff of *Hilton Obenzinger Magazine* at Schreiber High School in Port Washington, New York—Josh Berman, Carol Blum, Robin Dissin-Aufses, and Victor Seidel; the Columbiana archives of Columbia University; the American Studies Association listserv; and Joe Barthel, Paul Cronin, Ron Dudum, Sara Ferry, Leslie Gottesman, Elisabeth Hansot, Sara Martin, Bernice Mast, Beverly Parayno, Mark Rudd, Alan Senauke, Kevin Scheirer, Joseph Shapiro, Paul Spike, Ben Weiner, Barry Willdorf, Bonnie Willdorf, Mark Williams, Helen Wilson, and Rick Winston. I thank all of the people who appear in this book, no matter how disguised in fictional garb, and all my students at Stanford University who have kept me refreshed in their constant stream of revelations. To those I have forgotten to mention here I also give my thanks, and my apologies for inadvertently overlooking their contributions.

I especially thank Stephen Vincent for his editorial and publishing acumen, and for years of friendship.

I also thank my agent, Elizabeth Wales, for her effort to bring *Busy Dying* to life.

Finally, I thank my wife, Estella Habal, for her years of love and support, and my son Isaac.

This is for all the ghosts, especially Ronnie.

Hilton Obenzinger writes fiction, poetry, history and criticism. His most recently published works include *a*hole: a novel* (Soft Skull Press, 2004), *Running Through Fire: How I Survived the Holocaust by Zosia Goldberg as told to Hilton Obenzinger* (Mercury House, 2004), *American Palestine: Melville, Twain and the Holy Land Mania* (Princeton University Press, 1999), *Cannibal Eliot and the Lost Histories of San Francisco* (Mercury House, 1993), *New York on Fire* (Real Comet, 1989), and *This Passover Or The Next I Will Never Be in Jersualem* (Momo's Press, 1980), which received the American Book Award of the Before Columbus Foundation. Earlier books include *The Day of the Exquisite Poet is Kaput* and *Bright Lights! Big City!*, and he is one of the featured poets in *Five on the Western Edge* (Momo's Press, 1977). He is also co-editor, with Leslie Gottesman and Alan Senauke, of *A Cinch: Amazing Works from the Columbia Review* (Columbia University Press, 1969).

Born in 1947 in Brooklyn, raised in Queens, and graduating Columbia University in 1969, he has taught on the Yurok Indian Reservation, operated a community printing press in San Francisco's Mission District, co-edited a publication devoted to Middle East peace, worked as a commercial writer and instructional designer. He received his doctorate in modern thought and literature from Stanford University in 1997. Currently, he teaches advanced writing and American literature at Stanford.